Why the Sparrow Cries

The Sparrow Duology

Book One: Why the Sparrow Cries

Why the Sparrow Cries

The Sparrow Duology

By

Hope Bolinger

Why the Sparrow Cries
Published by Mountain Brook Ink under the Mountain Brook Fire line
White Salmon, WA U.S.A.

The website addresses shown in this book are not intended in any way to be or imply an endorsement on the part of Mountain Brook Ink, nor do we vouch for their content.

This story is a work of fiction. All characters and events are the product of the author's imagination. Any resemblance to any person, living or dead, is coincidental.

ESV Study Bible. 2008. Wheaton, IL: Crossway Books.

ISBN 9781953957-41-2

The Team: Miralee Ferrell, Alyssa Roat, Kristen Johnson, Cindy Jackson
Cover Design: Alyssa Roat

Mountain Brook Fire is an inspirational publisher offering worlds you can believe in.
Printed in the United States of America

DEDICATION

2021:
To my future Homer, are you lost? Do you need a GPS?
I can't wait to meet you and hope you exist.

2023:
Oh hi, Trey. There you are.

CONTENT WARNING

This book contains mentions of domestic abuse, ancient temple prostitution, a brief mention of sexual assault, alcoholism, and death. Many of these issues hit close to home for me and many close friends. In the case of any sensitive subject, I have tried to approach it with the utmost care and delicacy. However, this warning is included ahead of time for readers who have been affected by any of the above issues.

Part One: June

"My boy, beware the sparrow.
For you are a godlike eagle,
And eagles do not allow the company
Of ordinary creatures."

— Fragment from the Palikarian epic *Stroution*, author unknown

Chapter One
Why the River Nile Bleeds

The Tube jolts to a halt.

I suppress a grin. As much as I hate this—the Tube rattling, the people—at least I'm free. Free at last to explore London. I'm not complaining. Even with the number of bodies packed into this car.

The train jolts again.

My grip on the red pole slips, and I stumble backward into a man wearing a business suit that matches his fiery red hair.

I mutter a quick, "Sorry." He flares his nostrils in reply, but I imagine something like "stupid," "overweight," and "American girl," just fluttered through his thoughts. One to talk. Most Brits here wear gray or black. Who decided wearing scarlet was a good idea?

Oh well. I don't care about how many people are packed into this small Tube. Or what British people think about girls with blue pixie cuts in sweats and a hoodie. I'm in London. Lon-don.

And I'm away from my mom for once. Thank goodness.

A *ding-dong, ding-dong* emits from the sliding doors as they open to a concrete station. The smell of cigarette wind fills the car.

My heart plummets into my lower intestines when I see the large crowd gathered at the edge of the train platform. So much for optimism. I tighten my sweaty grip around the pole.

They'll get off soon, Harper. They have to.

I glance around at the inhabitants of the Bakerloo line. *Please tell me all of you wanted to stop here.*

Yeah, probably not. Nice thought, though. I squeeze my eyelids tight and try not to think about how many humans suppress the oxygen from the space between bodies. My eyelids fly open again when we jolt. Bad luck. I caught a nasty glare from a woman I almost bumped into. Raven hair, matching dark eyes where the irises almost blend into the pupils and pencil skirt.

At least *someone* got with the program, Mr. Redcoat. Something about his presence sends ants crawling up and down my skin. Alarm bells often ring for me around any man—thanks to Dad—but this feels different.

Like someone has wrapped their fist around my gut and given my organ a good squeeze.

"This is Baker Street." The crisp female voice from the overhead speaker layers itself over the backdrop of a flickering train light. A pitiful number of bodies exit the coach. Thanks a lot for your contribution, Britain.

"Change for the Bakerloo, Jubilee, and Metropolitan lines."

That's a lot of lines. You guys sure you don't want to get off? Especially Mr. Redcoat?

Focus, Harper. Eyes on the prize. You get an adventure, a day out of Uncle Laran's apartment. You'll be out of this crowd soon.

The swarm of bodies filters through the doors like gnats by Lake Powell. Uncomfortable, I press myself against the wall on the other side of the train as the oncoming Tube-goers squish against me. A woman in a severe bun grips a Costa coffee cup with French manicured fingers. It fills my nostrils with the dizzying scent of caffeine. Breakfast feels like forever ago…

A passenger lifts her arm to check her watch. Last I checked my phone, a few minutes ago, it was 2:13.

Thought I caught the Underground during an off time. I

frown. Guess no "off-time" exists in England during the summer. It's Phoenix all over again.

Heat rises in my cheeks and droplets of sweat break out on my forehead and upper lip from the number of humans packed in here. Not the best day to wear a hoodie…but London in June feels freezing compared to Page, Arizona. Weather app said it was a high of ninety-five back home.

With what little room remains left, by accident, I elbow a bystander, the same woman in the pencil skirt—she scowls at me—as I reach into my bag. I fish out my phone to distract myself from the cramped conditions for the next two stops. "No Service," reads the top of my screen.

I chew on my lip.

Got lost in Phoenix once as a teen during foot traffic rush hour. Haven't recovered since, I guess.

Then again, if I scroll on Tumblr, I might not hear the next stations on the overhead. Don't want to miss the stop. Don't wanna do Phoenix all over again.

Never again.

When we reach Oxford Circus, I squeeze my way through the crowd and release a brief gasp of relief. I clutch the cool white brick wall next to a sign for *Wicked* on West End. This break from bodies disappears in a moment as what seems like half the train empties itself.

Next to the *Wicked* sign, another poster with a TARDIS arrests my attention. Wonder if Uncle Laran likes time travel shows as much as me. He talks a lot about football, but I have a feeling he doesn't mean the type where men dogpile just for funzies.

Bodies sift and bump past me like wayward inner tubes on a lazy river.

Guess everyone wanted the same adventure today, since we

all let off at the same station.

I follow the signs to the Central line. Ride this for one stop. *Just one stop, Harper.* My heartbeat echoes the click-clack of the train on the tracks.

One stop later, one funneling through a thin hallway later, one escalator ride later…I seek refuge against a wall that leads out of a station and consult a map. I made sure to screenshot the image on my phone before I left Uncle Laran's place.

Thank goodness I did that. The battery appears to be draining quicker than my patience, if I'd pulled up my GPS to walk me the rest of the way there, that app would siphon the rest of the phone's stamina.

Don't know why the phone's so exhausted. It doesn't have to walk as much as I do here. Fiery pains in my feet grumble in agreement.

But hey, we'll be there soon. Think of all the cool stuff you'll get to see, Harper. Think of all the awesome photos you can take.

At long last, the crowd disperses, and I peek outside to spy a street sign and get my bearings. But before I recognize anything, a group of tourists passes me—a tangled mess of sunburnt women, college-age students in New York University tees (all loud, way too loud), and some teenage girls letting out peals of laughter which bounce off the sheer white walls.

Good ol' Americans.

Clutching my camera bag tightly against me—as I had done on the Tube to avoid pickpockets—I trail behind them, knowing they, too, will be heading toward the British Museum. It's the only thing nearby to visit. Although Uncle Laran mentioned something about a cartoon museum also being in the area, who wants to turn down seeing the Rosetta Stone and mummies and stuff?

"Maybe they'll have Mallard Fillmore at the comic museum," Mom had said on my way out of Laran's apartment. "You might want to stop by on your way back home. Get a picture with Mallard."

Mom loves that comic. I'm not really a fan of birds. Not since a hawk tried to carry away our terrier back in first grade. Ah, Arizona, how I miss you.

Eh, at least here birds can't carry away small pets.

Clusters of pigeons rev their wings as we filter past them. I think I remember seeing a little bird or two with iridescent green and gray wings back at Paddington this morning when I scarfed down a pastry. Hope we don't stumble into too many more birds in this country.

A soft breeze catches us on the way down the road as the group consumes the whole sidewalk. Before I can inhale the welcome coolness, I smell a whiff of cigarette as we wait at a crosswalk.

I cough. Forgot they smoke more here.

We walk a long way and then flood the road in front of the museum, halting a poor red double-decker bus due to our group's size.

Having reached our destination, I weave through the loud mass, trying to bypass them and reach the exhibits before the whole United States population does.

Success!

I dodge around the group leader, a stout man in metallic sunglasses carrying a strawberry umbrella, and veer left to join a line for a security check. A guard behind a table beckons me over, and his gloved hands prod through my Persephone Books bag. Mom bought it the other day. She likes stories with female characters. He sifts through the contents—my inhaler, camera, sketchbook, and wallet.

He waves me forward as if wafting away a bad smell, and I scoot to the right as fast as my calves will take me to beat the crowd. My feet halt at the bottom of the stone steps. I stare at the skyward columns, chin stuck in the sky. Just look at how the edges of those columns spiral like snail shells.

This would make a gorgeous painting. The back of my neck aches, and I drop my gaze.

That is, if several tourists weren't posing on the stairs.

I glare at one of the said guilty parties as I scale the steps. He doesn't seem to notice, his two bandaged fingers in a peace sign for his wife snapping the photo in the courtyard.

"Take another one, sweetie, of me holding up the roof." He groans as he squats and places his palms flat above his sweaty head.

The woman snorts into the phone. "You look hilarious." She claps a hand to her purple lips and lets out an unruly giggle.

Man alive. Listen, I don't want to dislike people. However, tourists are a whole different breed. Like birds. Most people are pigeons. But tourists, they're hawks about to prey on small dogs and coupons.

Speaking of—

The atrium hosts even more humans than I thought possible. Their voices bounce all the way to the glass ceiling. I crane my neck and trace the triangular shapes until they disappear behind a rounded corner.

Near the large, circular staircase, a gaggle of British school-children in neon-yellow safety vests congregates. Next to them, several Korean tourists huddle in front of a sign carrying the map of the various exhibits.

Remembering the number of Americans behind me in

security, I pick up my pace and rush across the tile floor, past the welcome desk and a naked statue on a horse, looking for *one* spot without people.

Yeah, good luck with that. Deep breaths. Find pockets of air where there aren't crowds.

I can't breathe in crowds.

Eyeing a stool by the food court and a Native American totem pole, I dash over there and slide into the metal chair. What a steal.

A sweet odor, coming from the Court Café, prickles my nostrils. I clutch at my stomach when it gives a soft moan and a rumble.

Haven't eaten since this morning.

Nutella and flaky croissant still linger in the back of my throat from the meal I had earlier in Paddington station. I parked on a bench and ate and sketched landscapes for three hours there, hoping to snag the train during a less busy time. No such luxury exists here.

I leave my sketchbook on the seat to reserve it and head toward the café. Hope no one kidnaps it during my two point five minutes of absence. I left my nice notebook at home. This one's torn in the corners and fraying. Not much of a loss if someone steals it. Plus, the pictures in it aren't all that good. Just rough drafts.

As always in London, there's a line, so I join the queue. Decadent chocolate cakes with Malteser balls on top catch my attention, but I balk when I see the price printed on a white tag.

"Five pounds for dessert?"

Mom only gave me fifteen for today, and I spent four on breakfast, so skip the sweets, Harper. Not that you need them anyway, flaca. I pat the rolls on my abdomen. *Yep, definitely don't need it.*

We call skinny people "*gorda*" in Arizona and not skinny people, well, you know. At least, some of my Hispanic classmates do this. It's supposed to be ironic or something. Apparently when you say the same epithet here, for any of those who actually understand Spanish, they pass you a weird look. Like you've stuffed onions up their nostrils or something.

It's probably the blue hair.

As I scan the menu for a moment, one of the only vegetarian sandwich options doesn't appeal to me. I hate Dijon mustard. So, when I reach the counter, I order the other one instead and pluck some gold-silver pound coins from my wallet.

Returning to my seat, I take off the wrap's casing and pick out the pieces of chicken. Right after, I launch into the bread, noticing how a British woman a few seats down eyes me with disgust. Didn't even call her *gorda.*

Then she returns to her sandwich with a fork and knife.

Oh, right, Uncle Laran also threw a conniption when Mom and I ate without utensils at dinner last night. They have some strange customs in London.

A sickening, sweet taste of apple and mayo fills my mouth, a strange combination. I force myself to swallow the mouthful and shudder as it goes down.

Well, at least they have pretty exhibits here.

Disappointed and still hungry, I pull out a sheet of paper from Uncle Laran from my bag, watching a group of tourists coo at some key chains in the shape of owls from the shop across the way. Might want to save my money for a *Doctor Who* shop housed somewhere in London. I return to the paper.

"Uncle Laran's list of things to find in the British Museum," the paper reads, breaking up twenty items amidst all the available floors.

He claimed he wanted me to look for these artifacts to enhance my overall London experience—and promised to give me a box of Maltesers candy if I took a picture of at least half of the exhibits on the list. How could I refuse? Turning down free chocolate? Could I even call myself a female if I did?

But with the way he ushered me out the door this morning, his usual clean shirt untucked and his graying hair a staticky mess, something tells me he wanted some peace and quiet at home without needing to look after a sixteen-year-old kid.

Can't blame him. With Mom on her tour group expeditions, she expected her brother to play babysitter. Neither of us liked that arrangement.

And as much as I can't stand tourists, I hate cabin fever even more. One summer too many stuck at home with no ride and no friends taught me that lesson well. I consult the sheet of paper again.

"The list of items to find on the ground level:

The Rosetta Stone—Written in three tongues (hieroglyphic, demotic, and Greek), this stone helped archaeologists crack the code for the language of the Ancient Egyptians.

Hoa Hakananai'a ('lost or stolen friend')—This Easter Island figure, made of basalt, was created sometime in—"

"Rosetta Stone it is," I decide, pulling my camera out of its bag. Bet it'll make a gorgeous photo. Twenty pictures in two and a half hours, and then I can show them to Uncle Laran back at Paddington.

Mama wants her chocolate.

No sooner do I rise from my seat than someone else slithers

into it. Ah well, at least no one kidnapped the sketch book.

I speed walk to a map display across the room and hoist myself on my tiptoes to read the inscriptions beyond the wall of people. Rosetta Stone. Exhibit four, got it.

My tennis shoes squeak when I make a brisk stride toward a room flanked by columns similar to the ones I saw outside. Ducking into the entrance, I stop right away because a barricade of humans surround a glass case. Ah man, so much for the picture. Squinting, I spot the tip of the jagged black rock. The tourists pack themselves into such a tight space, there's no way I can maneuver through them.

Spotting no one at the other end of the display, I race toward there and soon learn why the back of the artifact draws no crowd. It has nothing on it. Slick as Mom's granite kitchen countertops back home. Same dark color as them too.

I feel my cheeks grow hot with frustration. *Guess we'll skip this one and go to that Easter Island thing. You only have to get ten out of twenty pictures for those Maltesers anyway.*

Back to the white map with the colored exhibits and around to another room on the ground floor—and yet another reprise of a stuffed-full place. I tuck my elbows into my chest to snap a picture of the gray, eyeless figure of Hoa Hakananai'a.

Pretty, but not a stone-translated-into-several-languages pretty.

I bolt out of the exhibit. As little physical contact with people as possible and I can breathe again. I return my gaze to Uncle Laran's paper.

Let's go for something more unknown.

My sweaty index finger trails down the page to one of the top floors. People hate to climb stairs, after all. The higher the thing is, hopefully, the fewer the tourists.

"The list of items to find on the third level:

Cleopatra's mummy—This famous Hellenistic and Ptolemaic queen's corpse can—"

"Nope," I say, "not obscure enough." I blink away imagined images of the crowd around that artifact.

"**The head of Augustus**—A Roman emperor and—"

"Absolutely not. Everyone's heard of him."

"**The Palikari Laver**—This ancient artefact, taken from a Palikari temple to the god of the dead, was used during the Greek Dark Ages to supposedly bring about eternal life or reverse the effects of time. Historians struggle to figure out its true meaning given no written language existed during this time. The only evidence we have of the use of the laver was in a documentation of the Festival of Sparrows by Herodotus. He wrote about the event hundreds of years after it took place. When the Palikarians were faced with an imminent invasion from their Greek neighbors, they used the laver as a last resort."

I've never heard of Palikari in history class, and a laver sounds just boring enough to keep sightseers away.

Finally, we have a winner. Because, well, it's really a loser.

Hope swells in my chest. I race up the stairs, darting around a couple taking a selfie on the winding steps. I heave breaths and wheezes and clutch a hand on my side, which has begun to burn. I reach the top and scoop my inhaler out of my bag.

Good old asthma, kicks in whether or not I'm standing in a

crowd.

I inhale two puffs of medicine that tastes like chicken soup and follow the signs to the Greek exhibit—no markers exist for anything Palikarian in nature.

Good, so obscure the museum doesn't even put up a sign for them.

I enter the Dark Ages exhibit and notice the crowd has thinned a significant amount from downstairs. I guess people are more into Light Ages. Make sense with the phone glow that consumed the faces of tourists in shadier spots at the train stations.

A single visitor catches my attention for a moment—a man in a burgundy suit coat and pants.

Didn't I see him back on the Tube? Then again, maybe crimson suits are all the rage in London right now. And I didn't get a close look at the man on the train, not after my gut squeezed.

The clothes are what stun me, not the person.

He stares at an Etruscan grave with a creepy sort of smirk plastered onto his face. The painted, carved woman atop the grave, shrouded by a burial cloth, looks on at him with a mixture of shock and disgust. Almost as if this man with the blood-colored clothes placed her in the tomb in the first place.

My intestines tighten again. Huh, maybe I have a thing against men in scarlet suits.

All right, Harper, let's get back to the mission at hand. No use spending too much time looking at a tourist, not at the British Museum. You see plenty of sightseers here.

So I scurry back to the blank room with only one person inside it.

Nobody studies this period in their history classes. No one cares about what happened during the Greek Dark Ages, except for Uncle Laran.

He mentioned, on a constant basis, his dissertation. Apparently, he included a section about the first Dark Age in it.

On the wall above a British Museum worker in a neon vest, I see a dark blue sign for "Palikari Exhibit: 70.5."

Seventy *point* five? The poor little guys don't even get a full room, just half.

But, hey, that means fewer people come to this place. Yay, we get to breathe.

A faint flutter of light fills my lungs, my chest, and I feel my lips tug across my cheek into a smile. One, *one,* bored tourist in square glasses remains in that half-room dedicated to Palikari. She shuffles around with her hands shoved into her pockets, casting disinterested attention to some of the larger items on display.

She sighs and exits, nudging the museum employee with her elbow. "Where's Cleopatra's mummy?"

Bless, I have the room to myself. I waddle with giddiness into the empty carpeted exhibit to finally find one of Uncle Laran's items from the list.

Not sure what to expect of a laver. Uncle Laran's Anglican, so I think it has something to do with water? I venture toward the largest artifact in the back corner—an iron cauldron-shaped tub, large enough to hold a man.

You could pour some water into that thing. Jackpot, I think I found it.

I pivot in place to catch a glimpse of the other objects, in case I missed something, but none look like laver material. Some of the other items in the room do hold my interest for a moment. A bronze bull with foot-long horns in a charging position stands atop a square coffin. Did they bury their livestock or something?

No way could they fit a cow in there. The casket could house a child, a small man perhaps. Maybe the dude who was buried really liked his pet bull or something. I mean, I'm a fan of our neighbor's chickens. Even if they are birds, at least they wouldn't try to snatch a stray puppy like hawks do.

And they're not people who want to hug you and touch you all the time, which is always a plus.

Nothing else catches my eye, so I return to the laver.

A couple carved calves hold up the vessel, but besides those, not a single decoration adorns the thing. Plain as my face. I peek inside the bland artifact, but the whitewashed pot contains just as much on the inside as out—nothing.

I glance at the dark blue label beside it to make sure I haven't gone to the wrong part of the room. "Palikari Laver," the placard states.

Right place, I guess. No wonder not a single soul wanted to pay a visit to this exhibit.

Oh, well, a picture is worth a thousand Malteser balls.

I raise my camera. The harsh lighting renders the image on the camera far darker than in person. Fluorescent bulbs flicker, and for a moment, the one right above me shudders like a flash of lightning.

Then calm rushes over the room. Weird. Maybe they had a power surge. Better get the photo before everything goes dark.

The camera snaps before the lights can have a second opinion.

Pulling the viewfinder away from my face, I jerk back when I glimpse the photo. The bottom of the laver, in the picture, is filled with blood—or some scarlet liquid.

What in the—? Was that there before?

Heart thumping in my chest, I stare at the tub and watch with horror as the wine-dark fluid fills the cauldron, bubbling with steam wisping off the edges. I twist my neck to see if the museum worker on the other side of the wall has detected the strange turn of events, but she, engaged in a conversation with the tourist about Cleo's mummy, takes no notice.

Gut writhing with an anxious pain, I return my gaze to the Palikari pot when I hear a sickening splash.

It's not quite the sound water would make, not the kind of noises that would come from a neighbor's pool. It's softer and slower…and more bizarre.

The cauldron has emptied itself of all its liquid, leaving the inside once again chalky white.

But in the middle of the laver sits a man in a dark blue tunic.

Chapter Two
Why the Deer's Feet Run

His stench hits my nose first.

The pungent combination of onions and urine overwhelms me to the point that I stumble against a glass display case containing some shattered remains of a pottery vase.

Can't breathe again, stupid asthma. Fiery thorns wrap around my lungs. I'm tempted to dig out my inhaler, but my body won't move right.

I pinch my nostrils and gaze at the specimen afresh. Where did the blood go? The liquid disappeared like magic.

Mom hates that word, magic.

London does have that extra edge, though, with Mary Poppins and Harry Potter. Fifty bucks says Hagrid will pop out of the bull coffin thing and tell me my Hogwarts letter got lost in the mail.

Focus, Harper, back on man who suddenly appeared.

Clean shaven, dark skin, black curly hair, about my height—a foot taller in the elevated tub—he could be fifteen with such youthful eyes, but something about his hunched spine and weathered face ages him a handful of years.

Some part of me really wants to hug him or pat him on the back to support him as he stands. I usually assume tubs are slippery, but maybe this one isn't.

Ugh, human touch. *No way, Harper. You must be going crazy.*

Not after what happened in Phoenix.

His deep brown eyes flit from one end of the room to the

other, confusion stamped into his furrowed eyebrows and frown.

Yeah, this situation perplexes me as much as it does you.

Once more, I pivot in the direction of the museum worker, but she seems fixated on the group of British students from downstairs. They now flood the Etruscan exhibit. Their neon yellow jackets glow in the low fluorescent lights.

Shrieks from a student in a black Sikh turban pierce from one room into the other. At first, I think he's seen the man from the laver, but he points to a sarcophagus with the shrouded woman atop it. I notice he's gesturing at a girl with fiery red hair who has her hands pressed against the coffin. "Amelia, you can't do that."

The museum worker bolts into action.

She rises from her chair against the wall and marches toward the disobedient schoolgirl. She'd been standing before, but I guess she sat at one point. Even against the carpet, her black shoes clump like an earthquake. "Do not touch the exhibits."

How about splashing in a laver full of disappearing blood? Does that go against the rules too?

The tourist in the burgundy suit, in the other room, catches my eye for a moment, and I spot a glint in the pupils. Why do I have such an icky feeling about him?

Again, maybe it's the red suit. Kind of reminds me of the blood in the laver.

But he turns around, disinterested, toward a Dark Age weapon—a triangular dagger—behind a glass display case. Perhaps he stands at too sharp an angle to notice the phenomenon going on in the half-room.

I whip around and find the tub empty. Oh, shoot, he's out. Where'd he go?

The not-bloody man crouches a few feet away from the grave with the bull on top, hunching his spine more than I thought possible. He opens his mouth and lets out a pained sort of moan, as if someone had just punched him in the stomach. Like the splashing of the blood, his scream comes out quieter than water, but somehow the stifled shriek hurts my ears more than a horror-movie squeal would.

He rocks back and forth on his knees in front of the coffin with the bull on top.

Oh, man alive, my abdomen burns in what I can only assume is pity. I wonder if he somehow knew the guy from the tomb. Maybe he'd lost a friend when he arrived at the museum. A family member, even.

After all, I do know what that feels like.

I shake my head at the thought. Knew him? How did he get here in the first place? No, this can't be real. *You watched one too many* Doctor Who *shows, girlie.*

Bet the museum puts this on as a prank, to scare the few poor visitors who come to 70.5. Or he's some method actor who wants to pretend he lived in the Dark Ages, so this place hired him. With enough prodding, Uncle Laran would do that.

Okay, actually, with *no* prodding whatsoever Laran would do that. He'd show up and have to have guards drag him out, tunic and all.

My teeth press into my bottom lip as I convince myself that's what *this* tunic-clad fella's deal is. Yes, he works here, and they channel food-colored water into the cauldron thing. The pipe must come from against the wall.

Seems like tampering with historical artifacts, though. Plus—

"How do they keep the inside white after it drains?" I lean over the laver to spot a hole through which they can channel the red liquid. Not a single crack or crevice shows itself in the container.

Bizzare.

He groans again, louder this time, and I shush him, uncertain of what else to do. My fingers itch. To what? To pat him on the back? Why do I want to touch this kid?

And shouldn't he wait to put on this performance until he draws a larger crowd? Why not go to the atrium downstairs? He'd have plenty of an audience there.

The worker has returned to her spot, with her back turned toward us. With an absentminded hand, she scratches at her dark curly hair. The man in the tunic—either ignoring me or unable to hear—pounds his fists against his chest, then grabs clumps of his hair and gives a hearty howl. This one sounds like water instead of blood.

At last, he catches the museum worker's attention.

"Everything all right in here?" The walkie-talkie on her hip chatters as she rises and heads toward the stooping figure on the floor. She doesn't seem to notice me in the corner, all the color going out of my arms, and by the cold feeling on my face, I can assume my cheeks.

No answer from the sobbing man. She repeats her question and reaches forward to place a hand on his bare shoulder, where the dark blue tunic doesn't cover. The second her skin grazes his, he lurches forward and breaks out into a sprint through the Etruscan exhibit and out the doors.

"Sir, there is no running through the museum."

Yep, definitely not a museum worker. I think I just witnessed time travel.

The guard shadows him, her pace far slower. She pulls her walkie talkie to her lips and shouts something into the speaker, too far away for me to hear. I can easily guess the message, though—a hooligan dressed in funny garb, running around the exhibits, casual stuff.

A hysterical laugh bubbles in my stomach.

You just saw a man out of time, Harper. Freak out a little. I try scratching my arm to produce some sort of emotion other than humor. Nothing happens. I claw at my skin harder until a dull sort of pain comes and then two words flit across my mind—

Poor guy.

Ah, empathy. I don't feel that little friend very often. Haven't for some time. The sensation is a mixture of nice and tragic.

Poor guy, if he does come from a different time period, everything he sees must shock him. And now, I bet the whole staff will surround him and force the time traveler into some sort of research lab. Typical.

I roll my eyes. Claw at my skin again. No pain comes. *Man alive, you watch too many TV shows, Harper. Why are you so casual about this?*

Probably because of Tumblr. The popular site has trained me for weirder situations than this.

After some of the fan theories and creepy original stories I've read, a live artifact is nothing. My generation has been prepared for the strangest circumstances because of our TV shows and social media sites.

Except Tumblr taught you nothing about sneaking people out of museums. Or even what a diet looked like for people thousands of years ago. The aftertaste of the sandwich lingers on my tongue. I swallow. Let the museum workers here take care of this.

Yeah, they'll "take care" of it just like Mom "took care" of her marriage with Dad.

Then, something strange happens. I find myself moving forward, as if in a trance, toward his direction. Interesting, considering I can't stand other people.

So why follow him?

Some foreign reason prods me past the group of uniformed school children in the Greek exhibit, past the golden Babylonian lion on a sapphire background. Rooms wind like mazes, with so many possibilities of hiding places and dead-end corners.

I notice the museum worker has stopped her pursuit and retreated into her seat. Perhaps she's lost him. Or sent someone on another floor to scout the situation.

Think, Harper. If you wanted to avoid people in a new environment—like you do here in London—where would you go?

I stop and squash my eyelids shut.

Where would you go?

Visions of my church back home dance across my eyes. Images of the labyrinth hallways full of drawings from the children's classrooms, of stick figures grasping the hands of their parents. Of rainbows and cacti sunsets. Where on Sundays, after service, I would retreat into the lone stairway that led to the storage rooms downstairs. Almost no one would use it on a given church day. Everyone liked to hang in the fellowship hall to down weak coffee and donuts from a local bakery.

There I would huddle into a corner and wait as my mother chatted with every member of the congregation who couldn't avoid her gaze and beckoning hand quick enough. The first time I found my haven in the stairwell, she spent two hours searching for me. During those two hours, I could finally breathe.

He would go there. I don't know why I'm so confident—ask some Greek or Palikarian deity who might have an idea—but it seems like the right answer.

My eyelids fly open, and I inspect the wall for any staircase signs.

One reveals itself when I turn the corner, and I speed-walk in that direction, pumping my arms and puffing short, shallow breaths. Finding the doorway to the staircase, I dip inside and scan the area.

He doesn't appear in my line of vision.

I galumph down a few steps, swinging my arm and body around the railing and bumping into a man snapping a picture of a relief on the wall. Wow, nice, Harper, way to be a tourist.

I stop myself mid-swing to utter a half-hearted "sorry" to the man I bumped into—and because I hear a soft whimper.

At the bottom of the steps, I spot the blue-tunic-clad figure with his head buried in his knees.

The outfit rides up his legs, so I try not to observe anything in great detail. I imagine underwear had no place in the Greek Dark Ages. That could explain the urine smell. A few tourists waver nearby to pass him up or down the staircase. None seem to toss more than a confused, annoyed glance at him.

Heart thumping in my ears, I approach him on tiptoe, worrying anything too surprising could set him running again.

When I reach him, he jolts a bit, sensing me nearby. I remain still, and he recommences his moans. After a few moments, I slide down the wall and sit a couple feet away from him. Once again, he hesitates in silence, peeking out of his elbows to watch me with his dark eyes. Something about the way the dim stairwell lights reflect off his pupils warms my insides.

"Go ahead." I nod at him. "Let it all out." Breathe, kid. I'll be here to help you breathe.

He raises his head and cocks it to the side. He doesn't understand.

"Yeah, that makes sense you don't speak English. Guess you're really out of time, huh?" Come on, Harper, freak out.

Shriek like a woman from an '80s movie. Go ballistic, darn it.

Why does this feel so normal?

His mouth opens and he answers with a strange, throaty reply. Even if I knew his language, I would not know how to replicate those noises.

"And I can't speak Dark Age-ish, or whatever your people talk in. Palikarian? Either way, the only other language I know is Spanish. *¿Quieres salir el museo conmigo?*"

Do you want to leave the museum with me?

A dirty hand reaches forward, and he pinches a piece of my hair. Why don't I recoil like I usually do when someone touches me? Something about this feels innocent and kind of funny. I even let a grin tear up the side of my cheek. I try not to inhale the dusty scent of his fingers. "Never seen blue hair before, huh? Bet the women also don't cut theirs so short where you come from."

Guess blue hair gets you attention anywhere you go. Should've gone for red. I think back to the Palikari tub and the man in the crimson suit. Nah, blue's fine.

He says something in a loud voice that sounds like, "Kyane."

"Uh huh. Blue." I say the color in a clear voice, hoping *kyane* has something to do with the hue.

Groups of tourists balk as they pass us on the way to the staircase. I offer them a smile and wave of the hand as if it's a normal occurrence to talk with someone from another time in the British Museum stairwell.

The tourists do not appear to think so and continue to gawk at us. Can't tell which of us stands out more, the American with blue hair or the dude in a tunic. Tightness squeezes my chest.

"All right, pal." I place a delicate hand on his shoulder. He flinches. "We need to get you out of here before some British government official, or whatever, puts you in a lab or something."

Tumblr posts I follow have had a certain bent on government experimentations lately.

"Kyane."

"Yes, we've established my hair is blue. Just like your outfit." I point at his tunic, but he continues to stare at my forehead instead of my finger. "Now, the exit's around the corner, but I think I spotted some British Museum workers there earlier, so we should figure out how to not catch their attention."

I eye his tunic, a dead giveaway. Bet the one lady with the walkie-talkie told everyone about his outfit.

Then, my attention shifts to my red hoodie. He looks smaller than me. The garment could fit.

Without hesitation, I tear off my hoodie and shiver. I'm not used to sixty-degree summers, not coming from Arizona's climate, at least. I toss the sweater at him and try to avoid the expression of horror stamped onto his face.

Women don't take off items of clothing in front of men in his culture, I guess. Oh well, there's a *lot* more he's gonna have to get used to. Oh boy, how will we explain cell phones to him?

"Put on the hoodie." I grab the garment and shove it against his chest.

Wrinkles form on his forehead as he frowns, not comprehending.

I sigh. "Fine. Put your arms up like this." I raise my hands toward the ceiling, and when he remains still, I grab his arms and force them into the air. With purposeful speed, I shove the hoodie over his face and pull the cloth down. I make sure to keep the hood over his head, so we can keep the museum workers from recognizing him.

"You know"—I chuckle as he stares at the new outfit like a child—"most couples do this in reverse. The girl wears the boy's hoodie and never gives it back." Then I remember that his onion stink will get all over the garment. "In fact, let's stick to tradition. Please don't give me that back."

Does he need pants? I pause. Nah, I've seen people walk onto the Tube in kilts. His tunic looks like a skirt.

The Palikarian lets out a whimper. Sounds familiar. Like me back in Phoenix that one day.

"I know it's confusing, little guy." I stand, grab his hand, and try to pull him to his feet. "But we gotta rush out of here to get you to someone who won't hurt you." Why does my voice sound so high? I cough to clear my throat.

"Okay, let's see who we should get you to." Nope, the tone still comes out an octave higher than usual. "Uncle Laran, maybe?"

The idea occurs to me now. Uncle Laran does know a lot about the Greek Dark Ages. Why not bring this dude to him?

Although stronger than me, the guy relents and lets me lift him up. I guide him by hand through the atrium that leads to the main entrance. His hand feel warm. Oh, St. Olga, I miss Arizona's warmth.

Doing my best to avoid eye contact with the workers stationed at each end of the room, I force our way toward a group of tourists in matching hot pink T-shirts. We meld into that crowd until we reach the outside stone steps, and I refuse to stop until we approach the outside gates. For some reason, I remember to breathe in this crowd. Something about concentrating on the warmth from his hand aids me. The weak early-summer sunshine spills onto our cheeks, and the smell of a fresh breeze wafts, feeling out of touch in the middle of a city.

I pull out my phone to find a map back to Paddington. No way should I drag him on the Tube. His stench alone would give someone cause to pull an alarm.

Then again, that could keep people from standing close to us. That's a bonus. Maybe I should keep him around for the whole London trip in that case.

My thumb clicks the power button, but the screen stays dark. I press again—nothing.

"Did the battery die already?"

Mom mentioned something about our phones draining faster here, but I remember reading "55%" at the top of my screen when I arrived at the museum.

"Perfect." I can feel the headache swell in my temples. "Guess we're riding the Underground, then, since I can't pull up a map to help us walk back to Uncle Laran's apartment."

Hand in hand, we cross the busy street. He gapes at the cars and shouts, "*Harma, harma,*" the "h" pronounced in the back of his throat, as if he needed to hock a loogie.

"Yes, cars."

We cross the road and head our way up the street, passing scattered leaves and pigeons bobbing at a piece of stale bread that someone must've dropped. I dig into my bag and pull out my blue Oyster card. Mom put enough cash on this for today's trip on the train.

Uh huh, but how do you plan to get him on the Tube, Harper? No way you can scan the thing twice. The machines would know and wouldn't let him in.

I remember seeing the ticket machines—wall-ATMs of sorts—at each station. I could buy his ride there with my leftover money Mom gave me for the day. Thank the Arizona stars I didn't get that dessert at the museum.

Besides, if I bring Uncle Laran back a live exhibit, maybe I'll get those Maltesers after all. Chocolate and a new friend—not a bad day in London, no siree.

After turning down a few wrong streets and consulting a large white sign with a map in the middle of the sidewalk, we find the red logo for the Tube station. Already, before we arrive, I spot a massive crowd of people. Of course. Why did I ever imagine anything else would happen?

I flick a glance heavenward. A perfect cerulean blue sky fills gaps between puffy clouds. Oh, Lord, how am I going to do this?

The Lord doesn't seem to answer. Or if He did, I couldn't hear Him in the buzz of the people packed into the station.

Clinging to the Palikarian's warm hand, I pray as we enter through the doors.

Chapter Three
Why the Tunnel Runs Deep

The Phoenix Incident

"MOM." I CAN'T BREATHE.

I'm huddled on the sidewalk as the crowd filters around and over me.

"Mom, where'd you go?"

I lost her. Fire fills my lungs and I crumple myself into a ball as I watch the shoes of pedestrians step over me through my fingers. Forming my hands into a bubble around my mouth, something I read on a Tumblr post somewhere, I breathe.

Touch, everyone is touching me. The feet, brushing legs, touch, touch, touch. Someone claps a hand on my back. Not Mom, I assume. This doesn't feel like her cold fingers. Maybe they meant to comfort me, but I couldn't hear over the cars honking on the street, the buzz from the foot traffic, my moaning.

She takes ten minutes to find me. We head home right after that, but I can't catch my breath until we've returned to the car, away from the crowd.

* * *

London, Present

My fingernails dig into my palms. I'm face-to-face with the Underground ticket machine. I click the English language option and glance over my shoulder at the trailing line behind me, and beyond them, the Palikarian against the white wall. When we arrived in the station, I pressed his shoulders against the tile and placed a palm in front of his eyes.

"Stay."

He appeared to understand. Hasn't moved from his spot since.

I return to the machine and hit the "Buy Tickets by Destination" button. I enter the zone—I think Uncle Laran mentioned something about Paddington and Zone One…hope I heard that right—and pay about five pounds for a ride to Paddington station. A bright smile slices the Palikarian's cheeks in half when I approach him, sliding the slip of paper into his sweaty hand.

"Let's get out of here before it gets any crazier, kid."

Turning toward the ticket-taking machines, I dig my Oyster card out of my bag and place it on top of the yellow scanner. The metal barrier lets out a beep and the doors slide open. The Palikarian guy tries to trail behind me, but the doors close on him.

He mirrors me and places his ticket on the scanner. Nothing happens.

Whoops, forgot Oyster cards and tickets work differently.

At the ticket machines, I was half-tempted to buy him an Oyster, but the five-pound deposit prevented me. Wish I'd spent less money on lunch.

I reach over the barrier to grab his hand and place his ticket in the machine. His shoulders jolt a little when the paper slip suctions into the silver machine and out the top for him to collect as the doors open.

Red catches my eye for a moment as the man from the exhibit flies down the escalator. Huh, maybe the British school kids got out early. He must've been one of their chaperones.

That also means we have a crowd coming, yikes.

Not taking any chances of losing my new friend in the crowd, like in Phoenix, I snatch his fingers into mine. Ah, warmth spreads across my palms again. Something flickers through me like the electric spasms of the Tube lights.

Man alive, Harper, you weirdo, stop enjoying this.

We arrive at the platform, and he races to the colorful tile mosaics on the wall. He releases my hand and presses his palms against them, rubbing his fingers up and down.

Passengers nearby shuffle away from the man marveling at the murals. They clutch their bags closer to their bodies.

The Palikarian man continues in an ignorant bliss, eyes wide with wonder, as if he's never experienced artwork before. Maybe they don't have murals in Palikari.

Wind whips through the tunnel with the screeching sounds of an approaching train. Goosebumps and a shiver roll up and down my spine.

Since when did summer become so cold?

Then again, at our house, Mom always tried to conserve AC and would only flick the cooling systems on during the hottest of days. It will take me a few days to adjust to London.

A bright clock dangling from the ceiling informs me of the time in blazing orange numbers—four in the afternoon. Right before the rush hour hits. Well, the more intense rush hour, anyway. Every o'clock here draws a crowd.

I lace my fingers into his warm ones and force him off the wall. He lets out a groan of protest.

"I know, but we'll get to a safe place soon."

Instinct kicks in, and I glance over my shoulder and catch a flicker of the red coat before the fabric disappears. I guess the school kids and that chaperone are taking the other line at the other end of the station. Weird that men in red suits have appeared out of nowhere in London today, and that something about the color has caused my stomach to burn.

Dad did like to wear a lot of red tank tops and T-shirts.

My hair tickles the bridge of my nose as the train rushes into the station, whizzing past the posters of London's destinations and performances of *Twelfth Night* in the West End.

We duck through the beeping doors, and I yank the Palikarian over into one of the remaining open seats. Even if he held onto a red pole in the aisle, something tells me the unexpected speed would send him flying into the back of the train.

I stand beside him and offer a smile.

"Hopefully you'll like my family when you meet them." My voice jumps sky-high again. "They both like history. And you're basically history. So they're going to like you. Uncle Laran is all about the ancient stuff, and Mom's down for anything before the 1950s."

A man beside the Palikarian scoots toward a woman in a tan blazer on the other side—to avoid the stench, I guess.

When the doors slam shut and the cars tumble over the bumpy tracks, the Palikarian's fingers snatch the pole beside the seat. I watch his dark knuckles whiten from his tight grip. He clenches his eyes shut and grimaces.

"The next station is Oxford Circus." The overhead crackles with a cheery voice. "Doors will open on the right-hand side. Change for Bakerloo and Central lines."

Let's hope people get off at those stations.

He releases a sigh of relief as the train slows. I tap his arm, and when he at last deems the situation safe enough to open his eyes, he sees my hand outstretched.

"One more train we gotta hop on, little guy."

His chin bobs in a nod, as if he understands. With his fingers in mine, we both trudge out the door behind a throng of people.

Down a corridor, we hustle toward the next platform. When he sees us approaching the yellow line, his teeth bite down hard on his upper lip. He stares at me wide-eyed with an expression hinting at betrayal. As if to say, *"I don't want to ride that horrible, shaky chariot-thing again."*

Yeah, he didn't understand me at all back on the other train.

"Just one more ride, kid." I squeeze his hand in comfort. "We'll let you sit on this one, too."

I feel his hand release from mine.

"No, no, no." I try to keep my fingers clamped down in a cage, but he's bonier, and quicker, and manages an escape. "No, hold on to me."

He clenches his jaw and balls his fists. Saying nothing, he faces the opposite wall containing a colorful mosaic of the various Bakerloo stations. He spreads his feet shoulder-length apart, like a football player preparing for another to crash into him.

Trying to prep himself for this next ride?

The train whooshes in, and when the doors slide open, he rushes into the car before the passengers can exit. Classic tourist, he fits in already. I wait for the people to disembark, step on, and see the Palikarian kid—slash man? Hard to tell his age exactly. Maybe he's a teen like me—in a seat. He rises and beckons me with an emphatic wave.

"You want me to sit?"

With no other chairs remaining empty, that would leave him on his feet. Nevertheless, he continues to gesture me over. After five seconds, he shouts something at me that almost sounds like "Kathy." Probably not Kathy, of course. Kathy sounds nothing like an Ancient Greek—or wherever he comes from—sort of name. Really seems more like the kind of woman who complains about coupons at the local Walmart where some of my friends back home work.

"Kathy, Kathy, Kathy." He pounds his fist against the seat.

My arms spring into a calming gesture. "Okay, okay, little guy. I'll sit." I shake my head. "Man alive, you're more uptight than my mom." Still, I fight a smile crawling up my cheeks.

"Kathy."

I shake my head as I slide into the chair, gesturing toward myself. "Harper. Har-per." I pronounce each syllable in a clear voice.

He tilts his head to the side. Yep, didn't comprehend what I said again.

Train doors glide together, and he grips a scarlet pole in the middle between two of the doors, ensuring enough space between us. Perhaps to prevent me from grabbing his hand and forcing him to take my seat. Smart kid. If my legs weren't so tired, I'd put up a better fight, though.

A woman in a tight dress a few feet away from him shuffles more in my direction—away from the smelly passenger in the middle of the train. Her nostrils wrinkle to make a point of her unfortunate placement.

She bites into a fish and cream cheese sandwich. The lunch (or dinner?) fills the air with a sour, salmon scent. Talk about horrible smells, oh my Arizona stars.

The train trembles as it takes off.

My brave little man stares out the window, clinging to the pole like Tarzan on a jungle vine. I feel the train start to slow as the wheels glide into the next station. He tilts his head at me and jerks his chin toward the door.

"Time to go yet?" I imagine he asks me with those wide, dark eyes.

I shake my head. "Few more stations."

He frowns and sucks in his cheeks as the doors open and a few passengers rub shoulders with each other coming on and off. Determined, he resumes his firm stance, arms wrapped around the pole, as the train commences once more.

I suppress a laugh bubbling in my stomach at the sight. A skinny man in a Page High hoodie, with a tunic skirt dangling from underneath it.

Mom wouldn't approve of that illustration. So I approve of him even more.

We reach Paddington station, and he offers me a smug grin as I rise and join him at the center pole, about to disembark. The smile reminds me of an elementary kid who, for the first time, took a jump off the diving board at the local pool.

"Yes." For some reason, I'm fighting an urge to tousle my fingers through his curls. "Very, very brave."

* * *

We arrive at Paddington during rush hour, and when I see the disastrous number of people in line for the escalator, I opt for the stairs. With a resolute pace, I scale the steps and toss a triumphant glance at those on the moving steps to my right. I'll beat you guys to the top.

Turns out—I learn twenty steps later—they all chose the non-stairs option for a good reason.

Acid fills my chest, and my sides ignite in fire. Welcome back, asthma. I did not miss you.

Nearing the top, I gasp a *heh-uh-heh-uh* and reach into my bag for my inhaler. I'm not supposed to use it this much, but desperate times…

The tunic kid-slash-man passes by me but stops when he notices I've halted on the steps to take a few puffs of briny medicine. He asks me something in a higher, crackled voice, but I raise a hand, sucking in air.

"Fine," I pant. "Need a moment, that's all."

After the fire dies in my lungs, we continue the trek up the rest of the steps.

"Uncle Laran said he'd get here at five." I clutch my sides, arching my back toward the milky ceiling of glass. "Thirty minutes now. He usually arrives early to things, but that still leaves at least twenty minutes. I say we find a chair near the meeting place." Uncle Laran mentioned a Korean bakery place called Soboro. Wonder if they have chocolate anything. "We can wait for him there."

Whether the kid agrees with the plan or not, he follows me behind some glass doors to metal chairs across from the bakery, which wafts a strong green scent of matcha. It lies right across from a Paddington teddy bear shop and a grocery store. Even I can't suppress a grin at the little stuffed bears with the red caps and blue duffle coats sitting on display racks in the windows. You could live at Paddington station if you wanted to. I could take plenty of beautiful pictures here.

By habit, I reach into my bag and pull out my phone.

"Oh, right." I glare at the dark screen. "You died so fast." Rest in peace, poor little device.

I crane my neck at the Palikarian, expecting him to stare at this mysterious contraption in awe, but his attention fixes on the pastries behind the glass displays at Soboro. A pink tongue rubs over his crackled lips.

"Wonder how often your culture eats." My stomach growls from the lack of a substantial lunch inside its walls. Now the bakery smells of ginger and cinnamon.

"Let's check my arsenal." I pull out my wallet and find seven British pounds worth of change in there. "That could get us about two pastries from Soboro. Don't know what people eat in Palikari, but sugar is a universal language, in my opinion."

Eyebrows furrowing, the Palikarian stares at the coins in the zipper pouch of my wallet. One grubby index finger, dirt caked under the nails, extends to rub the rigid texture of a pound.

"You guys must have currency that looks different from this, huh?"

He continues to stare. Something tells me the shininess interests him more than the actual value. Who knows? Maybe he comes from the days of bartering. Where one caveman traded a tortoise for a bag of grapes, or something like that. Did they have grape bags?

I motion for him to stay in his seat as I approach the bakery, ordering two chocolate and ginger muffins. They cost less than two pounds each. A lady with a French accent collects the money at the register, asks me if I will "take away or eat in my order," and tells me to have a nice day.

The Palikarian almost jolts out of his seat when I return, approaching with food.

Oh, man, something about those puppy dog eyes warm my insides, like a toasted muffin from a bakery.

Suppressing an odd, giddy joy, I slide the treat into the Palikarian's lap and park beside him. Something so satisfying about sharing food with others. As I unpeel the wrapper from my pastry, I notice he doesn't touch his. Instead, he gapes at it.

"You are too funny." I reach over and shed the paper parchment off his muffin. I return to mine and do an emphatic impression of taking a large bite of the treat.

Still staring.

"It won't poison you." I pinch a piece of my muffin and plop it onto my tongue. The floodgates drown it in my mouth. "See?" I swallow. Spicy sweetness lingers on my tongue. "Tastes delicious."

Biting his lip, he mirrors me and squeezes the top off the pastry with his index and thumb. It glides through his lips, and the whites of his eyes show and his whole face lights up.

With lightning speed, he tears off chunks of the muffin and stuffs them into his mouth, as if he hadn't eaten in weeks. I think back to the woman in the British Museum mess hall and how she ate everything with a fork and knife. Wonder what sort of reaction she would have to the man lost from time. Already, a few British gentlemen in the area wear expressions of disgust after seeing my friend devour his muffin. They tighten their grips on their newspapers and briefcases.

Bring on the hatred, people. I like this kid.

Another woman, with the same raven hair and pencil skirt as the woman I'd bumped into on the Tube earlier, parks in a chair near the store full of Paddington teddy bears in duffle coats. Wonder if she went to and left the British Museum at the same time we did.

I turn my attention back to the time-traveling teen.

While he devours the pastry, a small pigeon lands by my feet and bobs its beak against the floor to catch any spare crumbs the guy drops. I nudge the creature with my foot, but its stomach wins out over fear, and the bird continues to eat.

Why do the British let birds into their buildings?

Either way, all three of us didn't get much of a lunch today. I allow the winged creature my pity. At least until it's had enough to eat.

I return to my treat and attempt to savor each warm-spice bite. Halfway through my pseudo-meal, I notice a lanky man in a worn tweed suit with a salt-and-pepper beard—withering like his hairline—standing in the doorway.

Uncle Laran.

He spots me and swings around the glass doors with a brief-case in hand. I rise to meet him, holding the remainder of the muffin in my right hand.

"Wotcher."

Oh, man alive, he tries too hard to be British.

Can't blame him a whole lot, though, for why he left. I'd retreat to London too after being engaged to his last girlfriend who cheated on him. She and manners got along as well as day and night, orange and a rhyme.

He sets his bag near my chair. "Didn't expect you to arrive here early as well, Harper. Thought you took after your mother in her tardiness." His voice feigns a proper accent. But three years of working here can only do so much to the American drawl.

"Take after my mother? Man, Uncle Laran, what an insult."

He tightens his lips. "Get all twenty photographs at the museum?" He gestures toward my bag, which he must assume has the list in it still.

I shake my head and my lips curl up my cheek. "Even better."

I rotate just enough for him to get a view of the guy licking his parchment paper. What a beauty.

"Uncle Laran, meet a Palikarian man."

Chapter Four
Why the Twin Doubts

UNCLE LARAN'S SALT AND PEPPER BEARD makes a scratching noise as he massages his fingers through the bristles. I hate that sound. Causes goosebumps to ripple up my arms every time.

The noise reminds me of Dad when he used to scratch his facial hair. Touch, touch, touch…ugh, can't stand that.

"Uh huh." Uncle Laran winks and nods his head in a slow bob, up and down. "I can see he comes all the way from the Greek Dark Ages. They wore hoodies back then, too, mmm?"

"I let him borrow it to escape without the museum workers noticing."

"Oh, dear." He presses his palms against his cheeks in mock surprise. "Not the museum workers."

Great, he doesn't believe me.

"I can prove it." My voice shrills in desperation, clawing at my throat. Sliding into the seat next to the Palikarian, I pinch a piece of my hair and nod at him to touch the lock. "Go on," I coax. "Tell Uncle Laran what you called this. Remember? Something like kya—kya something."

Blank stares greet me from both the man and my uncle. All that fills the silence for the next few minutes is the sound of a group of men wheeling their bags onto the escalators that lead upstairs to a Starbucks. The woman with the raven hair has vacated her seat near the Paddington store.

My cheeks flush with fire.

"Most people call it hair." Uncle Laran clears his throat. "Or in this case, an intrusion of personal space." He chuckles to himself. "Thought you of all people would understand that. Don't you have an aversion to touch or something?"

"Just smell him."

Uncle Laran wrinkles his nose and looks rather taken aback. He coughs and changes the subject. "Harper, how many photographs did you take at the museum?"

Ah, a more proper topic. Guess they don't talk about body odors much here.

I frown toward a woman juggling her groceries in her arms from the store behind the bakery. "One."

Then, the realization hits me. The one photo I took was of the bleeding cauldron-thing. It doesn't often turn red. At least, let's hope not.

I thrust my arm into my bag and pull the camera out, whacking the Palikari guy with the strap by accident. I flick the device on, press the triangle button to get to my camera roll.

With heat building in my cheeks, palms sweaty, I pass the camera to Uncle Laran. "Worth a thousand words."

The glow of the screen lights up his face. Even in the dim station lighting, I catch a twinkle in his left eye, a little spark. "Good Moore, is that blood?" He sounds way too excited for a fake-British man talking about something, well, bloody.

Also, "Good Moore"?

"Dunno, the liquid drained soon after it filled the tub. But the laver thing deposited a little gift." I gesture in the direction of the Palikarian.

"And the blood simply vanished from him as well?" He surveys the spotless tunic. Well, if you call brown stains with no scarlet "spotless."

"Like magic."

By now, no longer distracted by his muffin, the Palikarian

surveys Uncle Laran with a mixture of doubt and wariness. Even his legs shift a couple inches to the left away from him.

Maybe Laran reminds him of someone nasty back home?

Maybe he has an aversion to something too. Not touch, but perhaps Laran has surfaced an unpleasant memory in his brain.

Uncle Laran does something unexpected. He bends down, knees crackling, until he kneels right beside the Palikarian—who still tries to scoot away, but the chair arm prevents him. How very improper of you, Uncle Laran. Two clean cut fingers snatch the end of the tunic to observe the pattern on the bottom. *Oh, please don't lift that thing too high.* Crude white triangles alternate on a navy-blue backdrop.

"Wool." Laran rubs his thumbs across the thick fabric. "The pattern matches those I've seen in tomb paintings."

He turns to the man and says something in the back of his throat. His husky voice drops a couple more notches than normal.

I cross my arms. "What are you—?"

He holds up a hand. "Communicating in Ancient Greek. Studied it in my master's at Arizona State University. Granted, he looks a bit confused. Perhaps we never learned the correct pronunciation in school."

Weaving his eyebrows together, the Palikarian listens for a moment when my uncle tries another attempt at the ancient language. Then the wrinkles in his forehead relax when he seems to hear a phrase he recognizes. He replies in a tongue that comes out hoarser.

Uncle Laran pinches his chin like a thinker deep in his thought. Teeth flash a yellowish tint as he smiles.

"Sounds like a mixture of Etruscan." Uncle Laran snaps his fingers to recall the rest. "And Greek, definitely Greek, about the right combination for his culture." He bites his lip. "And the purpose of the laver could, in theory, be to bring someone from one time to another. They did practice magic in their culture, like you said. Not Harry Potter magic though. Something darker. More sinister. Unreliable."

So time travel is real. Maybe I'm accepting it pretty easily, but I do watch a lot of *Doctor Who*.

Pressing his hand on his thigh, my uncle forces himself to rise, knees cracking again. He glances over his shoulder to make sure no one had stared at his un-British behavior of kneeling on the floor. Then, he raises his hands at me as if to say, *Fine, you got me.*

At long last, an adult trusts my judgment.

"From Palikari." He gives the diagnosis.

Ha, told you.

And then I proceed to relay the events at the congested museum from the Palikarian man kneeling at the sarcophagus and crying to his mad dash through the exhibits and into the stairwell.

My pish-posh uncle stops me halfway through. "And you clearly didn't report this incident to a worker."

"They could've—I dunno—experimented on him or something."

"Good Moore, you watch too much telly, Harper."

"Duh, I'm American." *And so are you, so enough of this "telly" nonsense.*

We glower at each other for a moment, not sure whether to break out laughing or raise our voices into a debate. I break the staring contest. Nearby, a woman in a hijab thanks the bakery worker for her green matcha cake.

My uncle slides into my previous metal chair. "Since when do you want to invite more people into the two-bedroom apartment?"

"He can sleep outside."

"Harper." Warning shoots through his voice.

"Kidding. But what else could I do? If I was in his situation, I would rather a teenager found me than a government authority."

"What else could you do? Not have chased him and let a professional handle the situation. Like any decent human would."

I shrug, avoiding Uncle Laran's gaze and eyeing the teddy bears at the Paddington bear shop. "Well, I promised to get my family members souvenirs. Thought I would give you yours first."

He frowns. "How do you mean?"

"Haven't you always wanted a Palikarian friend? You like all that Greek Dark Age stuff."

Even he can't prevent a wry grin from forming on his face. He shields his eyes with his palm to massage his temples.

"What I don't understand"—his neck purples from suppressed laughter—"is why *you* helped him. Your mother calls you a misanthrope."

"That's not completely true. I don't hate people. I just don't trust them."

"And you trust him?"

"Give it time. But for now, he hasn't given me a reason not to."

Although he doesn't wear glasses, by the way Uncle Laran looks at me, he reminds me of a professor giving a student an eyebrow-raised expression over a pair of spectacles.

"All right." He relents, rising. "I suppose you expect him to sleep on the sofa or share my room?"

I lift and drop my shoulders. "I hadn't thought that far yet. In and out of the museum and to this station." I snap my fingers. "Just like that."

"No plan?"

"None."

"How surprising." He says this in an unsurprised tone.

"I guess we should get him back home at one point. Maybe visit the British Museum tomorrow and plop him back into the laver." The clock on a sign behind the glass doors reads a quarter till five. Beneath the timepiece, a large board announces in burnt orange letters the times for trains and destinations. They close the museum in fifteen minutes.

"Yes, I suppose we ought to do so." His square jaw nods at the Palikarian. "For now, we can afford him a bed tonight. The flat's a little under a mile away."

Uncle Laran offers his wrinkled hand to the Palikarian, but the latter shrinks away. Ah, maybe he doesn't like touch either. But why did he have no problem holding my hand?

Better yet, why did I have no problem holding his?

He tosses a helpless glance at me, and his lips form the word, "Kyane." Maybe *kyane* is my nickname or something.

"Doesn't like you much, Uncle Laran." Or doesn't trust him. Maybe this kid and I have more in common than I thought.

"No." His nostrils widen in a sniff. "I have a strange, horrible feeling I remind him of his master."

"Master? Like, he's an apprentice or something?" For like, a town crier position? The kid wails a lot.

"If he's learning how to be a slave, then, I suppose."

Oh.

I learned about slavery in my American history class, of course. From Bible readings in church, I know slavery existed for the Hebrews in Egypt. But the Greek Dark Ages? Did enslavement happen everywhere?

"Without a doubt, a slave," Uncle Laran continues, his eyes

brightening with intellect, voice raising at the opportunity for a teachable moment. "No higher standing based on the pattern in his garments. His dark skin tone indicates he worked outside, at least, according to tomb paintings. If he obeyed a woman—with very pale skin, I might add—it means he did not live in a high enough part of society to turn down your commands."

I glance at my arm in the greenish station lighting. "Pale skin?"

"Yes, to him that indicates you never go outside. A sign of luxury. But Palikarians weren't exactly egalitarian. So, for a man to obey a woman meant he was of a low rank. Hence, a slave."

My heart sinks as I watch the Palikarian's dark legs bounce up and down with tension when Uncle Laran paces near him—sometimes they bobble a little too high, couple close calls there with the commando thing.

Scared out of his mind, and no wonder.

We can't send him back home now. Not with the awful slave business development we just learned.

"Maybe we shouldn't take him back to Palikari." I grab the seat which Uncle Laran rose from, and the Palikarian's shoulders relax as I sit between him and Uncle Laran.

But what else would we do? Keep him? Kidnap him from his time?

No, no, Harper, not kidnapping. He came with you.

Laran rubs his face. "We ought to return him to Palikari, Harper. Even in less-than-ideal living conditions, he doesn't belong here. Think of all the films you've watched about time travel. You've seen *Doctor Who*. Any time someone disrupts historical events, disastrous consequences ensue."

The Palikarian scratches an itch buried in his oily curls.

"But." I hate it when my voice goes high. It crackles and

burns my esophagus. "The Doctor also breaks some of those rules in the show. He rescues people from all periods of time."

Puce crawls its way across Uncle Laran's face and into the corners of his eyes where the crow's feet indent his skin. That color appears on my mom when she struggles to think of what to argue next.

I mean, does he have a different plan? If we left our visitor out on the streets, someone could abduct him or hurt him.

For a brief moment, I think I catch the flicker of a familiar sheath of raven hair and a pencil skirt darting into the grocery store. I blink, and the black disappears. I need sleep.

Uncle Laran smears his palm down his face. "What place does he have here? In British society? Does he speak a word of English?"

"Look around you." I spread my arms wide. "On the road up here, I passed Greek, Italian, Indian, who knows what else restaurants. England accepts visitors from everywhere. You would know."

"Now, Harper—"

"If England took you in from America, why not the Palikarian from the Greek Dark Ages?"

"Kyane," the Palikarian adds.

"What he said."

Uncle Laran's forehead moves an inch up, an indication something intellectual and boring has piqued his interest. I recall seeing him do this on FaceTime. The same call where Mom asked him if we could stay at his apartment for the summer.

"Did your friend say *kyane*?" He attempts to mimic the inflection used. Like his English accent, he tries. He fails.

"Yeah, that's what I was trying to get him to say to you earlier."

With his thumb pressed into his chin, he mutters to himself again. "Sounds like the Greek word for *kyaneos*. The two languages do have similar roots, after all, so that makes it ninety percent certain he meant the color, as he gestured toward your hair. Considering it's light blue rather than dark blue, and *kyaneos* usually indicates dark blue, he can distinguish between hues. Most scholars thought this impossible in his historical context."

"English, Uncle Laran, please."

He presses his fingers to his lips. "Suppose he could inform us about the secrets behind the Palikarian Festival of the Sparrows mentioned in a papyrus fragment written by Herodotus—I think I remember someone finding another piece of the fragment with the date, but they never revealed the contents—which later inspired a Catullus poem."

Swiveling shoes squeak as he pivots around to face me. "Suppose we could keep him for a few months to answer some questions about his society."

If that prevents him from going back to a life of slavery, sure.

Laran continues, "My dissertation dealt with a comparison of the Palikarians and Etruscans. He could define correct pronunciations for his language, explain the use of the so-called Palikarian pantograph—oh, brill, the possibilities."

Fingers press together and then smoosh against my uncle's lips. They remain there in silence for a moment as his eyelids wrinkle shut and he lets in a deep breath to either control his excitement or soak in "the possibilities."

His eyelashes flutter open.

"Well." He claps his dry palms together and rubs them, creating an unpleasant sound. Dad used to do that too. "No time to waste. Let's get your friend home."

* * *

Aches throb in my legs from the amount of walking I completed today. Not to mention, by the time Mom arrives home for dinner, the jet lag has overpowered me, and I feel as if someone has dropped barbells on my eyelids.

I hear her enter through the whining door and catch a glimpse of her silhouette from the couch. I'm lying down, feigning sleep.

She seemed to pass every trait down to me, except for her high metabolism. The woman makes a skeleton look overweight.

Through a slit in my eyelids, I spot her jutting collarbone as she leans down to kiss my forehead. Man alive, woman, why? She knows how much I hate touch.

She stiffens before she can reach me. I stop twitching.

"Laran?" She's still bent over me and blocks my view of the television. "Good day at work?"

His voice calls from the kitchen in the next room. "Not terrible. No surprises. Yourself?"

"Good Saint Olga, no."

Mom likes to pretend we're Catholic. We go to a Baptist church, but close enough. At least that's what Dad told her when she migrated from Immaculate Heart of Mary Catholic Church to his home place of worship.

Don't know why she never switched back after…everything.

She likes the grape juice at communion better than the wine though. I don't blame her.

Mom groans. "My group thought it best to create a forest of selfie sticks at Kensington Palace. So no one saw the Queen today." Pause. "Laran, did you bring an intern home from work with you?"

Intern?

Then, I remember the Palikarian had pressed himself into the corner of the wall—right underneath the framed cross-stitch "God Bless This Home"—after we coaxed him to wear a pair of my red sweatpants. Not quite a crimson suit, but half-vogue.

Uncle Laran seemed hesitant to use his closet not only because he stands six inches taller than the kid, but also because the Palikarian refused to dive into the bath when Uncle Laran offered him a tub full of water.

"You would think he'd embrace that chance," Uncle Laran had said in a cheeky voice when the kid cowered in the main room's corner, farthest away from Laran. "He appeared to us from a laver, after all. Close enough to a tub. And the Ancient Palikarians and Greeks were obsessed with bathing."

Yeah, like Catholic and Baptist churches, lavers and bathtubs. Close enough.

"Intern?" Uncle Laran echoes my thoughts as I hear his dress shoes thump across the kitchen tile toward the main room. They stifle for one step when he passes over the circular carpet at the kitchen table.

"The teenage boy in the corner," my mother prompts, voice stern yet shrill. Her voice is father away. Through my squint, I see she's straightened. "Or…early twenties? I can't tell. Not that it matters." Her neck twists toward the Palikarian. "Tell me what you're doing here. Well?" Mom sucks in her breath after a moment of silence. "Young man, how did you get into this apartment?"

"He can't speak English." Uncle Laran's shoes reach the soft carpet of the main room and cease to make noise again.

"Did you pick him up off the streets? The number of beggars

we passed today…by Kensington, no less."

"No, Livy, your daughter found him at the British Museum."

She continues to lean over me. Tangy peach perfume prickles my nose. The scent churns my stomach.

"Oh, Olga. Harp brought a tourist home?" The peach smell dissipates when she straightens and steps away from me toward Uncle Laran. I relax. "Did Armageddon start, too? One of the tourists in my group acted like it when they couldn't see the changing of the guard."

Uncle Laran chuckles with his mouth closed, sounding more like hiccupping. "No, Livy."

He tells the whole story, and when he finishes, my mother's deadpan "hh" yields no hint if she believes the narrative or not.

"You do plan to return him to the British Museum soon, Laran?" Mom travels to the TV stand and runs a finger over a blue ceramic house heirloom. "Obviously, we can't keep him. You can't just kidnap—"

"He came willingly."

"Whatever, even if he is from some other period of history, we can't let him stay. Probably misses his family back home. His mother."

Fight her hard, Uncle Laran. We say no to slavery in this house.

His voice cracks. "Thought he could stick around for a few months."

"Months." Anger shoots up in her voice. I imagine her face has gone beet red but can't tell through my squinting.

"For research inquiries, of course."

Through my slit eyelids, I spot Uncle Laran claw at his neck, a nervous habit. "Livy, you must understand. No archeologist in his right mind would pass up this opportunity."

"What opportunity? To steal an artifact from one of the world's largest museums?"

"I *mean* to see how correctly we interpreted the evidence found in his time. Think of all the confusions he could clear up about the Greek Dark Ages."

Mom pinches her nose and shuts her eyes in disapproval. She releases the expression after a moment. "Wouldn't take a bath, you said?"

"Yes?"

"Let me try, Laran, to get him to clean himself."

"Livy, he howled for five minutes straight."

"Trust me. Besides, if he dirties any more of Harp's clothing, you will pay for every trip to the laundromat. Four pounds a load. And I know you already shell out enough for this apartment."

Seven hundred pounds a week, no kidding.

Through my limited vision, I glimpse her lifting a finger. Her voice always goes up when she does this. "Another reason why you can't keep him. You really want to feed him for who knows how long? Think of another plan. I'll work on the bath."

Uncle Laran relents, and Mom's voice softens when she speaks with the Palikarian. He answers with a few croaky whispers but eventually rises and follows her out of the room. Sandals squeak on the tile, and then the sound disappears.

Something inside of me wishes he would distrust her instead of Uncle Laran. After all, the kid and I have so much in common. And as far as people go, I trust her the least.

Minutes later, she returns. A subtle hint of bubble bath wafts from her, and I can hear droplets drip onto the floor.

"Deed, done."

"How?" Laran echoes my thoughts again.

"Motherhood is a universal language. And no matter what your age is, fifteen or fifty, you always miss your mother. No one is immune."

Right, Mom. No one but me.

Chapter Five
Why the Flesh Tears in Half

BEFORE THE HARSH LIGHT GLOWS BEHIND the white room curtains, I push away my covers and groan as I rise. Mom rolls over to the other edge of the bed and carries with her what remains of the red blanket. She stole most of the covering around two in the morning.

I sit at the edge of the bed for the moment feeling claustrophobic in the small cell of a room.

Sliding my suitcase from underneath the bed, I unzip the bag, letting the noise penetrate the air. Half of me wants to wake Mom up for keeping me shivering all night. Cool metal grazes my fingertips as I grab the laptop. Mom doesn't stir.

The door whines when I open it, and I pad in my green fuzzy socks out to the couch in the main area. A heavy weight from inside the bedroom releases from my chest. It even smells nicer out here, like a fresh hint of English Breakfast tea and subtle-sweet digestive cookies.

Alone at last.

I flip open the laptop and the screen's light floods the small room.

Though larger than the bedroom, the room still restricts any exaggerated movements. Uncle Laran, Mom, and I find it difficult to squish in the three of us amidst the compact love seat and armchair by the lampstand.

My mouse clicks the internet icon and spins the wheel of blue death—indicating my computer will take its sweet time to resurrect. Of course, nothing comes easy to me in London, does it? Ten seconds later, the browser pops up in my window. A gray pixelated dinosaur appears with the phrase, "There is no Internet connection."

Thank you, England, for the amazing Wi-Fi.

I type the Tumblr address and press enter once. No internet. Once again. Click, click, click, click, click, click. I bang my palms against the keyboard.

A door creaks and a silhouette with curly hair approaches. The Palikarian.

Before I can say anything, he turns the corner and bolts out the front door. What the—? Why? Where? Should we have locked the door?

Part of me wants to follow him, but part of me understands why he'd want to run. To get outside, to get back home, to breathe. After all, even though Uncle Laran insists we didn't kidnap him, I had grabbed his hand and paid for his ticket. And he didn't understand English. Maybe we *have* stolen an artifact, like Mom said.

Someone in one of my history classes mentioned how the British Museum is full of stolen artifacts. So if we took one of those, how does that make us any better than those museum curators?

Maybe I should let him go. I'm basically a tomb robber if I force him to stay here.

I coerce myself to peruse Tumblr—to distract my mind—until my eyeballs burn and I steal a glance at the door again.

But what if he gets lost? Or hurt? Or accosted by someone on the street?

Itches pull at my toes. I should check outside. See if he ran out there to get some fresh air.

I chew on my lip, sigh, and slam the lid on the laptop. Might as well say I tried.

After a groan and push off the couch, I slip on my ballet flats nuzzled near an umbrella stand at the front door and shove my hand into my PJ pockets to ensure I put the key to the apartment there. Don't want to get locked out.

The soft jangle fills my chest with relief. I creak open the door and shiver down the hallway, down the stairwell, and out the main glass doors.

Smoke fills my nostrils as a man stationed by a hazel tree puffs a cigarette. I bury my arms deeper into one another and scan the street near the apartment for any other signs of life. A pigeon bobbles its head near a scraggly bush, but nothing else fills my line of vision. Wind brushes my arms as goosebumps find their way up to my exposed shoulders.

So he has run away after all.

Heaviness fills my chest. Should've run after him. Grabbed his hand and—

No, that would've been kidnapping. Everyone should get a choice. We can't make him stay in the apartment. And after having some random woman dunk him into a lukewarm tub of water, I can't blame him.

I press my fingers into my pockets again and let the warm metal on the keys smooth into my fingertips. Time to go back inside.

As I turn, I hear footsteps. They slap the pavement. Swiveling back, I spot a silhouette with bouncing curls pumping his arms. *No way.* He beelines to me and halts when he reaches the steps by the entrance. Scents of pine shampoo from his bath filter through the cold, humid air.

Smells nice.

"Chose a weird time to exercise, my dude."

He doesn't return my smile. Instead, the whites of his eyes glint in the darkness and he makes a frantic gesture at the door with his arms. Then he throws a glance over his shoulder, as though he'd run away from some hawk that wanted to snatch him and bury him in its nest.

"*Thura, thura.*"

Yet another frantic motion toward the entrance to the apartments. The words probably mean "door."

I throw up my hands and hiss. "Okay, okay, calm down. Can't wake up everyone else in the flats." Keys jangle as I twirl them around my index finger. "We'll get inside." I glance at the sidewalk and notice the man with the cigarette has disappeared.

We march up the steps and I pull open the door. He darts inside and slams himself against the wall. Whites still showing in his eyes, he directs his gaze at the sidewalk. I follow his line of vision until he lurches forward and shuts the door.

"All right, pal. Now just what were you running from?"

* * *

"Had fun out there?" I feel something like a gasp of relief fill my chest. He still hasn't answered my questions, seeing that he doesn't speak my language. But the silence that fills our walk up the stairs and into Uncle Laran's flat forces the whisper out of me.

He doesn't reply but shifts toward the windows in the family room and motions to the lame celestial backdrop. Didn't have a chance to take a gander when I went downstairs. Not that I missed much.

"With all the light pollution you can barely see the stars." My eyes feel dry and begin to burn. Not the best idea to scroll on Tumblr for who knows how long before I went outside. "They've got nothing on Page, Arizona. Now, since you decided to come back, after giving me a heart attack, why don't you go to bed?" Part of me wants him to stay out here in the room with me. Mom would be scandalized.

"Kyane," he croaks, throat full of cotton.

"Go back to bed." I wave him in the direction of Uncle Laran's room.

Mom's brother refused to let him sleep in the main living area. "Might sneak away in the middle of the night, wandering the London streets." He had suggested this over dinner.

Sweet dates and salty olives still linger in the back of my molars from dinner. Laran wanted to replicate the sort of meals the Palikarian would eat back in his country. Cheese, bread, fish, the whole shebang.

Didn't seem to make much of a difference. He ate everything as if he'd not eaten in years.

Well, not exactly true. He didn't consume the fish. Uncle Laran later explained he comes from a culture which must not have eaten animals of any kind. Nice, kid's a vegetarian like me.

I noticed during dinner how flustered the Palikarian appeared throughout the meal. When I asked, Uncle Laran almost choked on a date from his laughter. "Used to eating with males only."

One other thing did intrigue me about the meal. Uncle Laran refused to serve the Palikarian water. He rummaged through his fridge and heaved a sigh when he saw no alcoholic beverages.

"Apple juice'll have to do. Either that or beer."

"He allergic to water or something?" I watched Uncle Laran pour the golden liquid into a glass. Mom also uttered a protest at the thought of a young man sipping on an alcoholic beverage. She always displays uneasy reactions around anyone drinking.

"To drink water in Palikari opened you to a world of diseases." Uncle Laran reached for a rag after spilling some juice on the table. "If we offered him water, he might refuse and die of thirst." He paused. "Come to think of it, beer would do no good. Nowadays drinks have a much higher alcohol content than back then. Don't think he's reached a university age yet."

So the apple juice supply diminished at dinner.

The Palikarian takes cautious steps toward me and tiptoes over to the corner chair.

Come on, Harper. Let him stay. He's not hurting anything.

Yet.

Can't really blame him for wanting to run away either. But what could've chased him?

Before we ever visited a major city, my mom would drill me on what to look for in a stranger who would want to abduct me. She packed pepper spray in her purse and a keychain with a rigged alarm. Maybe our Palikarian friend stumbled into a shady character who wanted to steal kids on the street.

Happens way more often in Phoenix than I want to think about.

Sigh. I haven't had personal space this whole trip. I should probably ask him to leave. "No, that's not what I said. You're doing the complete opposite."

Sinking into the leather seat, he cranes his neck to steal a glance at the computer screen.

"Look, kid, you're cute, but Tumblr time is sacred time. And you're lucky you didn't wake up Mom and Laran with your whole 'I'm gonna run away' stunt." I snap my fingers, and he jolts in his seat. I point to Uncle Laran's door. "Back to bed. Now. Before you run away again and anything else chases after you." Ugh, I hate myself for doing that. Wish I could take the snap back.

Sorrow and fear fill his expression. Troubled, he hunches his head into his chest, either in a half-bow, or to hide himself, and proceeds to stand and make a solemn trudge toward Uncle Laran's door. He halts and tilts his jaw long enough to catch my eye, enough to give my gut a cold, swift stab of pity.

His mien seems to say, *"Please don't hate me."*

Two seconds after, he ducks into the sleeping quarters.

As soon as he closes the door, the air leaves the room. So much for breathing.

* * *

"So." Mom avoids my gaze and busies herself with tossing her dirty laundry into a bag by the closet. "Uncle Laran and I talked at breakfast. He thinks you should join me on my tour group today."

As I sit up on my mattress in our bedroom, I don't reply.

"I also thought it was a good idea." She straightens from the bag but still refuses to turn toward me.

'Course you did. Fraternal twins must operate on the same wavelength.

"Thanks, but I can just stay here today." I lean over my laptop and refresh the browser. Still no Internet. It seems to go in and out. Last night, Tumblr central. Today? Nada.

She turns and takes two paces in my direction, feet shuffling on the red carpet. "You won't go?"

"Why would I want to?"

"Mother-daughter bonding time, of course." Her scarlet-painted nails shut the lid of my laptop.

I afford her one glare before I reopen the computer.

Mom continues pacing back and forth, four steps at a time.

"He suggested you accompany me because he needs you out of the house—"

Well, can't blame him. It's a tiny living space.

"—says Homer might trust him more without you as a crutch here."

My shoulders stiffen as I freeze and pull my eyes away from the bright glow of the screen.

Mom raises her eyebrows at me as if in triumph of at last catching my attention. Well played, Mom. The only other thing that could draw me away from this is a certain Palikarian running away again.

Images from last night flash across my mind. Did that really happen mere hours ago?

"Homer?" I flit my gaze toward the only object behind her, a 2012 Jeffrey May Award in a wooden frame. Anything to avoid eye contact. "As in the dude on *The Simpsons*?"

"As in the writer of the *Iliad* and *Odyssey* during the Greek Dark Ages."

Man alive, why did we let the nerds pick the name?

Pain shoots up my nose from wrinkling my nostrils so high. One of the English teachers at my school assigns seniors the *Iliad* and *Odyssey* for their reading. From what I've heard from my peers, the former put them straight to sleep.

"Ho-mer," I repeat, but the name tastes foreign on my tongue.

"Darling, we had to call him something other than 'the Palikarian.' Laran never had kids and hasn't named anything in his life. Apartment forbids pets, you know."

Oh goodness, think of all the terrible names he could give to cats—Great Catsby, Catniss, Harpurr Lee.

What did Harper Lee write again? *To Kill a Mockingbird?*

That's right, we read it for eighth grade English.

"Anyway, back to the tour. I hear there's a lovely portrait gallery nearby our stop today. Has a painting of Shakespeare, Henry the Eighth, and loads of other famous figures. Thought you and your photography eye might appreciate it."

The adults are going to drag me every which way no matter what I argue.

"Fine." I click my computer shut. "Where does your group go today, slash, can I avoid them except on the ride over there?"

"To the National Gallery, and yes. We leave in five minutes."

* * *

We jolt to a groaning halt and park a decent walk away from the pillared building. Our tour guide informs us that we have two hours at the National Gallery and will meet on the sidewalk at twelve sharp to travel next door to the Portrait Gallery, as Mom had mentioned back at the apartment. He offers to give a tour to some of the highlighted exhibits, but for today's excursion, the group will spend most of the day on their own. I thought my mom would lead the tour, but she blends in the crowd somewhere between a ten-year-old on her iPad and an Asian man in a suit and glasses. When the crowd disperses, I nudge her with my finger.

"So what do you do again?" The whole reason you dragged me with you to England in the first place?

"I participate in the tours with the group and inform the agency about what areas they can improve at various sites."

"They pay you for that?" I suppress a laugh as we pass a man dressed like Yoda by the entrance. He squats crisscross applesauce mid-air on some optical illusion staff.

"I should hope so."

"Why don't you give tours? I thought you liked history and stuff."

"Sometimes I wish they would let me. The tour guide they gave us is awful. We've gotten so many complaints about him."

Dozens of street performers congregate by the green and gold fountains near the museum steps. A guitar player serenades the stairs with an Ed Sheeran song. I shiver in the slight June breeze.

"And I still like history." Mom wrinkles her nose when she catches a whiff of one of the performers who stinks of weed, like the man with the cigarette outside the apartment last night. "Not as much as your uncle. He's more into ancient artifacts. I like older times when they promoted family values and good morals."

Not to mention slavery.

A guard in an oxford shirt and dark tie rifles through our bags inside the doors. Entering the wan light of the museum, we embark up another flight of steps as a museum worker encourages us to donate ten pounds in place of the free admission.

Spotting a massive amount of people within the walls, I trail behind my mother and catch glimpses of beautiful paintings behind visitors snapping pictures on their phones. Wow, can you imagine having a photograph in here? What an absolute dream.

We enter a spacious room jam-packed with people. Much of the clump congregates on the right side of the gray walls.

Hmm, let me guess, we found the Van Gogh paintings I heard about on the ride here.

The guide had garbled about them into a faulty intercom that released static after any word that contained an "s". But I did manage to catch the name *Van Gogh*. It appears everyone else did too.

I dive into the remaining seat on the wooden bench near his

paintings right before another traveler, a man in a turban, can take the spot. I wait for five minutes to catch a glimpse or more than just a mere spiral of a pine tree or the tips of golden sunflowers. But the visitors keep pouring into the room and crowding around the paintings. Mom wavers beside me on the bench and launches onto her toes to try for a better view.

"Portrait Gallery?" I shout up to her in the noisy room. Oxygen has all but escaped from my lungs.

"Sounds like a plan."

We burst out of the doors and into the cooler air, able to breathe at last. Rounding the corner of the building, we amble a short handful of strides to the Portrait Gallery—a gray stone building just behind the National Gallery.

Another bag check, another entrance, this time without as many visitors. Although I dislike portrait painting compared to landscapes, fewer people wins over waiting five minutes to see a single artwork.

Mom, twinning with Uncle Laran in his desire for older pieces of history, begs to see the paintings of old kings and queens. She slips her arm into mine and forces me to join her on the journey before I can object. She tugs me along like I had Homer yesterday. Maybe we *had* kidnapped him.

Then again, he returned after running away.

Scaling the stone steps, we reach the second floor and enter a dim room dotted with people and oil pastel portraits. One in particular catches my eye in an instant—a larger ginger man in a flat cap with a feather and a coat dotted in pearls.

In my periphery, I see Mom press a red fingernail to her chin. Beside her, a woman with raven hair and a tight black dress brushes past her to take a gander at a portrait with some other dude in fur and a cape.

"You know something crazy?" Mom's shoes do a little dance on the mosaic wood floor.

Yes, many things.

"If portraits existed during Homer's time, he would never have had his painted. Know why? Only the rich could afford the oldest version of a selfie."

Ignoring her, I continue to stare at the painting. He reminds me of someone I saw back at the British Museum. A certain ginger man in a burgundy suit. Didn't I also see him at the train station?

Noticing my gaze, Mom jabs a nail at the portrait. "King Henry the Eighth."

I recognize the name from history class. "Didn't the dude marry, like, six wives?"

"Uh huh." She nods, enthusiasm building in her voice.

"And he didn't stay married to five out of six of those wives, right?" I stare at her, allowing myself this once to meet her gaze. "Divorced some of them?"

The light in her eyes dims. "Uh huh."

Back to the portrait. "Some of those wives died, didn't they? Horrible deaths."

Her silhouette shrinks in my peripherals in the dim lighting. A heaviness fills my chest as soon as the words slip off my lips.

Yikes, I crossed a line.

I hate hurting people, even Mom. No wonder I don't trust people. I can't even trust myself to say the right thing.

Tears brim on her waterline. She turns away and mutters something about seeing a Shakespeare portrait. Angling away from me, her blonde hair seems more ginger in this odd, darker lighting, like the King Henry VIII portrait.

Chapter Six
Why a Horn Breaks a Wall

SCATTERED BOOKS AND DOG-EARED PAGES LITTER the main room floor when we return from the excursion. Very improper indeed, this mess.

In the center, surrounded by an army of academic articles, Uncle Laran sifts through leaf after leaf. I can only guess that he wants to find a certain document.

In the corner of the room, on the lampstand, a scarlet-hued cinnamon candle burns, wafting its sweet-spiced scent in our direction. I notice Uncle Laran has shut off all the electric lights in the house.

To help Homer adjust, I imagine.

On the blue leather love seat, Homer rests his chin on his fist as he gazes out the window. He offers us a fleeting glance before returning to his outside world. Beside him, on the armchair, his period clothing lies in a crumpled heap. By the looks of it, no one took it to the laundromat.

They might never do that. Could spoil archeological evidence or something. Images of George Washington's coats circling in a washing machine spin through my mind and confirm my thoughts.

Like so many time-travel movies state, we can't step on butterflies. Any major changes to our timeline could have disastrous effects.

My eyebrows pinch together. I remember what Uncle Laran had mentioned at Paddington the other day. *Should we get Homer back to Palikari? He did want to run away yesterday and only came back after something seemed to chase him.*

What *had* chased him the other day?

My gaze follows the Palikarian's to the outside world.

"Home." Mom tosses her purse on the kitchen table, extra loud to catch her brother's attention.

Uncle Laran tilts his head toward her, and a warm smile spreads from one half of his face to the other. "Morning," he calls in a cheery voice.

"Afternoon, actually." Mom checks her watch. "Four fifteen if you want exact numbers."

His black and white beard bobbles in a nod before he returns to the stack of papers. "Gathered lots of information about our Palikarian friend today."

Mom set a hand to her hip after she smooths out a wrinkle in the fabric. "In four hours?"

"Eh, more like three. He tired from trying early on. Surprising, really, given his staunch line of work. Nothing about the Festival of Sparrows today. He didn't seem very keen to talk about that."

He waves us over, and we tread around the paper labyrinth. Seconds later, pulled out of a deep thought, Uncle Laran realizes a stack of books traps us. The top one declares its title, *Art and Identity in Dark Age Greece, 1100–700 BCE,* by Susan Helen Langdon.

"Quite a collection you have here." I try to catch the names of the other titles before Uncle Laran scoops books into his hands to free up sitting space.

His cheeks redden.

"Thank you, but I'm afraid even with what you see before you, many gaps exist which archeologists—such as myself—cannot decipher—"

Oh no. Uncle Laran, no. It's summer vacation, please no lectures.

"—not yet, at least. As far as his history goes, we know so little about it, so authors write about other more interesting and important time periods. Wish I had a larger paper menagerie, though."

"Did he learn any English words today?" Mom directs this at Homer, in a high-pitched voice, while my uncle picks up a book titled, *Unwritten: The Rebirth of Written Language in the Post-Dark Age in Greece* by K. Johnson.

Uncle Laran wags his chin to indicate no.

"Comes from an auditory culture, though." Uncle Laran taps his ear with a finger. "They had no written language at the time, so I believe he shall pick up words within the next few days, sentences in weeks, and by the end of summer, fluent as a flautist in an opera."

The books now form into columns, providing space that hadn't existed when they were sprawled. A place to sit opens at last.

We kneel on the carpet. My legs let out a gasp of relief from standing and walking most of the day. A large book Laran holds makes a *thwap* when my uncle flips it open. Yellowed pages let off a scent of vanilla and dust.

"Even with the language barriers, we discovered Homer's occupation through pointing at a lot of pictures in these books and comparing his garment"—he jerks his chin in the direction of the clothes on the armchair—"with the patterns of archeological finds at Palikari temple sites."

Pages fly across his thumb until he stops at a black and white picture of a caved-in roof, bearing a triangle pattern matching the bottom of the blue tunic.

"Temple to Leinos—the Palikarian god of death."

Man alive, what a place to work. Thought my friends' stories of scooping ice cream during the summer sounded bad enough.

"How…interesting." Mom chews on her lip.

She tends to use "interesting" when she can't think of a more pleasant synonym. Out of the corner of my eye, I see her rub her thumb across a tarnished cross necklace in a mechanical motion.

"The little hunch in his back threw me off." Uncle Laran curves his neck for a moment, to demonstrate. "Most temple workers stayed inside and remained upright during rituals. But the Leinos Temple maintained a vast area for gardening outside. I assume he worked out there."

The god of death likes *living* plants, cool, cool.

Homer's silhouette glows against the backdrop of the tangerine afternoon light in the window. He gazes at the green world of a park near the apartments, an emerald in the city. The light stings my eyes, but I think I catch a hint of a content upcurve of his lips. Moments later, I realize I, too, am smiling.

Glad you ran back to the apartment last night, kid.

Uncle Laran pipes up, interrupting the tranquil moment. "Think we figured out his age, too."

"Teenager or adult?" Mom looks relieved at the change of subject from the god of death unpleasantness. Lines release from her forehead, leaving behind pin-straight imprints.

"Around the age of fifteen."

She clutches at her chest. Whatever wrinkles line her skin show their faces tenfold now. "So young."

"True, by our standards." He pushes an index finger up his nose, even though he doesn't wear glasses. Something tells me he just recently adopted contacts. Maybe in the Skype call he wore them. I try to resuscitate the memory from spring. Everything was so fuzzy then. "But in Palikari, he would start his mid-life crisis in about a year. Slaves and servants would've been lucky to make it to thirty."

"Must've grown up so quickly." Mom's wrists crackle when she rests on them.

Amidst the temple ruins in the pictures, I spy stone statues of various animals—a bull's head, a decapitated bird, a foxlike animal with its snout chopped off.

"Did they worship animals or something?"

An involuntary shudder ripples up my mom's spine when I ask this.

Uncle Laran purses his lips and stares at a water stain in the ceiling as if deep in thought. "Not quite. Some historians surmise, based on later Etruscan finds of sarcophagi, that Palikarians believed they would take on a form of an animal in the underworld."

"Really?"

"They revered bulls the most." He taps the bull in the picture with his finger. "So those standing highest in society would hope to take on that shape."

Not a bad gig. If everyone turns into an animal, they wouldn't have to deal with humans down there. Granted, no one wants to end up a gnat forever, either.

Wonder what kind of animal I would've ended up as.

At the mention of a bull, my mind flashes back, again, to the museum where Homer crouched by the grave with the bull on top and wailed. I explain the incident to Uncle Laran. "You think he knew the guy? Cried so much, you'd wonder if he was related to him somehow."

After all, I sobbed for a month straight when my dad died.

Random incidents would send hot tears spilling like loose

magma trails down my cheeks. A line in a movie, a crimson poppy in our neighbor's planter. A Mediterranean Sea poured out of me throughout that month.

Since then, I think my body ran out of tears for a lifetime. Couldn't even form a droplet of briny water if I tried.

Uncle Laran answers in the negative. "I researched the subject in the museum, but the rich tomb dweller lived two hundred years before Homer. Even if they existed in the same time, they resided on completely separate social strata. As a poor temple slave, Homer would not receive the time of day from that man."

My thumbs grapple with the short, fuzzy carpet. "Why react like he did, then?"

"Two reasons. First, the Palikarians shared the belief with the Egyptians and Greeks that if you remove a sarcophagus from its tomb, the person cannot survive in the afterlife. To Homer, whoever lived in that box died forever the second someone placed it in the British Museum."

Oh, man alive, that's rough. At least Dad thought he was going to heaven and all.

"Second, the temple to the god of the dead was situated on the necropolis."

"Necropolis? Like the Acropolis in Athens?" I tilt my head forty-five degrees. "We learned about that in history class."

"No, 'necropolis' means a city for the dead."

"Oh." Sounds like a fun place.

Homer lays his head on his arms and gives up his view of London.

"That means"—Uncle Laran says with a sniff, taking in a heavy whiff of cinnamon candle—"all the temple employees worked a double duty of maintaining the building and protecting all the buried bodies from tomb robbers. Seeing the bull-decorated tomb in the museum told Homer that someone in the temple failed at his job."

"Homer couldn't help it." I tuck a strand of hair tickling my nose behind my ear. "How could he protect a dead guy when traveling through time and space?"

Uncle Laran sniffles again and rubs his nose with a pocket tissue. "They had a different mindset back then. People worked more as a collective whole. Failure of one meant failure of all."

Arizonans kind of work that way, too. At least people of certain groups within Arizona operate this way. But Dad came from New York. Didn't acclimate all that well, and, it appeared, neither did I.

Homer's moans from the museum echo in my head.

"Do you think Homer worries he won't end up like a bull in the afterlife if he botched his job, Uncle Laran?"

A solemn sort of laugh gurgles in his throat. I've decided that I hate every sort of sound that comes from this man.

"Harper." His whisper sounds like a flicker of candlelight. "Homer was so poor that he would've ended up as a worm at best in the underworld. Good and bad people didn't really matter much where he came from. There was only the rich and those who couldn't afford to live forever."

* * *

Half an hour after our meeting in the main room, Uncle Laran sends me and the Palikarian on an expedition to Kensington Gardens and Hyde Park.

"Good exercise, and back home he lives in the outdoors. Could make this whole journey less foreign to him."

I accept the chore quicker than he expects, and he raises his eyebrows into a sea of wrinkles. "No reserves?"

"Need the exercise," I lie.

The truth—I don't mind spending more time with this kid.

Homer slips into another hoodie of mine, a green one with the Arizona flag in the middle, a copper star with beams of red and yellow jutting out in every direction. He uses the same sweatpants from the day before. I can only hope he borrowed a pair of underpants from Uncle Laran.

On the way to the gardens, we pass a beggar sitting cross-legged against a brick pub on a sleeping bag. She smells a lot like Homer did the first day I met him. She peers at me through a tangled clump of graying hair.

Homer halts. He tosses an expectant glance at me.

My skin tingles with the urge to leave the area.

This spot feels too much like Phoenix. When I had a panic attack in the middle of the sidewalk, a homeless man sat five feet away. Maybe he had been the one to pat my back. Reminded me of the way Dad did. Three hard pats after he—I don't want to think about the *before*.

The beggar, an older woman with a weathered face, cranes her neck toward us. Dark pupils bore into me until I feel my skin burn and fists sweat.

"Spare change?"

I make a move to cross the street, but Homer remains stationary.

"Sorry, Homie." The nickname rolls off my tongue in an odd way, but Homer doesn't feel right yet. "Left my wallet at home." I toss up my hands to indicate "no money."

He bites his lip, bows his chin, and we renew our amble.

Guilt wells within my chest for a moment, but I shrug off the feeling. Teachers back home say some people fake being homeless. We ought to give them a granola bar or food, but never money, they claim.

Uncle Laran's words back at the apartment burn my ears.

Good and bad people didn't really matter much where he came from. There was only the rich and those who couldn't afford to live forever.

Well, then it's a good thing we aren't taking him back home, right?

I chew on the inside of my cheek until I taste blood.

What if one day, Homer decides he wants out of here, and runs away again? I hate to admit it, but maybe Mom has a point. We can't keep him here forever.

We could make it work. At least, for a while. Not like we have a deadline or someone from back home in Palikari who wants to kidnap him and take him back to his timeline.

We best hope Homie doesn't have to run away from anything again, like the first night.

The road within the park is flanked by trees and grass. Living in the desert my whole life, the idea never occurred to me that so much green could exist in the world. Everything smells fresh, too. Like the world is awake and alive for the first time in its existence.

Joggers, pedestrians, and cyclists pass by every which way on the path.

We pass a round lake dotted with swans. When the birds flap their wings against the water, the movement creates a loud sound. Jumbled in the noise, a cyclist in a skin-tight T-shirt dings a bell, a lady jangles a few pound coins to a man in an ice cream truck, and a child shrieks as a chartreuse parakeet lands on his fingertip.

A statue of a weathered bronze man on a horse salutes us. We bypass it. I trail Homer's line of vision toward the robin-egg-hued sky.

"Want to go longer, Homie?" His stride has not slowed once since we arrived. My legs ache from the day before.

He gazes at each attraction wide-eyed and glowing so much one would imagine him exploding in a sunburst, a gardener through and through.

I try to take in the statues with the same enthusiasm, but 3D art fails to thrill me.

Homer breaks into a gallop when a certain statue nabs his attention.

I trot over in a half-hearted jog through a pair of foot-high gates and onto a circular stone platform. Atop a bronze mountain decorated with fairies, a little boy in a dress presses a bugle to his lips. The trumpet reminds me of a bull's horn.

A circular placard beneath the statue reads in dark letters:

"PETER PAN
The boy who would not grow up."

With his hands shoved in the sweatpants pockets, Homer bobbles on his toes and stares. Even when tourists dive in front of him to snap a picture, he refuses to budge. I stand next to him and glower at a tall woman blowing lip-pierced kisses at Peter as one of her friends captures the moment on a phone.

"You're kind of like him." I nudge Homer, who flinches in surprise. "A lost boy. The question is, should we keep you in Neverland? Or get you home?" My lips twitch. "At least you don't have a Captain Hook after ya, eh, Homer?"

He opens his cracked lips and forms a word. Then shapes the word again. "Homer."

His first word. Homer.

Something explodes like a light in my chest, as if I've gone supernova. And suddenly, for the first time in months, I feel—something. That's new.

My skin prickles when someone taps my shoulder. I twist around and see a man who looks like the King Henry VIII portrait. His smile splits his cheeks, and he pulls his daughter—at least, I assume she's his daughter based on the red hair they share—by the hand. She looks a little too old for that.

"Mind taking a—" He holds up a phone and gestures to the statue.

"Oh, sure." I drop my shoulders. Hadn't realized they'd gone up to my ears, but that happens when someone touches me. "Wish I'd brought my camera. I mean, obviously I can take photos on a phone, but not the same."

The man and the daughter approach the statue. He pauses before he twists around and cranes his neck at Homer.

"Mind if we include this lad as well?" He clears his throat, seeming to catch my narrowed-eye expression. "School project for Amelia." He nudges his daughter who has her arms crossed. "Has to take a photograph with twenty strangers in the park to show the importance of acceptance and friendship."

What a bizarre assignment, but maybe the British schools do things way differently. Stranger danger warning bells whir in my head, but I untense my shoulders again. English folk are polite, Harper. They aren't as prone to violence as Americans. At least, from what I've heard.

I motion for them to stand together, and Homer's shoulders skyrocket to his ears when the man drapes his arm around the Palikarian's shoulder. Discomfort crawls in my abdomen, and I hold up the phone camera.

"Smile."

Only the man does when I snap the picture. I pass him the phone and instinctively clasp Homer's fingers with my free hand. "Good luck on your project, Amelia."

She rolls her eyes.

The man dips his chin in a sort-of bow. "Thank you. We'll treasure this." He slips the phone into his pocket.

"No problem." A nervous giggle bubbles in my throat. I yank Homer along and trip on rocks as I speed-walk down the path. Better hope we don't run into anyone else like that guy. Otherwise we might have a real reason to get Homer home, so some creep doesn't come after him.

We both don't breathe until we return to Uncle Laran's apartment. Call me crazy, but something about that man reminds me of Captain Hook.

Chapter Seven
Why the Drunkard Starves

AMBER ALERT

My heartbeat thunders in my ears for a split second until I see Homer emerge to use the restroom in his—well, my—SpongeBob pajamas. The notification disappears from my phone.

Relax, Harper, who would want to abduct him? Nobody knows he exists.

I slam my laptop lid shut and rub my itchy eyes before succumbing to sleep. I dream about pirate ships, and fairies, and I forget the rest.

* * *

"What Palikarian delicacy will we consume today?" I stifle another yawn as I step into the kitchen. Uncle Laran has donned a pair of plaid green pajamas.

"Pancakes."

"Ah, how exotic."

In the dim kitchen, he pauses in stirring to squint at me, like a librarian scrutinizing a student who drew over lines in a book in highlighter.

"Figured we would introduce him to other foods. Since he plans to stay for a long time." His voice comes out short, like Mom's when she gets less than eight hours of sleep.

"Not to mention." He drizzles honey into the batter. "The Ancient Greeks ate a form of pancakes called 'tagenites.' Kind of similar to the dish we'll eat today."

Yeah, but he travels from Dark Age Palikari, not Greece. Maybe Palikarians ate seaweed for breakfast, for all we know. Dad did like cold pizza in the mornings. The thought of our little visitor eating cold food makes me think of my father and his own munching habits.

I clear my throat. "Cool. I'll set the table."

With an emphatic yank of the wrist, Uncle Laran pulls open the silverware drawer. "Don't forget the forks and knives." I swear I hear him add, "You Americans."

A moment later, Uncle Laran pipes up above the noise of a sizzling pancake on a griddle. "We plan to leave for Southwark Cathedral around ten."

Oh, right, I forgot about church.

"We as in you and Mom?" Hope causes my eyelids to crinkle. Much as I love the good Lord, I've gone on enough walks and been through enough crowds at museums to fill my people limit for the week.

His frame stiffens. He freezes mid-pancake flip. "As in all four of us." Glad to see his stern tone woke up in time for our family breakfast.

The image of Homer wrestled into a tie and suit flashes through my mind. The boy who gripped the pole of the Tube with such fervor. How on earth would we get him to hop on a train ever again?

"Even Homer?"

"Unless your mother counts as two people."

I mean, the woman has enough personality for five.

With a sizzle, the pancake flops over as wisps of smoke billow in the kitchen. Honey and sweet flour perfume the room. Ah, smells like the home country of Arizona.

"Again." Uncle Laran nods at the digital clock on his oven. "We depart at ten. Want to catch the Underground at a good time in case they cancel a line or two. They do that sometimes. Especially on the weekends."

I picture Homer on yet another train ride to Southwark Cathedral. Uncle Laran said the church resides on the other side of the muddy Thames.

And what would he wear? If the British clothe themselves in suits on the everyday, a hoodie will not do for church. Already, I need to excavate another dress from my suitcase since sweat stains the armpits of the olive green one.

"We might not want to start him at church the first week." I make sure to place the forks and knives in the wrong place setting to frustrate Laran. "He might not adjust. Not understand. Maybe we should start him off with something easy, like a VeggieTales movie."

Who wouldn't like stunning visuals about singing vegetables?

Plus, if someone dropped me in a mosque, synagogue, or Hindu temple, I would have no idea how to act. How much worse would it be to take someone to a church thousands of years after his own time?

"You said he comes from around 800 BC, right? Christianity didn't show up, for him, for another eight hundred years." I put the napkins on top of the silverware instead of on the bottom, too tired to do this right. And an itch in my chest wants to observe Laran's reaction.

A spatula flips an anemic pancake onto a plate near the stove. Is it even cooked right if it's that pale? Paul Hollywood would yell at Laran for serving us such an undercooked pastry.

"He'll adjust."

After a breakfast that results in Homer knocking over a glass jam jar, Uncle Laran coaxes him, with way too much difficulty, into a suit and dress pants. Although the oversized oxford drapes on his chest, Homer cringes at it as if the outfit corseted him too tight. Plus, he made choking noises when Laran knotted a blue tie around his neck. *Poor guy.*

The long Sunday morning commute across the river allows for a few open seats on the Tube. Homer insists my mother, uncle, and I sit before he slides into a plush carpet chair. I do notice, however, he chooses a spot nearest to me.

Little victories, our elbows touch on the seat rest. How can elbows also be warm?

He seems to flow with electricity. Weird for a kid from 800 BCE.

We exit the brick London Bridge station and I find my hair rising with static in the air. My dress also sticks to my skin despite the cooler temperatures outside.

Curse the humidity here.

As one of the first groups to arrive at church, we grab a handful of hard bronzed-hued seats toward the front of the nave on the right side. My protest that taking up a spot close to the front might draw more attention to our foreign friend than the back stifles as I crane my neck toward the stone arches that swoop toward the ceiling to join hands. I'll give Britain this, the place is beautiful, even if the building smells like a combination of old, wet, and stony.

Uncle Laran motions to Shakespeare's memorial statue. The bald bard, made out of copper or some similar metal, reclines, resting his head on one of his hands. "He attended services here during his day."

"No wonder English teachers love his plays, if they're half

as pretty as this place. How in the world did he ever pay attention to the sermons?"

Laran clicks his tongue. "Given some of the content in *Two Gentleman of Verona* and *Titus Andronicus,* something tells me he didn't listen all that much."

Homer rises and stares at the dedication to the Bard for a long time. Images from the Peter Pan statue dance in my memory. He didn't want to move from that spot, until the weird dude in the red suit wanted a photograph.

"Why does he like statues so much?" I lean over Homer's empty chair to poke Uncle Laran in the shoulder. "I know the Greeks had a lot of them. Did the Palikarians, too?"

His chin shakes left to right.

"Very little art existed in his time. And almost none of our excavations from the Dark Ages contain artwork with people in them. No statues, no tomb paintings, hardly a brushstroke. Anything with the depiction of a man must enthrall him."

Artwork without people tends to be most beautiful, though. I had begun to think that the dark Shakespeare statue was the only ugly thing in the whole sanctuary.

Homer returns to his seat beside me, and we take in the rest of the surroundings.

Stained glass windows speckle the sanctuary with blue, green, and yellow light. At the sanctuary front, a wall cradles life-sized stone figures. Saints, maybe? I wonder if good ol' Olga is up there. Instead, I spot a golden mother crouching next to a child, most likely Jesus.

Members file in until the clatter of the metallic bells indicates the start of service.

As one of the members swings incense, I cough at the burning scent. Do people from England have no asthma?

We rise when the choir in white robes fills the stone walls with high, pure voices. The word "Jerusalem" repeats in the refrain. Goosebumps ripple up my arms.

I gaze at an even older relic than the church, Homer, as he echoes the movements of the congregation members. He emerges and recedes into his seat along with the crowd. When the choir sings, and the members join in the chorus, he listens. I watch as he shuts his eyes and attempts to concentrate on the words, trying to absorb them, comprehend them.

Tears sparkle in my mother's eyes when she spots this phenomenon. Something tells me she thinks we're "getting through to him" on the evangelism front.

She does like to hand out church pamphlets to strangers at Sam's Club back home.

One step at a time, Mom. We gotta teach him words first.

The pastor—or whatever Anglican churches call the person talking up front—gives a sermon from 1 Corinthians about greed and how certain church members used to gorge themselves on the bread and wine of Christ while others in the field received nothing at the table. He applies this to taking care of the poor and all that, but I zone out within the first five minutes of the sermon.

No wonder Shakespeare never paid attention. I could fall asleep to this monotone voice.

We reach the communion part of the service where everyone files into a line and approaches the front of the sanctuary. The recipients kneel, and a priest or some sort of high official in the Anglican church—don't quote me—places a round slice of bread into the participant's hand. Then, everyone takes a sip of red wine from the enormous communion chalice.

Oh, gross, everyone's lips touched that. Touch, touch, touch. Shivers dart up and down my spine.

Sitting to my left, Homer goes in front of me, mirroring Uncle Laran ahead of him. Isn't there some sort of rule against non-Christians doing communion? Either way, the adults don't seem to mind.

Homer kneels beside Uncle Laran and plops the bread slice into his mouth same as everyone.

But when a man approaches him with the heavy communion cup full of wine, his eyes widen. When the gold rim reaches his lips, he snatches the goblet from the man's hands, tilts his chin back, and begins to drain the entire draught.

Mirth bubbles in my stomach.

The attendants watch in horror as his Adam's apple bobbles to the scarlet liquid pouring down his throat. He finishes, hands the cup back, and wipes his mouth with his sleeve. That stain won't get out anytime soon. Good thing he didn't wear a white choir robe.

I suppress a snicker, and can feel my face turn pink.

I watch him stagger back to his seat when I stoop at the altar. They slide a piece of bread into my palm and have me take a "sip" of the wine, even though only a few rosy droplets remain at the bottom.

"The blood of Christ."

Not too terrible. The mixture tastes like sour grape juice.

I take my seat and notice how my mother's cheeks have blanched. Meanwhile, Uncle Laran's face grows purple as he tries to suppress laughter. I join him in his reaction. Can I take this kid back with me to Arizona?

That could solve the Captain Hook problem. No more running away from things, and no worries about sending him back to a world of slavery.

Homer, on the other hand, appears rather pink. He drapes

himself over the chair and bellows a laugh at a woman in the row behind him. She's an older lady in a gray dress, and she gawks at him, petrified. Her grip tightens on her brown handbag.

His giggling ceases.

Homer propels himself forward and bellows what sounds like a tune to a song, or a chant of some sort, but I would not propose Homer try out for any singing competition any time soon. His notes sound sourer than the wine served for communion. He slaps his knees in a rhythm and bobs along to the beat as the congregation files in a stiff line toward the front to receive communion. What's left of it, anyway.

Uncle Laran collects himself and motions for us to leave the service. Got it. We've upstaged the pastor.

Laran and I each grab one of Homer's arms and lead him toward the doors. He slumps like a dead weight and belts out a song which might've sounded like "His Eye Is on the Sparrow" if you tried hard to believe it followed the same tune.

On our way out, we pass the man who I saw in the park the other day, accompanied by his daughter Amber. No wait, Amelia. He seems to be the only one grinning, amused.

I give him a half-salute and march out of the sanctuary. So long, Captain Hook.

* * *

"Keep him a day longer, Laran, and Harper and I are going to stay somewhere else."

Through the shut bedroom door, my mother's voice still carries well from her place in the family room.

It always did, especially in her arguments with Dad.

Interspersed between her shouts come moans from Homer. Right when I left him to seek refuge in my room—before Mom and Laran's impending fight—Homer crouched into a fetal position on the blue love seat and rocked back and forth from a terrible hangover. Palms covered his eyes to block out the light, but he switched them back and forth between his eyes and ears to form a barricade against any noises.

To make matters worse, he puked on the Tube on the ride back home. And, of course, he carried that stench with him all the way back to the apartment until Mom forced him into a pine-laden bath.

I love the scent of pine, though. Five stars, I do recommend.

Glad Uncle Laran ended up cancelling our reservations for a Sunday roast at the Southwark Tavern, a supposed Sunday tradition. Homer may have upchucked the blood of Christ all over the food in that case. Not to mention the roast part of that involves meat, and so I would not receive much of a meal today if we went.

"Come on, Livy. He was a little greedy at communion, that's all. Those in his social strata would never have been allowed near wine, let alone tasted the drink."

"You know why that whole episode upset me."

I crumple my fists into balls. How typical of mom to want to get rid of the only human I trust.

"A world of difference exists between that boy and your husband, Liv."

I sigh and rub my fingers across the comforter on the bed to distract myself. By touch, the blanket offers no fuzzy warmth, but the fabric does help to clear off the sweat on my fingertips.

Then, I graze the cool lid of my computer. But as soon as I open it, I clam the device shut. Don't feel much like scrolling. Don't feel much like doing anything, really. I sprawl out on the bed and entomb my face into the itchy comforter.

My mother's shrill sobs bounce off the tight apartment walls. Her last defense to get anyone to submit to her will. "Never, never did I experience as much embarrassment as in church today. Be glad he didn't invoke the wrath of God, which could have struck him dead on the spot. Be glad we haven't either for keeping him in our apartment for so long. There are severe consequences to messing with timelines, Laran. It's demonic. Unnatural."

An odd noise comes from her mouth which resembles either the crack of a whip or a bolt of lightning. I hazard a guess at the latter, and picture her accompanying her warning with a hand gesture.

"Something tells me God has a sense of humor these days, Liv. Maybe he enjoyed the scene."

Bless your soul, Uncle Laran. Glad you're actually sticking through this argument.

Mom lets out a loud huff, followed by a short, "Well!"

Wow, great defense, Mom. A thud draws my attention to the window. A pigeon cocks its head at me and zooms away. Fly, Peter Pan, fly far away from here.

"Liv, even if we desired to take him home, we don't know how to replicate the process that got him here. It could involve Palikarian rituals."

Speaking of Peter Pan, why did Hook come to church today? Bizarre bumping into him at the park and then church. London has more than one active church, right?

Cold shock ripples through me. Has he been *following* us?

I palm my eye sockets and groan. Relax, Harper, you're acting like you did back when you learned to drive. Any time a car followed you down more than three streets you thought they'd come after you.

Besides, no one knows about Homer, right?

"It very well may not involve rituals, Laran. Let's think of something else."

"Herodotus thought the opposite in his fragment. It most certainly involved some sort of dark magic. Are you, of all people, willing to replicate that? To get him back home?"

Dark magic. Huh, that could explain why the blood disappeared from Homer and laver in the museum. Maybe that's how he traveled in time.

I shake my head at myself. Time travel is one thing. But magic? Then again, when it came to Harry Potter, many of my youth leaders warned that all fantasy has a basis in fact, and quite a few students in my school have Wiccan parents.

A moment later, someone slams their hand against what sounds like wood…maybe one of the kitchen cabinets? "If you do nothing about him, Laran, I will go to the British Museum myself to figure out how to expedite the journey back to Palikari."

Oh, woman, must you ruin everything?

"You know you can't keep him forever, Laran. If someone from the museum isn't after him soon, some other professor with an interest in the Dark Ages is going to come nab him. Not to mention any number of government officials who would be happy to get their hands on a time traveler. You've told me plenty about archeologists and tomb raiders. How much time until you think someone's going to knock at that door and take him away from you?"

"Paranoid as always."

A rustling movement outside the door indicates Mom's arms wrestling themselves into a light jacket. Light mauve, scented with her peach perfume. I hear her clack in heels toward the front door and squeak it open.

"Careful, Livy." My uncle clicks his tongue against his teeth. "Herodotus says the ritual involves a possible blood sacrifice, and definitely chanting dark magic. Quite certain you want to risk invoking the wrath of God just to send him back to Palikari?"

He follows this up with the same din of a lightning bolt my mom made a minute ago.

The slamming of a door answers in reply. Because, even if we gave Mom a handful of hours, she could never articulate any words to formulate a clever comeback.

My lips glide up my cheeks

I don't quite trust Uncle Laran—not like Homie, anyway. But as far as adults go, he ain't half bad.

Chapter Eight
Why the Secret Slander Slips

Two hours after the episode, Mom returns from the museum. Her blonde hair flies in wild directions either from the London wind or from speed-walking. I hazard a hypothesis at both.

Something inside of me wishes Uncle Laran gave his spare key to me instead of Mom so we could lock her out of the brick building and prevent her from taking Homie. He asked me to give the key back after I'd gone out to retrieve Homer the night he ran away.

"Shall we grab Homer's suitcase, Liv?" Uncle Laran places some crackers on a green plate and slides the dish onto the lampstand near Homer, who's sleeping on the couch. "For Homer when he wakes," he tells me.

He returns to Mom who bears a rosy glow in her cheeks from her brisk strides. Although it would make most humans look attractive, she reminds me of the color of tomato juice.

"Well?" Uncle Laran raises his eyebrows as he pops one of the crackers into his mouth.

I follow suit and let the buttery saltiness electrify my taste buds. Homie might not get any of these if they taste this good. When did I last eat?

Mom huffs at Laran and drops her purse on the table. "I spoke with a helpful man at the Palikari exhibit."

"Who gave you a satanic ritual to recite?" Uncle Laran makes a lightning noise through clenched teeth.

Mom affords him one eye roll. "No." She pauses. "Although he did have red hair."

"Like the devil?"

"No. No curls. Pin-straight."

Okay, who came up with the idea that Satan has red curly hair anyway? Probably some guy who hated orphan Annie or something. We put on that play during my seventh-grade year. Yours truly worked on the deck crew, moving around sets during the show for extra credit. Can never get those forty hours of my life back.

"A ginger without a soul, Livy…definitely the ritual type." Laran's whiskers twitch when he grins, taunting.

Fingers on hips make Mom's hand look like spider legs sprawling across her abdomen. She faces me. "Nice day?"

"Indeed." I stick a pinky out and mock a British accent— one thing Mom warned me not to do here. "Your brother and I chanted satanic rituals in your absence. Jolly good fun, dark magic is."

I catch a quick glance of approval from Uncle Laran. He winks. I think we just bonded.

Mom groans a similar noise to what I imagine a musk ox would make. Closed mouth, moaning through the nostrils. "All right." She throws up her hands. "I won't tell you two about my experience at the museum."

Fine with me.

Not fine with Uncle Laran, because he presses a palm on her shoulder. "Forgive us. Just wanted to lighten the mood."

Mom slides into a chair at the table and juts her nose in the air, refusing to utter a word until her brother apologizes three times. After the third *mea culpa,* Mom sniffs, exhales, and begins her tale.

"What surprised me most about the exhibit was how many workers they had in that little half-room for such an obscure period in history. They stationed a security person at every corner."

Panic seizes me. Did they sees us? Increase security because Homer had escaped from that exhibit? How long until they would axe down our door?

Squeezing my eyelids shut, I try to envision the small exhibit. A bull shape forms in the blur of darkness.

My eyelids fly open. "When I visited, only one woman worked nearby, in the Etruscan room." I imagine the woman sitting in a chair with her back to us, discussing Cleopatra's mummy. "And I feel like they should fire her, because she took her sweet time in figuring out a *live human* came out of one of the exhibits."

"Maybe they caught Homer's entry on camera and increased the security there." Mom wipes a stray hair off her forehead. Despite her wishes, it flops back to the same place it started. "I saw signs about CCTV security when they checked my bags. Bet they placed cameras all over the building."

Or maybe they had those before Homer showed up. You don't really think to observe those kinds of things when you have no intention of stealing artifacts in the first place.

I picture two men in white oxfords in a dark control room watching a computer screen as blood fills the iron laver and a teenager emerges from the artifact.

With his laver watched by four guards, no way we can just dunk Homer in and hope no one tackles us before we can chant the right ritual. I imagine dozens of wanted posters with illustrations of a man in a tunic plastered on the columns at the entrance. Even if we could get past the security check without drawing attention…

So much for needing to get him home. Fine with me. That

means no slavery today.

"Welp, I guess that's too bad. Can't get Homie home. Plan B?" I reach for a nearby pillow and dig my fingers into the cotton. It feels nice to claw at something, to squeeze the life out of this cushion.

"You didn't let me finish." Mom glares at me from across the room. She taps her foot and waits for an apology.

I shrug and meet her gaze. *You will not get one from me.*

She breaks the staring contest. "Anyway, the fellow in a suit with the non-devil red hair—I assumed a museum worker—approached me when I was staring at the laver. He said he knew a little about the history behind it. He told me a few facts, and when I pressed him about the rituals behind it, we traded emails to be able to run through my dozens of inquiries."

Eyebrows raised, she watches each of our reactions. Neither seem to impress her, because the lights dim in her cheeks. She clears her throat. "So that means, we got a personal historian from the British Museum to give me the information to help Homer on his journey home."

"Personal historian, eh?" The wrinkles in Uncle Laran's forehead deepen. He looks a little hurt. "Too bad this apartment didn't provide you one."

"A historian who shares my interest in protecting history." Mom lifts a finger as she corrects him. "The sooner we send him back, the sooner everything goes back to the way it's supposed to be. All this tampering with timelines is"—she shudders—"unnatural."

She rises and snaps her fingers at me. Irritation prickles throughout my skin, heat rising on every inch of flesh.

"Where did you put your laptop, Harper?"

I stare at my hands and refuse to meet her gaze. Then my

attention shifts to Homer passed out on the couch. With a huff, Mom rushes into our room and slams the door. Emerging seconds later, she thrusts open the laptop. Angry fingertips prattle against the keyboard.

"Password, Harper."

"Pretty sure the password isn't 'Harper,' Mom, but nice guess."

"Password."

"Forgot the magic word." Oooh, magic. She hates that word. Nice one, Harper. Wish I could give myself a high five. Maybe I can teach Homie how to do one later.

A palm crashes on the tabletop, causing all the legs to wobble. "If I ask a third time, you lose the laptop."

"Password's Phoenix."

She stiffens. "Phoenix?" She chokes on the word.

By instinct, I glide my fingers over the scar on my left wrist. Her gaze seems to follow my movements.

"Phoenix. Need me to spell it for you?"

Her lips tremble for a moment as silvery tears brim beneath her eyelids. Heat burns in my gut. I crossed a line again. How many more will I pass before I snag my foot on a tripwire? Before I cause an irreparable explosion between the two of us?

I duck into my room and lock the door.

Chapter Nine
Why the King Hunts a Mountain Partridge

Right before the Phoenix Incident

"Harper, how about we go to Phoenix today?" Mom asks this.

I grip the bandage on my wrist. The other day, he'd barely nicked me, by accident with the broken end of a beer bottle. Had a little too much alcohol last night, but three pats on my back later, he promised never to hurt me again.

And asked me to please not tell Mom.

I didn't, but she found out anyway.

"What do you say? You and your mom in Phoenix? A day trip, full of shopping, good food, and one-on-one time." She wants to go out today to get away from him. She'd found out about the cut and couldn't even look at him this morning. Mom reaches for my other wrist, the unbandaged one.

A whimper escapes through my nostrils. "Don't."

"You don't want to go? We can always try tomorrow."

"Don't touch."

* * *

London, Present

Morning brings the clattering of the calming computer and a wide-awake Palikarian, staring at the couch in a daze, as if confused how he got there in the first place. Not going to lie, it's kind of adorable.

"Laran." My mother rubs a pair of bloodshot eyes. "Remind me of your apartment's address."

"Peek outside and you tell me."

"I'm asking because the man from the museum wants to ship us a book on the Greek Dark Ages. From the museum's store, for *free*. If you saw the prices of the books in there…it's practically a steal. I want to get back to him fast before he takes the offer away."

That sounds sketchy.

I've had friends get fired from sneaking drinks on the job at fast food restaurants. Who would risk their job like that? Even if they could give away books, the merch doesn't come cheap in that store.

"Liv, you're talking to a man who wrote about the Greek Dark Ages for his dissertation. I probably have a copy." He moves toward a bookshelf nuzzled in the corner near the television.

Mom jerks her head, sipping coffee from a mug with a painted British flag design. "He says they came out with it a week ago or so. It covers rituals and temple practices, all new findings on the subject. Here, read the email."

Ugh, stupid curiosity, now you're making me get up from this nice, comfortable couch.

I rise and head over to the table, keeping my usual berth from Mom. I peek over her wrinkled dress shoulder to read the message:

"Dear Ms. Hesiod,

Thank you for your numerous questions regarding the Pali-kari exhibit. Never have we seen such interest in the Palikari Laver, a gem amongst stones in an archaeological sense. Believe me, we have a man who has visited every day for the past month, but he's never asked us as many questions."

I pause when I read this. Every day? What kind of nerd has that time? Or the finances to take off work for a month straight? Shaking my head, I continue to read.

"I was particularly impressed by the information you presented at the museum about Palikarian textiles and how they relate to the archaeology of the temple sites. No scholar has ever presented these findings before. Even that man who visits—who happens to know a lot on the subject—would have been surprised to hear some of these findings.

Although we cannot share as much information as you would like to know—as I excel more in Etruscan studies opposed to Palikarian—an archaeologist who works part-time at the museum published his most recent findings about religious activities during the Greek Dark Ages. He dedicates an entire chapter to Palikari, which includes a subsection about the ritual use of the laver.

If you would include your address in your correspondence, we would love to ship the book to your current residence. Although you may feel free to stop by and pick up the copy, we would like to ship the book to you to allow you to avoid paying a train fare or a long walk to the museum.

Thank you for your interest!

Regards,
Henry Whitley"

"We could pick up the book." Uncle Laran frowns at the screen before he scoops Mom's mug from the table.

"'We' meaning whom?" Mom clacks her fingernails one by one to the tune of some song I don't recognize. I notice the paint has chipped on a few of her nails. "I don't get a break till next weekend, and you teach classes all week."

Uncle Laran jerks his head in my direction, and Mom's nostrils flare.

"Absolutely not. I do not trust that boy to ride another Tube—still can't rid that awful scent of puke from my nose. And we will not send Harper on her own and leave him here to destroy the apartment."

Not to mention, last time I wound up alone in a city, I had a panic attack on the sidewalk. Sure, she let me go to the British Museum that one time, but now with Homie here, she won't risk anything.

It must be too early in the morning to put up a fight. Uncle Laran gives the apartment address before ducking out the front door to deliver a lecture to his college class. He teaches at Brunel University, a decent commute from his apartment.

Mom sends the email containing the apartment address to the museum worker and closes the laptop. She bites into a piece of toast drenched in marmalade and scurries out the door for her tourist group meeting.

I snag the computer the second she leaves and bury it under the mattress in our room. If she asks where the device went when she returns, I plan to hoist a shrug like a flag of victory, followed by, "Dunno. Ask Homer."

When I return to the main room to embrace my few hours with no adults, I notice the smelly blue tunic draped on the lamp table. Even the orange marmalade can't fumigate the onion smell from my nose.

A few hours after the garment made residence on the

armchair, Uncle Laran noticed the fabric begin to stink. He moved the cloth from the chair to underneath the green banker's lamp. The man refused to relocate it to his room, and Mom would not let the garment go within ten feet of ours. So, in the main room the tunic stayed.

I dig my perfume out of my suitcase and spritz Japanese cherry blossom all over the textile. I feel a bit like a destroyer of history, but if this thing's staying here for three months…

Homer, an almost-statue on the sofa, wrinkles his nose at me.

"You don't like this scent?" Moments later, the overpowering flowery fragrance punches me in the nostrils. "Oh. Whoops. Sorry, kid. Got overeager there."

I shuffle into the kitchen to avoid the Battle of Cologne. There I fix myself some toast with raspberry jam. When I reach the table to eat, I notice Homer hasn't budged these past five minutes. I plug my nose, rise, march toward him, and extend a hand.

"Come on, you need to learn more skills than just the English language. And in the twenty-first century, the females don't always do the cooking for you."

He slips a dry palm into my damp one, and we amble from the carpet to the kitchen tile. There, I teach him to place two pieces of bread in a toaster and how to spread butter or jelly on them when they pop up. He jolts when the slices of bread burst through the two holes, a slight char rimming their edges. We take a seat at the table, and I notice he parks at the other end, as far away from me as possible. Oh, right, he doesn't eat with women in Palikari.

"Not in my house, kid."

I stand and slide into the wooden chair nearest to him.

Whites show in the corners of his eyes, stunned, but he doesn't shift seats. After muttering a prayer somewhere along the lines of please-God-tell-me-we-didn't-burn-the-toast-too-bad, I meet his dark pupils. They remind me of a pigeon's eyes when the birds park outside my window. "Let's eat."

You deserve a seat at the table.

At the same time, we bite into the bread, the tart-yet-sweet raspberry jam spilling onto our tongues and glazing our teeth with a rosy tint. Seeds produce a weird chewy-crunch in our mouths. He offers a toothy smile, bits of jam crusted in the dents, and holds up his slice of bread with pride.

"Nice work, buddy." What's the use of learning a language if you don't have food in your belly, anyway?

After we eat breakfast, I suggest a walk in Kensington Gardens and Hyde Park to evade the various stenches invading the apartment—burnt toast, urine, and an acrid Japanese cherry blossom. I take Homer's lack of a reply as an agreement, and we head our merry way to the park teeming with joggers and dogs without leashes.

Right before we exit the apartment building, I check my bag for keys. It's difficult to peer into the purse with the dim hallway lighting.

"Oh, I forgot. Uncle Laran gave Mom the only spare." After the first night Homer stayed here, at least. Well, I guess he's gonna have to deal with the possibility his neighbors might steal his toaster.

We leave the door unlocked and exit the apartment. This time, I remember to bring my wallet and slip a few cool coins into Homer's fingers. He beams as we approach the familiar pub with a homeless stranger in a sleeping bag nestled underneath an awning. Homer claps a pound coin and a few pence into the weathered hands of the homeless woman.

The beggar smiles at us, missing one of her front teeth. "God bless."

Upon our entrance to the park, a building with Grecian-style pillars catches my attention. "They have a lot of Roman and Greek architecture here." I dig a pencil out of my bag and point at the graying stone. "Londoners really value history, or something." No wonder Uncle Laran wanted to come here.

A slight stab of guilt freezes my gut for giving him such a hard time about moving here. After all, the girl he'd dated up North, in the Midwest, cheated on him with some dude from Jersey. I'd want to flee the country too after that.

We slide into a rare open bench, and I dig a sketchbook out of my bag. With the pencil poised in my fingertips, I outline the scenery of the park mid-morning. The sprinkling fountains spurt deep blue water onto bright green algae. A pigeon army marches behind a man with a brown lunch bag—I exclude the man in the picture. The ovular heads of a vibrant purple flower sway just so in the cool breeze. I notice how gray rain clouds billow across the cerulean sky like a London fog.

"Hope it doesn't pour soon." I chew on the pencil eraser for a moment of pensiveness. But we're in London, the place known for its drizzle. I might as well be asking the city not to breathe.

Maybe this city doesn't like touch either. All the people who weave in and out of the historic buildings. Does London also hike up its shoulders and look for gaps in the crowd?

Homer taps his finger against my notebook and then points. I follow his arm and see him motion to a bald human by the round pond, kneeling in the sand to take a picture of circling swans.

"M-man." The word takes so much effort.

"Yep, there's no man in the picture. Isn't it nice?"

I finish my sketch and rise from the bench, only for a wheezing couple in jogger outfits to take the seat from us a moment later. We start to take the same path toward the Peter Pan statue. This time Homer leads the way. But when we reach a tree that cradles lime green parakeets, his sandals stop their clip clop across the stone pathway. I glance his shoes. They're ratty and about to disintegrate on his feet. He needs tennies.

A creature on a thin branch on the tree emits a high-pitched screech followed by what sounds like the constant smacking of lips. I spy the little birds with their blushing beaks and eyes, the source of the noises.

Homer kneels, as before royalty, and stretches out a shaky finger.

Nothing happens. The birds cock their heads at him as if to scrutinize his palms for food. At last, one flaps its wings—a darker green than the rest of its body—and settles on the landing pad of a finger. As the small parakeet perches, Homer's eyes light up.

"He's kind of like you."

With his other arm, he reaches forward to grab mine to form a bridge for his parakeet to land. "No." I yank away and shrink back.

"No?" His vocabulary now totals three words. "Homer," "no," and "man."

"I—I don't want to hurt him." I bite my lip and cringe. "He's so small, you see."

Not understanding my explanation, as I did not use any of the three English words he knows, he beckons me with a waving finger, saying something that sounds like "*ercho*."

By now, we've drawn a small, jabbering crowd of onlookers. A small child with a short bowl haircut tugs at a woman's leg.

"Mummy, I want to hold one." Some others in the semi-circle forming around us take out phones to snap a photo.

Breath escapes my lungs, until I look at Homie. Focus on him, girlie. Breathe.

"Fine." I kneel and reach out my palm. "To get out of this crowd."

Our fingers touch, and I feel electricity again. The kid's made of lightning.

The claws feel hard when they land on my fingers, but not as sharp as I imagined. Like a curled twig on a tree. A few half-hearted claps emit from the people around us, and Homer beams at me, cheekbones projecting out of his thin skin, as if to say, "I trust you with him."

"Don't." I raise my arm until it scares the parakeet into flight.

Don't trust me with anyone.

* * *

Half an hour later, the skies release a muggy drizzle, and we rush back to the apartment. Raindrops slap the pavement as we pass the pub. The beggar woman and her sleeping bag have disappeared. To find shelter elsewhere, I presume.

When we reach the door, in an automatic motion, I reach into my now-sopping bag for the keys to the apartment.

"Oh, right." I sniff as a glaze of water drips down my chin onto my shoes. Water bleeds onto the old, brown hallway carpet. "Forgot Uncle Laran didn't give us one."

Lucky for us, we left the door unlocked.

We open the door with a bang and a squeak and rush inside the dark apartment. Did Laran turn off any lights? He's at the university, right?

It's so cold in here. He'd mentioned his apartment was one of the few to have AC, because he purchased a boxed one for his windowsill. Most of London went without cooling technology in the summers. It's like someone turned up the AC while we were gone.

I swore we left the building with the lights on and the AC low. Uncle Laran gave up on the candle business in the main room when Homer almost knocked over the cinnamon-scented thing in his sleep.

Maybe Mom or Uncle Laran arrived early, cranked the air, and shut off the lights.

Silence hushes over the flat. Our soggy steps squish across the hardwood floor. We kick off our shoes.

"Hello?"

Nothing answers back.

Power outage, maybe? But I swear I saw the flickering glow of a TV in another room when we approached the apartment from the street. Someone forgot to shut their curtains.

Homer swings his arm back in a protective sort of motion, whirls around, and motions for me to stay in place with a jabbed finger under my nose. Like I had done to him back when we escaped the museum and I bought our train tickets. Before I can protest, he grabs an umbrella from its metal case by the front door and skulks toward the main room area.

For a few moments, my thundering heartbeat provides the only sound in the apartment. Then a shout of "No!" from Homer followed by "Man!"

An intruder? Had Homer run away from him his first night here?

Picturing a man in a trench coat waiting in the main room

corner with a gun, I race into carpeted space to find the armchair flipped over and couch cushions in disarray.

Oh, dear St. Olga, I let in burglars. Uncle Laran's gonna kill me.

I dash over to the sideways chair to pick it up when I realize the smelly tunic no longer rests on the lamp table. Twisting around, I see the television and some dusty antiques Uncle Laran placed on top of the TV cabinet remain in place, undisturbed. I do an attendance check, just in case. All accounted for, except Homer's tunic.

Why would someone steal a smelly tunic but not a television? Maybe the English are so polite that they don't know how to rob people right.

I ball my fist and chew on a knuckle. Deep breath…one, two, three. My eyes itch. I would say from tears, but I haven't cried in so long. Another inhale and I feel Homer's hand clapped on my shoulder. Warmth spreads across my skin.

"Homie, I don't know what to do. They're going to notice somebody stole the tunic. We can't lie about this."

"Man."

"Agreed, they're going to know some man broke into the apartment. Or a woman. Don't know if it makes much of a differ-ence." I bite down on a trembling lip. "This confirms what Mom said. That someone knows about you, or at least, has a weird thing for smelly tunics. You're not safe anymore. Even if we can't get to the laver at the museum, Mom'll find a ritual in that book and send you back to—"

I can't finish the sentence.

Whoever stole the tunic left us with no choice. We knew the rules of Hide and Seek. They found our hiding spot. Find a new one or lose the game.

Breathe. One, two, three…

Focus, Harper. What else did they take? Check all the other rooms.

Hope fills my chest. We could find a new hideout and—

—and?

And we'd have to figure out the rest of plan B later.

Rushing into my room, I find my black suitcase sprawled on the bed with clothing strewn in every which direction. Mom's bag lies some little ways off in the same condition. Taking a step into the men's room, I see books slumped on the ground, wings open like dead butterflies I've seen in glass cases at insect museums back home. I return to the kitchen and spy the eating table empty except for one item—a book.

Stones plummet from my heart into my abdomen. One yellow sticky note flaps off the book's cover, and squinting in the darkness, I can just make out the message:

"Regards,
Henry Whitley"

Time for a new hiding place.

Part Two: July

"Better to trust a woman than to trust a sparrow. At least the woman is not ordinary in music, in weaving, in the ordering of the household affairs. Lazy, the sparrow graces no one with its song. Beware, beware the sparrow."

- A Palikarian saying from oral tradition, original source unknown

Chapter Ten
Why the Eagle Grows Weary

Sunlight peeks through the patterned curtains on the window. I shiver under the light comforter the woman at the front desk of the hostel provided—she had an accent, maybe Greek or Russian? Seems odd to turn on the heater for the room, but lying on the top bunk, the effort to descend and click on the machine would take too much energy for its worth.

Plus, my mom, on the bottom bunk, would shut off the heater anyway if I awoke her.

Oh, the joys of sharing space in a new hotel. One with even less space than Uncle Laran's apartment.

I return to my musty, stained pillow and stare at the ceiling. In my periphery, Homer rolls onto his side to create a mummy-like garment out of his comforter. Something tells me Palikari, which existed in the Mediterranean, is much warmer than even England in July. Although we've adjusted this past month at the hostel, the cold mornings still propel goosebumps up our arms and legs.

"Homer?" I whisper to the silhouette across the room on the other top bunk. The light spilling from a crack in the curtains outlines his shape.

"Harper?" He rolls toward me. "What?"

Guess that answers my next question of, Are you awake?

"Nothing." Happy to hear your voice, that's all.

He rubs his thumbs around his eyes in circles and rolls back to face the wall. "Always something." Drowsiness clings to the last word, and his blanket bounces up and down in a sort of heaviness of breathing, of living.

He's not only been learning new English words, but seems to have picked up on sarcasm too.

Now wide awake, I place a precarious foot on the ladder and slap my palm on the mini-fridge by mother's bed to balance myself on the descent. When my bare feet reach the cold wood floor, I swing open the mini-fridge and grab my juice bottle from a Sainsbury run the other night. I dig through the suitcases on the other empty bed, the bottom bunk of Homer's side of the room, and pull out my laptop. There's no room for our bags anywhere in this room besides here. Luckily Uncle Laran didn't volunteer to take the fourth bed. He stayed in his apartment. Guess he'll lose the game of Hide and Seek with Henry Whitley.

Turning on the buttery bathroom light, I click the door shut. The water closet makes up the size of, well, a closet back home. Minus the water. They have so much water here.

Back home, grass grows in patches between rocks and sand. Rain falls seldom, and blue skies paint the long stretches of day during the summer. I miss the dry, and I miss home.

Wonder if Homie does too.

I swing the shower door open and squat on the floor, scattering a few bottles of shampoo. Could've sat on the toilet, I guess, but you can barely hold one human in here even with the bathroom and shower combined. My mouse taps the internet browser, but I receive the notification for no Wi-Fi signal again.

Once again, typical.

Eh, never mind, can't post anything about Homie on Tumblr anyway. Someone from the British Museum might flag the picture and track us down. Mom prohibited us from posting anything online ever since the day of the book incident in the apartment.

A rap sounds on the door. Ugh, so much for alone time. I

unhinge the lock and find Homer holding a towel in his arms.

"Shower?"

"Go right ahead."

I attempt to pull myself up by the sink, but the white basin wobbles, and I veto that plan. Almost broke the coat hanger rack on our first day here. Don't want a repeat.

Homer extends an arm and hoists me to my feet. My cheeks flush when I realize he has his shirt off. Didn't catch that in the lighting of the room at first. Even after a month's lack of garden work, he's still well-defined. Gotta do some temple work to develop my own washboard abs.

After I thank him, we do an awkward side shuffle in and out of the tiny bathroom. He shuts the door, and I return my computer to my suitcase. Drizzling water from the bathroom mixes with the sound of a sliding zipper. Right as I climb the ladder to catch a few more minutes of sleep, I hear Mom groan.

"He took the shower." She moans something indiscernible, muffled by her pillow. She chose the one without stains.

"In his defense, you have more hair than him and me combined. We take much less time in there."

"Still 'll steal all the hot water." Her words slur, indicating she had arisen, at best, a minute ago.

Mom rustles the sheets on the lower bed and reaches across the bunks to grab something from her suitcase. The light from a crack in the curtain reveals the item—a book. More specifically, the book Henry Whitley gave her after he broke into Uncle Laran's apartment and stole Homer's tunic.

The woman will not quit. She's gonna get Homie home if it kills her.

"Might as well give this another shot while we wait."

I roll my eyes. "Mom, let the thing rest in peace. You've

tried to decipher it for a good month."

"I think I have a theory that will work this time."

"Might as well get changed." I descend the ladder and suppress a laugh at Mom squinting at the pages of *Titans and Temples in the Greek Dark Ages* by T.H. Arrian in the dim morning lighting. "While Homer showers and all."

We often don fresh clothes in the bathroom, but I decide not to wait for Mom and Homer to complete their showers before putting on my *Daredevil* t-shirt and black sweatpants. Worn once already, both waft a faint smell of deodorant and sweat. But with Mom paying for us to eat out every night, our laundry budget plummeted.

"I think I might understand the first part of this ritual chant." She taps the book with a finger, like she enjoys doing with her e-reader back home.

"Translate it for me, then." I pull on a pair of Sherlock socks from Primark, but after wearing those ones for three days straight, they've begun to reek.

"Well, I can't put it into words." She bites her lip.

"Then we can't put him in the laver." *Check and mate.* I still haven't figured out the plan B to keep Homie here without running into that Henry dude. Hopefully the new hiding place will work out until I can figure out a way to keep him here long-term.

She sighs. "Something tells me Mr. Whitley didn't follow museum protocol. In America, you need a warrant before you can search through someone's home. Besides, he didn't seem like a security guard. Didn't wear the same uniform. Felt more like a tour guide or docent."

Ugh, I don't want to hear this again. "Even if he broke the rules, what will you tell the British Museum, Mom? 'Hi, we stole a live artifact from one of your exhibits and are really upset you tried to take it back from us.'"

She blinks several times as if to prevent an onslaught of tears. She cries easier than a chef dicing onions.

"Harp, let me borrow your computer."

"Dunno how much battery's left, but all right." Maybe there's something Homer-esque in the air, but ever since I've hung out with him, I've had less of an urge to argue with my mom.

Leaning across the beds, she digs the device out and clickity-clacks on the keyboard until she lets out another musk ox noise.

I bite a loose hangnail on my pinky. "Another email?" The guy from the museum keeps spamming her with messages, at least two per day.

"The nerve of this guy."

Water clicks off in the bathroom and Homer emerges in a steamy cloud a few minutes later with sopping wet curls in a plain white tee and jeans. His t-shirt soaks to the skin. Fire fills my cheeks again.

A few days after the apartment incident, Mom took him to Primark to purchase a new wardrobe. She bought the cheapest options, but he held the netted gray shopping basket with such delicacy, as if no one had handed him this many possessions in his life.

Before Mom enters the bathroom, the steam from the small chamber fills the rest of the room with warmth. But the cloud also brings out the moldy scent all the more. Lovely, can't wait to smell that all day.

"Nice shower?" I nod at his dripping curls.

"Cold."

He wipes his head with a damp towel and places the wet rag on the black bars of his top bunk. No towel hangers exist in the bathroom.

I attempt another go at conversation. "After Uncle Laran finishes his lesson, you wanna roam around Kensington Gardens?" A pause. "Homer?"

"Fine." He huffs.

What's with the attitude this morning? "Homie, what's wrong?"

"Nothing," he growls, climbing up his ladder, facing the wall, and sitting cross-legged.

"Always something." I mimic his voice from earlier.

He peers over his shoulder to glare at me. "Everything, then."

Man alive, I miss when he acted like he was five…instead of a hormonal teenager.

Before I can reply, knuckles rap against the door. Seeing that Homer refuses to budge, I slide down the ladder and click the lock. Uncle Laran swings the door open and steps inside to the din of water in the bathroom.

"Ah, your mother's morning routine lives on."

"As it does every day." I retreat to my bunk again, grunting up each step.

"Sorry I took so long to arrive." Late for Laran means right on time. "Felt like someone was following me today, a bloke in a bright suit. He turned down Gloucester. Good Moore, I was shaking with my heart pounding in my chest. Still is. Probably just paranoid."

For a month straight, after the mysterious Whitley broke into the apartments, Uncle Laran believed every man with a British accent wanted to follow him to the hotel and kidnap our Palikarian artifact. Can't blame him, though, with Henry emailing Mom all the time.

We need a plan B fast. Or plan C. Or whatever letter we're

on now. One that doesn't involve Laran extracting info from Homer and then leaving the two of us alone in the hotel room for days on end. If I go one more day without sunshine, I'll burst.

Mom lets us out, as long as I text her every fifteen minutes with updates. I've never dated a boy, but after all these precautions, something tells me I don't want to dive into that venture any time soon. Bet she'd make my curfew eight o'clock.

Uncle Laran kicks off his shoes and slides them into the nook by the door. He hangs his coat on the remaining hanger. "Chilly this morning, but the temperature will skyrocket to thirty-one—eighty-eight in Fahrenheit, I believe. Should feel more like home for both of you."

He drops his business bag on the spare bed and unlatches the top. He pulls out a notebook and a Greek Dark Ages book featuring a black and white picture of the temple to the god of the dead.

"Not too long a session today, mate. A few questions here or there about what you did for work back home, that sort of thing."

"Fine." Homer still faces the wall, now staring at a painting of water lilies decorating some sort of river.

Hmm, maybe I understand Homer's attitude. I wouldn't want to spend summer break having some stranger asking me constant questions about my life, like a never-ending counseling session.

Got lots of those because of Dad.

Having nowhere else to sit in the cramped room, Uncle Laran selects a place on Mom's bed after he shoves aside her crumpled sheets. He clears his throat and tries to pry a few answers out of Homer about the so-called Festival of Sparrows. He attempts and fails to do so at every lesson. Either the word "sparrow" registers nothing in Homer's brain, or he refuses to spill information about the *secret* rite. Whatever the case, he remains silent during this portion.

So, Uncle Laran moves on.

"Homer, buildings like palaces and temples seldom survived…your time." He avoids using "Dark Ages." Thinks it might offend him. "Do you have any idea how the temple to Leinos stayed intact?"

Homer clutches a handful of the bed sheet in his hand. "Survive because warriors guard gate." His broken English adopts a slight British accent when he speaks with Uncle Laran, opposed to with the rest of us.

"Did a leader command the warriors to protect the temple?"

"Yes."

"Was he a king or chief of some sort?"

Even turned around, I see him screw his eyes shut to recall. "Don't know word in English."

A graphite pencil screeches against the notebook as Uncle Laran, beneath me, attempts to write out whatever word Homer says in Palikarian.

"How did they employ you at the temple?"

"Emp-loy?" He sounds out the word and shakes his head.

"Who gave you the job at the temple?"

Homer bites his lips and presses his thumbs together. "Sad story."

Uncle Laran catches me leaning forward with interest. "He was probably exposed as an infant, Harper."

"To what? A disease?"

Long pause. "Parents who didn't want their children discarded them on the roadside to die. Happened in Egyptian, Roman, and Greek cultures, at least."

I recall one of my world history teachers lecturing on this.

"And childless parents who wanted a kid adopted those babies. They'd just go out and pick one up." At least, our textbook made it seem like that was the case.

"Mmm, not quite. Brothels and temples may have scooped up the babies to use them as slaves when they grew old enough—around eight or nine years old. That's probably what happened to Homer."

Man alive, poor Homie.

Heat burns in my cheeks. I shouldn't have grabbed his hand the first day. He doesn't trust people, or touch.

Homer quits his session with Uncle Laran early. As soon as Mom and Laran leave the room, he wobbles up the ladder and parks next to me on the bed. He tilts over and places his head on my shoulder.

I smile and lean into him. "I know. Thought they'd never leave."

Chapter Eleven
Why the Myrrh Mountain Sings

WITH A COUPLE HOURS TO KILL, we grab lunch at a Lebanese restaurant in the area. We wait ten minutes for an available seat. The smell of meat—a very strong, gamey sort of animal—fills the air, with the eye-watering aroma of peppers. A waitress leads us to a corner booth by the window. As I peruse the menu for vegetarian options, Homer gazes at passersby with a disinterested glaze sheathing his eyes.

"Homie, what's wrong?"

He cranes his neck toward me.

"You seem different, that's all." The menu flutters shut between my fingertips.

On the way to the restaurant, we passed two beggars. Homer's gray Converse knockoffs strode right past the homeless people without a second glance. I could ignore the morning episodes, but no way can I remain silent after that.

I mention the beggar woman to him and he gives a single nod, features darkening.

"Try to…" He presses his eyes shut to remember the correct word. "Be like Laran and Livy."

"You want to fit in?"

"Fit in?"

"You know, be like everyone else?"

His square jaw bobs in a nod so fast, I fear the sharp edges will slice right into his throat.

I reach across the table to grip his shoulders. He no longer flinches at my touch. "Do yourself a favor…don't."

"Don't what?"

A sizzle from nearby punctuates a silent moment.

"Homer, I trust you because you don't remind me of anyone else."

"Why?"

"Because every human I've met has hurt me in some way."

A waitress with a nose ring brushes past us to seat another couple in a tight corner table.

"Not Homer?"

"No, friend." Not yet at least.

Behind me, I overhear someone with a Scottish accent talking about something he read in the morning paper. I guess they do that here, peruse newspapers.

"Kidnapped her at Victoria and Albert, right in front of a huge crowd."

Icy panic seizes my chest. That word, "kidnapped," squeezes my stomach. Mom had repeated it over and over when she found me in Phoenix. "Coulda been kidnapped. What were you thinking?"

And how long until Henry finds the new hiding place?

Another Scottish voice answers him, a thicker one. "Can never be too careful these days."

Man alive, I don't want to tune into this conversation. I force myself to focus on the falafel listing on the menu.

Returning, the waitress interrupts my thoughts to take our orders. I motion to a random item without a meat listing, and Homer does the same for his food and drink since he can't read.

The waitress returns with our beverages after a minute. She hands me a Coke with a lemon wedge on the glass. Homer receives an odd thick, milky mixture. He stirs the contents with his straw.

"Think I remember there being a yogurt sort of drink on the menu." I nod as part of the liquid spills over the brim of his cup onto the wooden table. "Maybe you pointed to that when you ordered."

Homer hears the word yogurt and takes an eager slurp. We bought a sweet coconut version of the gloppy liquid from Sainsbury's. However, when he sips his straw, he recoils and his lips pucker. A retching noise burbles in his throat.

"Sour?" In an automatic motion, I hand him my napkin as the liquid spills down his chin. "Spoiled?"

He winces and tries another swallow. No better than the last time, he hacks into his napkin. I slide the drink toward myself, but he bellows a loud "no" in protest. Half the restaurant glares his way before returning to the world of conversation—I think we even draw the attention of a pedestrian in an Oxford University tee just outside the window of the restaurant.

Oof, gotta keep a low profile.

"Let me share in your pain, Homie."

"Bad." He points at the drink with an accusatory index finger, so stiff you could dip it in ranch and bite it off like a carrot. "Bad, bad, bad." He reaches forward and snatches the cup with an iron grip, matching mine already on the glass.

"I know. Let me try this to understand."

After a moment, he unhinges his grasp, and the grainy mixture glides toward me. I inhale a sniff, but the liquid offers no strong hints of its taste from the scent. The concoction offers a mere milk smell. I clamp my teeth on the straw and drink.

The sour mixture hits my tongue. I've tasted plain yogurt before, but never in beverage form. My face sinks into what feels like a crumpled wrapper shape before I swallow and lather my tongue on my napkin. Various visitors in the restaurant drill their eyes into me to signal their disapproval. Bring it on, people.

"See?" Homer frowns at the glass. "Bad."

"Agreed."

Every drink we've handed him besides water has tasted sweet. To venture back to something with such an acrid flavor would cause the stomach to curdle.

Would sending him back to his time create the same reaction? Would he taste and see that the Greek Dark Ages were bad and London good?

Even if we don't have another plan, that has to be better than a plan A.

I think back to Phoenix. What if a Harper snatched me off the streets? Away from Dad and his beer bottles, and from Mom and her obsessive need to control everything? Would I want to return home?

And did the stranger, or me, have the right to pull someone away from home and out of a less-than-pleasant situation?

Passing the time between our drinks and main dish, I scroll through the photos on my camera, deleting blurry images. Homer questions me about my activities, and I realize I never explained the device to him. Most places we visited didn't allow photography, and the ones that did…well, I think I had too much fun at those places to snap pictures.

My latest photograph dates to mid-June, almost a month ago. You forget to capture moments on film when busy having fun with a time traveler.

Homer gestures to the camera. "Its duty?"

Ah, he means its job. He's described his "duties" back at the temple at length. Including some nasty rituals tied with a love goddess or nymph. I couldn't figure that part out. Hard to tell from his muttering and the top bunk. The poor kid had to grow up way too fast.

"To paint an instant picture." I figure he understands paint and picture, not so sure about *instant*.

I press the cold lens to my eye and *click* a photo of the disgusting yogurt drink. Leaning over the table, I show him the image.

He scowls at the screen. "Bad, bad, bad."

"I know, Homie. So, I plan to delete the thing." I click a button with a little white trash can. The photo disappears.

"Del-ete?"

"Throw away, discard—to get rid of something you don't want."

"Ah." He nods. "My mother delete Homer."

Chills run through my blood at the mention of his mom forsaking him as an infant. Mom doesn't sound so bad now. If I didn't have an aversion to touch, I would give her more hugs. "Do you remember her?"

"Yes."

So the horrible stuff happened to him at an older age than that of an infant. My earliest memory, me taking a pair of jagged scissors to my bowl-cut hair, happened around the time I'd turned four.

"When did she leave you, Homie? Your mother?"

"Leave at temple?"

"Yes."

Veins jut out of his neck when he swallows. "When—delete Father."

"She killed your dad?" My heart pounds with such fervor in my chest, I no longer hear the kitchen grill sizzle or the laughter from a Middle Eastern couple deeply in love two tables down.

"No, warrior delete Father."

Oh, right. Uncle Laran mentioned lots of wars and fights happened during Homer's time. When the enemy murdered his dad, his mother had to make money somehow—a profit off Homie, I imagine.

Sorrow builds up in the corners of my eyes. Not enough to form tears, but adequate to cause my eyeballs to itch. How can someone go through so much pain and still emerge with the semblance of a happy human being?

I clasp his hands in mine. He flinches for a moment, but then relaxes.

"My dad died, too, Homie. He deleted."

"Warrior delete him?"

Darkness envelops my chest like a cloud.

"Harper?"

"No." I release my grip and smear my palms against my jeans. "Mom did."

* * *

We finish our meals and order baklava for dessert. Mom gave us some money for treats at the theater, but probably not enough for popcorn for the two of us. So we decided to splurge on the baklava instead.

Today's destination to get away from a hot, stuffy room.

Homer's face glows when he eats the sweet honey dish, and he arches his back so much in contentment, the hunch almost disappears.

"Good." He points to the plate. His gesture moves back to the yogurt drink. "Bad."

When I go up to the register to pay for the check, I rotate on my heel to find Homer scrolling through the pictures on my camera. Cheery lights from the screen glow in his dark eyes and cheeks.

"That'll be seventeen forty-five." The woman at the register flares her nostrils for a moment. I eye her septum ring. It looks just like a dragon.

I pass her a twenty and return to the table with my change. "Having fun?" Coins make a jingle noise when they slide into my pocket.

Homer jerks up from the camera and hands the device back to me, tucking his chin into his chest in shame. "No man."

"In the pictures?"

An abashed nod. "No man."

"An impressive feat during peak tourism season in London. Had to delete so many photos that got bombed."

"Why?" He rubs his hands against his jeans. "Why no man?"

A sigh deflates in my chest like a balloon. "Because humans, not beautiful."

Uncle Laran likes to yell at me whenever I leave out all the words such as "an" or "the" or, St. Olga forbid, a verb, when speaking to Homer. But I feel like the fewer words I use, the more we understand each other.

"Harper beautiful."

I freeze. Fire burns in my cheeks. "Oh."

He reaches across the table for the camera. I hand it to him, and he holds it upside-down to take a picture of me. I rush over to his chair to show him how to work the device. After a brief demonstration and a jolt from Homer whenever the lens shutters, he motions for me to return to my seat, and the lens snaps about twenty times with the rapidity of him pressing the top button.

"Okay, okay." I snatch the camera from him, laughing. "I think you took enough."

A sheepish grin splits his face in half. He gestures to the device in my hand as I flip through the very blurry pictures he captured. I might be able to spy some facial features in one if I squint hard enough.

"See? Beautiful."

Eye of the beholder, I guess. Uncle Laran did say the poet Homer had a visual impairment. "Your turn."

He attempts to replicate the smile I used when I posed for him. Unfortunately, my grin and grimace don't differ much, and so he looks like Uncle Laran punched him in the gut.

I tell him to relax, but this makes him look like he swallowed a gulp of that yogurt drink. So I tell him to remember the first day in Kensington Gardens when we stared at the Peter Pan statue for an eternity.

Well, before that man and his daughter Amelia showed up. Yep, never mind, Homer's shoulders skyrocketed when I said that.

"Okay, try to remember the day when we held the birds." I hold out a finger, envisioning a chartreuse flutter of wings and the hard claws. "Those little green wings."

His eyelids close enough to form a perfect portrait of a man.

The lens shutters, and I stare at the glowing picture.

"See?" He bounces in his creaking seat, eager to gaze at his portrait.

I point at the sour yogurt drink. "Bad." Then, I show him the photo. "Beautiful."

Chapter Twelve
Why the Darkness Haunts

"HOMER, I CAN'T BREATHE."

We'd run into a group of tourists on the way to the theater. They speak Korean or some language I can't recognize, and they spill through me and Homer like a river of people.

I'm back in Phoenix. Crumpling to the ground, I cover my nose with my palms to form a pocket of air to breathe.

Warm fingers grab my left hand a moment later. Homer's.

He squeezes and leans against me as we sit on the sidewalk and let the crowd pass us.

I breathe.

Panting, we reach the theater at last, but we have to take a breather by some metal tables at an Italian restaurant. And by we, I mean Harper. Thank our Arizona stars asthma came to join us for the superhero movie viewing.

"Ready for this, Homie? Your first movie?"

* * *

He was not ready.

I grab his arm and yank him out of the building. We reach outside, and he crumples against a nearby shop window with a sign for a cold medicine.

"Time to go home." A growl rises in my throat. I know leaving the movie early annoyed me, but my voice comes out a lot angrier than I expect.

Homer buries his head into his knees in sobs.

Wax fills my chest. I blink away the images of the people in the auditorium from moments before. When Homer screamed and a woman swung around in her large chair to shush us.

I sit next to him. *He helped you in the crowd, Harper. Your turn.* "Homie, talk to me."

He lifts his red-rimmed eyes at me. "Many man delete. Many, many, many."

"In the movie? Yeah. That happens in superhero flicks. People die."

His face contorts. "Harper not sad?"

"No, because it's not real. Actors play those parts." I roll my eyes at myself. He won't understand that. "It's just a story, remember? Like the Cinderella thing I told you earlier."

On our walk over, I'd described the tale of Cinderella and explained how we make up stories that sound like they're real. He claimed they often do the same in Palikari. Hence why we got Greek Dark Age stories like *The Iliad* and *The Odyssey*.

Shaking his chin from side to side, he warps his trembling lips into a frown. "Real man in story. Like Harper. Like Homer."

It takes me a minute to realize he means real people were playing the parts in the script. He thinks they died on screen.

"Trust me, okay? Those people did not delete."

He bites his chapped lips. "Why watch story that delete many, many man?"

How to explain this to him? Oh, Homer, we just watch people die for fun, for entertainment.

Then what feels like a brick hits my stomach. How many people did Homer watch get deleted back home? Uncle Laran had talked about lots of wars and famines and natural disasters. Homer had mentioned his dad at the restaurant, too. Maybe we should've watched a different flick.

Even if Homer did have stories like *The Iliad* back home—war tales—having someone read you a chapter out of a book's way different than seeing characters die on a screen in front of you.

Homer leans into my shoulder, and we wait until he stops shaking.

"That's it, darling. Breathe."

So he does, and I do with him.

* * *

At the steps of the hotel, I pull out a pair of keys and jam them into the front door to unlock it. We'll have to use another key the landlady handed us to access the room.

I crank the key the incorrect way. They always make this look so much easier in movies. "Makes no sense why Mom let you stay with us in the first place, Homie." I rotate the key in another direction. I can never seem to get keys right the first time. Plus, the knobs on the doors in this hostel don't seem to be like the normal doors we have back home. "She wanted to kick you out of the old apartment after the train incident, let alone take you with us to this hotel." Click, the doorknob jiggles open. "Well, I guess Uncle Laran does pay your bills. And maybe we did win her over with the whole 'slavery is *no bueno*' argument."

Or at least until she decodes that stupid book. Every part of me itches to throw the poor excuse of literature outside our hotel window and claim Henry broke in and stole it. But something tells me that'll backfire somehow.

In my periphery, someone in a scarlet suit ascends the staircase that leads to the upper rooms. Panic constricts my ribcage, and I peer around the corner and watch him. Relief pools in my stomach.

Brown hair on his head, not red.

It could be a wig, something deep inside me says. I squeeze my eyelids shut and shake my head, like an Etch a Sketch, to shake away the paranoia.

On my daily excursions to museums and parks with Homer, many a man wore a red suit of some type, a few gingers among them. Laran claims that most men in England don gray and black apparel, but I guess some of the males feel more frisky this year.

Laran suggested they're perhaps tourists or foreigners who work in London.

I rub the bridge of my nose with my fingertips to soothe myself. "Maybe some chocolate will help."

Homer and I snag a chocolate-dipped digestive cookie from the table in the hallway, and the landlady smiles at us, motioning to fresh British candies in shiny wrappers she placed in a bowl. We thank her and pluck a different kind of sweet. I plop mine in my mouth and a pleasant cherry flavor dissolves on my tongue.

One more key, rotating three times, allows us access to the room. They have so many locks in this place. No wonder Mom chose this as our hiding spot.

To our un-surprise, Mom and Laran have not yet returned to the hotel. With a couple hours of free time, I scroll on Tumblr, but a heaviness seeps through my head as if a doctor injected my brain with liquid lead. I don't get enough sleep here, not with Uncle Laran and his early morning lessons.

Before my head hits the pillow, I sink into a dream.

What seems like moments later, a shrill, "Hello?" awakens me.

"Back from the museum, Mom?" I groan, shielding my face with my arm to block out the buttery hallway lights.

Her bag slumps against the floor, and she, against the bed. She swings the door shut. "You'll never believe what I discovered today."

"A few ancient artifacts, I imagine."

"Unnecessary sarcasm." She waits a moment for an apology. None comes. She pauses. "Who gave you that bruise?"

Bruise? My arm throbs. Oh, yeah. That came from the crowd of people that trampled us. I didn't feel the throb until we bought our tickets at the theater.

Mom eyes Homer with slits for eyelids.

"I tripped off the ladder of this stupid bed."

"Oh?"

What's with the tone of disbelief?

We need a subject change. "You were telling me something you found in the museum?"

"I visited the Palikari exhibit today. To speak my mind to the guard spamming my inbox and breaking into our apartment. Don't worry"—her eyebrows rise—"Wasn't going to tell them about why someone broke in."

"Good." The word passes through gritted teeth. Wouldn't put it past the woman to throw up her hands and say, *"Just take the boy off our hands so we can get away from cold showers and mildewy rooms."*

"But when I arrived, Henry Whitley wasn't there."

"Took a day off?"

"My thoughts too. I stopped by the Information Desk on the main level to inquire when he would have a shift there. Just before the lady was about to tell me she couldn't provide information about her employees' whereabouts, she stopped when I told his name."

I roll over and shake the entire bed. One of these days, the wobbly bunkbed legs will collapse from my movements.

"The woman at the front desk told me no one under the name Henry Whitley works at the British Museum."

I bolt up in bed and about smack my forehead on the ceiling. Something frozen seizes my chest. "What?"

"No one with that name quit recently either." Her voice accelerates like a double decker on a downhill, perhaps to get all the information out at once before I lose interest. "Makes sense why he would break and enter. No British Museum employee would want to risk the legal consequences. Even if we had, as one would think, stolen an artifact."

Had we stolen Homer? Or did his choice to stay prove the opposite?

Focus on the problem, Harper. Some guy with a non-devil haircut wanted Homer's tunic. And this squirm in my gut tells me he wants more than an outfit. Our next plan better get here soon.

I lick my lips and taste sweat. "Then, who is Henry Whitley?"

"Almost afraid to find out, sweetie."

Chapter Thirteen
Why the Good Man Hides

MOM LOCKS THE DOOR AND SPEED walks—as she told me right before she left—two miles away before she sends a text message to Uncle Laran from a café about the latest update on Whitley. She returns, holds out her palm, and barks in a demanding voice, "Cell phone."

"Actually, that's your hand, Mom."

"Cell phone."

"Why? You think this Henry guy wants to track us or something?"

"Harper." Spit flies from her lips. "Phone."

I dig under my sheets and pull out the device with a Marvel Universe phone case. Mom claws me with her fingernails as she snatches the phone. She unzips her bag and drops in Captain America and Wolverine facing me, ready to fight.

She returns with her fingers outstretched. "Laptop."

"Mom, come on." Don't make me regret wanting to hug you earlier.

"Laptop, no questions."

"I haven't posted a single thing this trip. No way someone can track us unless we make ourselves known to the world."

"The second you open that thing, you tell everyone in London where you are and who knows what other sort of information. Now, for Homer's sake and the sake of your safety…Give. Me. Your. Laptop."

She had to pull the Homer card, didn't she?

Unpeeling my comforter from my leg, I unveil the silver

computer. So long Tumblr and Netflix. The delivery goes in the same pattern—her hands, her bag, crushing all the Marvel superheroes. I need a Wonder Woman now. She straddles the duffel to zip up the newest contents, and when she seals the tomb, she digs out a padlock and presses it between the ends of two zippers.

Wow, the woman *actually* locked her suitcase. My eyes grow itchy from what could've been an onslaught of tears if I still had the ability to cry. I can't.

I won't.

A mixture of anger and sadness swirls in my chest until it becomes hard to swallow. She has already taken too much away from me, and now this.

Mom orders us to stay in the room tonight as she ventures to Sainsbury's to buy dinner. She takes the suitcase full of electronics with her. Maybe to drop it off at Laran's apartment, or throw it into the Thames. Who knows?

A room-shaking door slam follows her exit. Homer, from his top bunk, tosses me a quizzical expression.

"Why Mom worry?"

"Because she's a mother." I huff, cheeks burning like coals. "It's her duty."

Half an hour later, Mom returns with plastic bags full of three-pound meal deals. She passes a cucumber and mayo sandwich to me along with a strange, prawn-flavored chips. Homer receives a sandwich with ham and cheese. Mom forgot Palikarians don't eat meat. To make matters worse, she passes him a beef-flavored chip bag, but lucky for us, he can't read.

Without complaint, he bites into the meal and chews, wincing. I wish I could tell him the grocery store used "pretend meat" to make the sandwich, but I can't bring myself to lie to this kid.

The next day, Mom and Uncle Laran establish the safety

pattern for the rest of our trip, until they figure out a way to return Homer to Palikari.

Plan A wins for now.

As always, Uncle Laran will enter the hotel room in the early morning for Homer's lesson and leave thereafter to teach at the university. Mom will deliver cheap breakfast—yogurt—and lunch in the morning, and after her tours, she'll bring us dinner in the early evening. Homer and I will stay put in the hotel room and listen for the five-knock code Mom created. Tap-tap, pause, tap-tap-tap.

Pat, pat, pat.

Knock, knock, knock.

Let, us, leave.

* * *

"Homer, we need to get out of here."

Restless, Homer tosses all the playing cards into the air and collects them when they all land, one at a time.

"If I eat another sandwich, I'm gonna puke all over Mom's suitcase."

He stoops to collect the two of clubs that landed near the fish-scented trash can. "How?"

"Quite easy. You lean over her bag and let loose all the contents in your stomach. Don't you remember upchucking on the Tube?"

"No, how we escape?"

"Already formed a plan. Lucky for us, we have way too much free time."

For the past several days, I've used most of our time telling him stories out of the Bible I packed.

We wait for the night. I listen for Mom's snores. They rumble like small thunderclouds. I ease off my comforter and slide each large foot onto the ladder with care. Each step takes five minutes, three in all, because each descent shakes the entire bed.

My soles hit the cold wooden floor after ages. I creep over to the coats hanging by the door and slide my fingers into her raincoat pocket. The fabric makes a scratchy noise upon contact. I tense and glance at the figure in the bottom bunk, but she rolls herself like a sushi toward the wall, undisturbed.

The woman sleeps way too well.

I pinch two fingers around her fabric wallet and ease it out of the coat. Then I click on the bathroom light to extract thirty pounds of cash from her—enough for the Tube ride and our meals tomorrow. Not enough to catch her attention as she withdraws three hundred pounds from the ATM every two weeks.

My hands glisten with sweat. I shove the thirty-pound wad into my Batman onesie's pocket.

Leaving the bathroom, I return the wallet to the coat and slide into bed. My heart races for the next hour. Or as long as it takes for the birds outside our window to begin their dawn songs.

The next morning, after Homer confirms in his lesson that, "Yes, some Palikarians kept pets. Rich Palikarians…"

And after Uncle Laran and Mom debate on the personhood of Henry Whitley—I could help look him up if Mom gave me back my computer and phone—

"Name sounds familiar." Uncle Laran's eyes dart toward Mom's suitcase for a moment. She must've brought it back at one point. Maybe when I was sleeping. Sounds like a lot of hassle just to keep us away from electronics. "Wonder if I stumbled across him in research. Perhaps a man interested in Palikarian history. Someone in my employment."

"I doubt he's an archeologist, Laran." Mom's spidery hands lay hold of her hips. "You've told me all the preventative measures you take before excavating a site. To try and steal an artifact, especially a live one like Homer, would go against any archeological code."

Uncle Laran scratches his stubble, face uneasy. "If you look at the history of my trade, it's filled with tomb robbers. Wouldn't put it past a desperate historian to kidnap someone."

And after the adults leave, we wait an hour before making our departure. In case Mom needs to double back for something she missed—motion sickness medicine, a book to read on the ride, my dignity, you name it. She never returns.

We arrive at Paddington, purchase our tickets, and waddle our legs fast as they can stride through the metal gates toward the yellow-lined platform.

Our destination? Camden Market.

Our reason? Mom spoke so poorly of the place. And with a thirty-minute commute to await us, we'll venture far enough away from the hotel that it will seem like a day's vacation, enough to make up for all the days Mom cooped us up.

Waiting in line at the concrete platform edge, Homer clutches his stomach and commences moaning. "Oh, don't feel good."

Fear ices my blood. I place my hand on his back and in a matted knot of fragments yell, "You okay? Gonna throw up? Oh, no. Oh, no, oh, no. Please don't. Please, please…tell me we don't have to go back to…"

He lifts his chin at me and flashes a mischievous grin. "Joke."

A cackling sort of noise, like an old man wheezing, issues from his throat. He doubles over in laughter, and I have to yank his gray shirt to keep him behind the yellow line. A man nearby with a plaid hat tucks his briefcase further into himself.

"You're the worst." I push his shoulder but shield a sheepish smile with my other palm.

We ride the whizzing train, no vomiting problems included, and arrive on a crowded road. Scattered clouds pepper a blue sky, and the street reflects a soft sheen of recent rain. Vendors on the walkway to the market call out to us, flashing merchandise and interspersing "'ello, darling" and various shades of catcalling.

I shove my hands into my hoodie, gripping the cash with clammy palms. No wonder Mom despised this place. Too many opportunities to meet what she likes to call "unnatural types" of people.

By the time we cross the street, I find my arm looped around Homer's. I'd forgotten I'd put it there when the wolf whistling got louder. I don't really feel much like moving it, even in this heat.

Squeezing through a throng of girls cooing at rainbow swirl bagels situated behind a glass case, we explore the various cramped shops in the indoors portion of the market. We fiddle with vintage signs at one place and leather bracelets at another. A corner shop dealing in old-fashioned cameras catches my attention, but I remind myself I only pocketed enough money for food and train tickets.

We peruse the food stalls and search for vegetarian options.

Cooks hold out samples on toothpicks and ask us if we want to try a bite of this or a skewered taste of that. When I ignore one who has a sweaty face, he repeats the question in Spanish.

At last, we find a stall where the vendor does not plague us for our attention—a vegan Indian place.

I order curry and naan, and Homer follows suit, looking

rather pleased with himself for ordering without obtaining a strange look for an odd accent or mispronunciation.

Seeing that all the tables in the area host the backsides of sweaty visitors, we grab a spot by a skeletal tree and inhale the spicy tofu and grilled cauliflower.

Garlic and some sort of spice, perhaps a chili pepper, pack my mouth full of heat. With enough pocket change left, we buy a basket of churros to split, equipped with chocolate and caramel dipping sauce.

"Mmm." My tongue licks some loose cinnamon. I wipe my sticky hands on my pants. "Sure beats sandwiches and weird chips."

Homer nods. The sugar coats his mouth all the way to his nostrils.

My stomach bubbles in warmth and I feel a ray of sunlight burst in my chest. Happiness at last, at least for another hour. "Nice to get away for a while, huh?"

He shrugs. "Sometimes."

"What do you mean sometimes? Your first night here, you left Uncle Laran's apartment. Only took something chasing you down for you to come back." I freeze. "Homer, what was chasing you down?"

"Man."

My thumb continues to rub on my pants, even though the sugar litters the pavement.

"Henry Whitley?" I jab a finger at my hair. Much of the blue dye has disappeared now and blonde fills in the cracks like sheaths of light. "Red hair. Not devilish?"

He shrugs. "Too dark to see. Man. Low voice."

A man with a stand full of patterned scarves cat calls to some woman on the street. For all we know, some creep like him could've chased Homer on his first night in London. They have a lot of dubious characters in these streets.

I unroll the parchment wrapper and take another bite. "So what were you doing before you ran into the man?"

Homer squinches his eyelids at a patch of blue sky. "I walk long way."

The bread grows soggy in my mouth. I swallow. "Do you mean you were trying to run away?"

My shoulders hike as I wince in expectation. Mom and Laran assured me on the daily that we hadn't kidnapped him. But I grabbed his hand. Pulled him along. Did we give him enough of a choice?

A ginger man passes in front of us, heading toward the churro booth. I would say Irish except for the height. He towers over much of the foot traffic. My shoulders rise to my ears and I scan what I can of his face. From what I remember, Henry didn't wear boxy glasses at the park.

My spine relaxes, for now. *He could've put on a disguise, you know.*

First wigs, now this? How far will my paranoia go?

The man disappears moments later, churro in hand, toward the street. His Oyster card flashes in the sunlight. *Harper, if that was Henry, he would've made a move.*

Homer shrugs. "No, just wanted to walk. Found way home, though."

Warmth spreads from my head to my toes. So we hadn't raided a tomb after all.

Home meant Uncle Laran's apartment. "How?"

"Followed stars."

Really? No way he can do that with all the light pollution here. Speaking of light, the blue sky looks a shade darker. Almost reminds me of a hyacinth, like the blue flowers in our neighbor's planters. We should get a move on soon, before Mom returns and finds us and thirty pounds missing from the room.

I ask a local vendor for the time, since my mom took away my phone, and when he tells me, I turn to Homie. "Gotta go."

Dark circles form in his eyes, likely at the thought of returning to the confined hotel room, but he nods. Off we go.

On the train ride back, he explains how Camden Market reminds him of a bazaar back home.

"Really?" I grit my teeth, bracing myself as the Tube screeches to a halt. Even with my grip on the yellow bar, I almost crash into Homer. "Uncle Laran always talked about how people during your time moved a lot. How could anyone set up a market? Or a temple for that matter."

He did come from around 800 BC, toward the end of the Greek Dark Ages. Maybe people settled down by the time he came around, a segue between the Bronze and Iron Ages. They lived on the cusp of something bigger and better, and yet, worse.

"More crowded, our market back home," he says. "Not as many choices. But food is food."

Agreed.

When we reach the entrance to the hotel, one of the workers scatters breadcrumbs for the flock of pigeons outside. Several birds that coo in the trees nearby rev their wings and land on the ground, hitting their beaks against the asphalt instead of the piece of bread.

Not the brightest bulbs.

Homer crouches on the steps leading to the hotel and watches them for a minute.

"You got any pets back home, Homie?"

His gaze never shifts, so I repeat the question. "Remember?

You talked with Uncle Laran about pets earlier. Does your temple keep any birds?"

In a huff, he stands without answering and enters through the green front door.

Love the kid until he gets moody.

Wait, did I think *love*?

I pass through the front door and grab a digestive cookie on my way. In the hallway to our room, I stop to prevent myself from stumbling into Homer. I assume he's waiting for me to unlock the door, but his wide-eyed expression remains fixed at the floor beside the entrance. His eyebrows knit at the bridge of his nose.

Following his gaze, I find the object and my blood chills, heart skipping a beat or two in my chest.

A book peers at us from beside our door with a yellow sticky note attached:

"Regards,
Henry Whitley"

Chapter Fourteen
Why the Fox Flees the Nest

"DID HENRY KNOCK AT THE DOOR? If so, please tell me you remained put."

Mom paces back and forth between the door and the other end of the crackled wall.

"We heard his knuckles rattle against the door," I lie, "when we ate the nice cucumber and ham sandwiches you bought from Sainsbury's."

I made sure to check the contents of the bag before pitching them into an empty grocery bag. The cleaning lady disposed of the deed. Mom narrows her eyes at me when I say "nice," a very un-Harper-like word.

"Because it wasn't the five-knock code, we stayed put." I rap my knuckle against the dusty wall. "After we heard him drop something by the door, we checked out the situation ten minutes later."

Wrinkles form on her forehead. *Should've stayed put and waited for me to find the book,"* I imagine she'll reply.

She presses her palms against her face. "And what if Henry lurked outside the door, Harper? Could've kidnapped you and Homer in the amount of time you took to pick this up."

She waves the book into the air.

Catch Me if You Can by Frank Abagnale and Stan Redding. Back home, Dad and I watched the movie with Leo and Tom Hanks. He and I liked the movies from the eighties more, Mom's least favorite decade. But no one told me the story came in book form.

"I don't know, Mom. We thought ten minutes was long enough. Sorry." I hate the last word as it falls off my lips like a loose boulder off the cliffs of Dover. I guess, on some level, she deserves to hear it.

For us leaving the apartment, not for picking up Henry's gift.

The shower sprinkles in the silence between us. Glad Homer decided to clean himself now. He felt so guilty for leaving without Mom's permission that when he saw the book, he fled into the room and buried his face in his pillow for half an hour.

Mom rubs the bridge of her nose and then the purple bags underneath her eyes. They droop so low, she could probably stow her wallet inside of them. Especially since it's missing thirty pounds now. "Guess I have to cancel my plans for the next week."

Does she mean, stay with us instead of going to work? St. Olga, let's hope not.

"Mom, go to your job. Nothing happened to us when we stayed put today."

"Until Henry grabs a pair of skeleton keys and breaks in here." She shakes her head. "My group planned a two-day trip for Canterbury. The plan was for Uncle Laran to bring you meals between work times."

As in tomorrow?

My cheeks redden with heat. "Why didn't you tell us this?"

"Because." She sighs. "There's ten hours between when I leave for Canterbury and when your uncle gets off work. I figured you might be tempted to leave the hotel with such a long time frame to yourselves."

Should've gone to Camden tomorrow instead of today.

"Let's stay with Uncle Laran for a few days, then. If Henry thinks we're living at this hotel now, it might take him a while to realize we left. Plus, your trip takes place on Saturday and

Sunday. Uncle Laran doesn't teach classes then."

She jerks her chin. "You are *not* going back to his place. On Sunday, he plans to go to church, and that leaves plenty of time for Whitley to find you and break into the apartment again."

Man alive, God crafted this woman out of marble. Or whatever material they made that Peter Pan statue out of—copper, I think.

Best hope Captain Hook didn't have any plans to come a-knocking again.

"When do you leave for Canterbury?"

"Tomorrow. Early morning."

I sit on Mom's bed, tired of standing. The mattress groans beneath my weight. I massage my calves. "Too late to cancel on your boss, Mom, the night before. They could fire you."

"But if I leave you here and Henry manages to access the room…no, I need to cancel."

The idea of our cabin fever days amplified by Mom's presence sours my stomach.

"Take us with you." The desperate words fly off my tongue with a spit that tastes like the cinnamon sugar from the lunch churros.

"To Canterbury?"

"Just like you had me tag along for the National Gallery Museum day."

She parks beside me, and I rise in an instant. "Sweetheart." She scrunches her face, preventing a Thames River of tears. "A trip to a museum nearby versus a city, more than two hours away, is very different."

"We could buy train tickets tonight. Let us come with you."

As I crane my neck in her direction, a loose piece of hair flies in front of my nose. Mom reaches to grab the strand, but I tuck it behind my ear before she can get a chance.

She folds her hands in her lap. "We're taking a bus tomorrow, sweetie. Not a train."

"Cheaper, right? And, if you're worried about space on the bus, we can squeeze into tight spaces." I glance at my stomach. "At least, Homer can."

"I don't know."

"Take away the money for my birthday and Christmas presents if you have to use that to pay for the bus ride for all three of us, but do not quit on your boss a day beforehand."

Tucking her legs under the bed, she leans forward into her hands to consider the proposal.

"He needs a new place to stay." I nod at the sweating bathroom door. Steam wisps from a crack. "At least, until we can figure out other arrangements."

"The company already booked the hotel rooms." Her voice comes out as weak as I take my tea. "They bought a double for me—took a nice chunk out of my paycheck, I'll bet—but not enough places for three people to sleep."

Silence spills over the room.

"Let me stay here and him go with you."

She snaps her neck up at me, face pink. "Absolutely not. I didn't let you stay in Arizona by yourself, why do you think I will in England? And not a chance I will share a bed with *him*."

"Him" spins the knob to the bathroom door and emerges wet in his Oscar the Grouch pajamas, borrowed from yours truly. He forgot a shirt again, silly him. Silly Harper, you need to stop staring.

A pine-scented fragrance fills the room along with warm steam. For once, the bathroom heat does not amplify the moldy-room scent. Something about whenever Homer exits versus Mom accomplishes this.

After massaging a towel through his wet curls, he drapes the sopping cloth onto the bed frame. He offers a warm smile to Mom. She returns a stern look.

Ah, friendship.

"Mom, unless you come up with a better plan that doesn't put your job at risk, I see no other options. Either both of us go, or you and him. I don't mind sleeping on the floor. Homer probably has no qualms with that either."

Slaves, from what Homer has described in Laran's lessons, didn't get real beds.

Her wrist cracks as she holds up her hand. "Fine, you can join me tomorrow. Only"—her eyes narrow at Homer—"because he needs a new place to stay since we haven't cracked the code in this book and we can't use the laver at the museum."

Our next plan accelerates to the lead.

Ecstatic, I relay the news to Homer, who had been busy trying to make out the words in *Catch Me if You Can*, holding the book sideways. When the words "we," "going," and "trip," travel across my lips, he engulfs me into a wet hug.

I toss a smug glance at my mom over my shoulder. "How can you not like him?"

She rubs a scar on her wrist, a similar one to match mine.

"You aren't the only one who doesn't trust people, Harper."

* * *

Paranoid, the next morning, Mom doles pink nausea pills to each of us. I notice how she doubled Homer's dose. Obedient, he crunches on the raspberry-flavored medicine, wincing at the bitter aftertaste.

"Any places we should hit up when we get there?" I mimic Homer's expression as the meds dissolve on my tongue.

"You will follow my group and my group alone," Mom growls, voice low and stern. "I want to keep a close eye on both of you at all times."

So much for avoiding Mom these next couple days. My tongue grazes over a remnant of the raspberry pill. At least we'll escape this cramped room.

And then what? I think, the cold morning air causing me to wrinkle my nose as we exit the hotel. Where will he stay? No doubt, Mom picked one of the cheapest hotels in Paddington. No way she can afford much more, even with the money Dad left behind.

We meet a crowd of eye-rubbing, yawning tourists at the bus stop and I grab a seat toward the front per Mom's instructions. "Motion-sick people, do *not* go in the back of the bus." She eyes Homer as if she expects him to protest. He doesn't.

"Train?" He nudges me in the ribs with his elbow. He clutches his tiny bag, the size of a pillowcase, against his stomach.

"No, a bus. You ride these a lot when you're my age. Except they come in yellow and with sticky spots on the floor instead of nice carpet like they have here."

Mom parks in the row next to us and motions for me to switch spots with Homer. "If you place him by the window, he might puke."

I roll my eyes. "Guess we'll cross that London Bridge when we get to it."

The bus bounces as we roll and swerve across the London streets, making wide swings when we approach curbs. Homer groans and buries his head into his knees as the vehicle continues to turn. With one hand, he shields his eyes, with the other, he clutches at his abdomen.

Mom raises her eyebrows at me. "Sure you don't want him in the aisle seat?"

Tempting, but if he pukes on you, you'll force the bus driver to go to the British Museum so you can dump Homer in the laver. Or worse, hand him to Henry Whitley.

Once, I experienced motion sickness on the Devil's Highway on a trip to visit some of Mom's friends in Morenci, Arizona. Route 191 curved over dusty cliffsides and through mountains until my brain grew fuzzy and heart throbbed in my temples. As I hyperventilated, blackness coating my vision, Mom plugged in a CD to distract me. Eyelids shut, I drowned myself in the music.

That could help Homie, now—some tunes.

"Give me my phone," I hiss to her across the seat. "So he can listen to music."

"Buried in my suitcase. The driver stowed it with the other large luggage." She says this in a holier-than-thou sort of way.

I return to Homer, who intensifies his groans. He rocks back and forth, cushion squishing with each movement.

"You know, Homie, for all the horrible conditions you experience back home, it surprises me that a little bus ride can take you out."

The pep talk accomplishes nothing, so I try another tactic by narrating the scenery as we glide by it.

Scarlet "Big London" buses whiz past. Cathedrals with spindling spires which almost look like drip castles, the ones I used to build from sand and water on a California beach as a kid. Dad used to help me. Trees arch their spines as we pass them. Cookie-cutter houses smooshed together in small villas remind me of the adobe houses back home, so smooth and clean on the outside.

But the inside, pat, pat, pat.

Just like that stranger patted me on the back in Phoenix. *Pat, pat, pat.*

Homer continues to groan when I narrate our surroundings, so I try to describe my home in Arizona for him. He enjoys the part about how we can never leave shoes outside because a scorpion might rent an apartment in a pair of Converse. How the summer oven conditions can singe the paws of a dog taken for a walk, or how the coyotes will snag small household pets left in the yard too long.

He smiles at the descriptions of juicy lizard tails and javelinas goring people, but Mom forces me to switch topics. So I use the last tactic in my arsenal to woo him out of his nausea.

This time, I tell the Bible story of this prophet named Elisha who bore a bald head. One day, a group of teenagers plagued him as he traversed up a mountain side—

"Tell a different story." Mom shields her stomach with her arms.

"Oh, come on. I really like this one."

"How can you choose such a terrible story when he's about to empty his breakfast onto the carpeted seats?"

"Nah, he'll love it. Everyone enjoys a great don't-talk-bad-to-bald-people-or-they-will-summon-bears-from-heaven-that-will-maul-you kind of story."

I twist the knob above his head, letting the cool A/C spill down his neck. Or it would, if Homer hadn't doubled over. "Not my fault you kept us cooped up in the hotel room to run out of Bible stories to share. Either I will finish this tale or tell him about Ehud, the left-handed judge."

Mom frowns as she takes a sip from a water bottle she purchased from Sainsbury's. "Pastor never covered that one."

"Well, basically, there's this really fat king, Eglon, who

takes over Israel. So this left-handed judge dude calls him into a secret meeting."

"No." Water trickles down Mom's chin as she makes a hand motion for me to stop. "I remember the story now. Don't tell him that one either."

"You ruin all my fun. Let me finish it for him."

"For Saint Olga's sake, no."

"Fine, Mom. Why don't you talk about Saint Olga, then, since you're so eager about telling us good and moral tales."

She glances at her lap, pale cheeks painted red in blush. "Oh, that's also not an appropriate story."

What?

"Now you *have* to tell it. You say her name all the time."

"Well, I'm not saying you should follow her example." A shy smile spreads across her sunburnt face. "But it is rather funny."

Turns out, a group of people murdered St. Olga's husband. She wreaked revenge in a number of ways, burying some of the men alive, getting some Drevlians drunk and having her men hack them to pieces, fun stuff like that. But her ultimate retaliation played out when she attached lit pieces of cloth and sulfur to bird's feet. The birds, of course, freaked out and landed on buildings to snuff out the fire, proceeding to ignite the entire city.

We all double over in laughter. Tightness in my chest releases. This is the way things are meant to be, a daughter and mother bonding over burning birds.

For the first time in months, I can look at her and feel something other than frustration. Hope ignites in my chest. I could hug her if the bus would stop bobbing up and down. Something inside of me wants to.

"Mom, that's a fantastic story. Why didn't you ever tell me

this before?"

The strong green smell of arugula breaks up the conversation. A passenger two seats back munches on the odd morning snack. Ginger hair peeks out from underneath a hat, and the rest of him hides in a striped coat.

Paranoia claws up my neck again. Relax, Harp, you can't panic every time you see a redhead—especially in a land so close to Ireland. He isn't wearing a scarlet coat. And something tells me Henry wouldn't get caught in plaid.

Mom's voice pulls me back.

"Harper, thousands of people died. It's really a sad story." Her lips draw into a thin line. "We really shouldn't be laughing. Even if they did deserve it. Those men."

I remember Homer back at the movie theater. Why had I gotten so desensitized to everything? Homer grips my hand and squeezes his eyes shut, maybe more motion sickness.

And then I allow myself to feel.

The window behind him blurs green. Didn't realize we were going that fast.

Chapter Fifteen
Why the Sword Fears the Soul

When the bus shudders to a halt and the engine ceases growling, Homer heaves a sigh of relief. He unbends himself and puffs his chest. "Survived." We both breathe.

"You always do, kid."

Our driver deposits us on a fractured sidewalk and promises to meet us at our hotel, a six-minute walk from today's destination, Canterbury Cathedral. After our guide instructs us that we will spend no more than two hours at the church, we commence a stroll, perusing brick and stone buildings, each older and crumblier than the previous.

Raising a yellow umbrella, our guide directs us to a stone gate that features shields of various colors and designs. One with a faded red horse and wings catches my eye. Our guide goes to inform the gatekeeper about our group's entrance, and I gaze at a green man on a throne with the golden words "EST ANNO DOMINI MELLISMO QUINCE."

Mom nudges me.

She nods at the group as they pass through the buttressed entrance and into the cathedral courtyard. My jaw plummets when I duck under the tunnel and pass into a large area with a hefty stone church.

Now that would make a pretty painting.

Aged spires jut into the sky, causing pains in my neck as I stare up at them. Arched windows swoop and join hands, like star-crossed lovers, at every inch of the building, and some metal scaffolding at the rear of the building creates an eyesore. Of course, humans had to ruin the beauty of the building somehow.

The gravelly voice of our tour guide forces me to return to earth. "We will meet back in this church courtyard in two hours to make our next stop, The Canterbury Tales Museum. Feel free to grab lunch on your own during the two-hour block."

He doles out the tickets to the group members.

It surprises me that he has enough for Homer and me We'd joined this trip as of last night. But as he hands me a paper slip, Mom catches my expression. "I told the tour group we have two extra guests and paid for your bus ticket and entrance fee for this, the museum, and the trip to Dover castle tomorrow."

My lips sag toward the stone pavement. "Did you tell them about us needing a hotel room as well?"

"Told them you paid for a separate room on your own." She winks. "Saved us a little money considering all three of us plan to squeeze into a room meant for two."

So, not much has changed since the last hotel.

We enter into the echoing sanctuary as pin-straight pillars, large as tree trunks, skyrocket toward a ceiling decorated in stone bars, the shape of diamonds, and geometric flowers. Stained glass covers every crevice of the walls, and deep purples, blues, and reds glimmer in the afternoon sunshine that's spilling through ever so faintly. And just enough scaffolding at every corner spoils the splendor.

Even though the outside wafts a cool breeze, the temperature drops even more inside the stony building. I clasp my arms around my waist and shiver. I nudge Homer with my hip. He leans closer. "Anywhere you want to go?" I whisper this so he has to lean even farther in to hear the question. There's that nice pine scent.

"Grab an audio guide." Mom motions to a station with radios on strings. "You can hold those up to your ear, and it will walk you through the cathedral."

"Great idea, Mom. Shall I get Homer an audio guide that speaks in the Palikarian language?"

Homer flips open a pamphlet the tour guide gave us and taps a picture. "We go there."

I squint at the map, leaning closer to him. "You sure, Homie? That exhibit's for a martyred dude."

The Palikarian understands neither "martyr" nor "dude."

"There." He taps the paper again. I hadn't noticed how clean cut his fingernails had become until now.

I shrug. "All right. Let's go visit Thomas Becket."

We make our way through rows of wooden chairs. Homer pauses when we reach a tomb inside the sanctuary. On top of the casket, a stone man lies on a rocky pillow, all draped in faded painted robes of some sort.

"How strange." Homer reaches out a hand for a moment and withdraws his arm, stuffing his fingers into his jean pockets. "You put man on tomb."

What? It takes a second for the images from the British museum of the Palikarian tombs to flicker across my vision.

"Instead of an animal? Yeah, we believe people remain people, even after they die."

He whiffs in a sharp inhale, and his eyes bulge, as if trying to comprehend such astounding information. We descend into the crypt, the dark hallways of shadows and silence and low-hanging walls. Dimly lit lanterns line columns which arch toward the ceiling, forming curtains of stone. In quietude, we spy various stone coffins along the way and rooms which split off with an altar of candles to some saint or cause.

I hear nothing but our quick steps as I attempt to ditch my mother and retain a moment away from her ever-watching eye.

My strides achieve nothing except sucking all the breath out of my lungs like a vacuum.

Wish my asthma would face an untimely demise like Thomas Becket.

Wheezing, I grab a wooden chair in what looks like a basement sanctuary of the church.

Homer slides next to me, and I notice Mom keeps her distance a few rows back.

"Who was Thomas Beck-ket?" The K crackles in Homer's throat at the pronunciation.

Sniffing in the musty air and trying to read the pamphlet in the gloomy lighting, I make out something about Thomas Becket being an archbishop in the twelfth century, appointed by Henry II. But the two didn't see eye to eye on how much independence a church could have. So Henry sent in four knights to hack Becket's head off. Lovely.

And turns out, the king probably didn't mean to kill off Tommy in the first place. His knights were really thick and didn't understand sarcasm when the king muttered about getting rid of Tommy-B.

My stomach sours at the mention of this. Maybe not all stories that involve dying are all that fun. Huh, maybe Homie has helped me become less desensitized to things.

"Guess any king with the name Henry turns out to be a jerk." I recall how the last Henry we encountered, of the eighth sort, married six times, killing two of those wives. His fiery hair flashes across my vision in the dim lighting of the room.

No wonder redheads cause shudders to run up and down my spine. Even if Henry Whitley didn't exist, they still would.

Creasing his brows, Homer *fla-laps* the pamphlet against his leg when I return it to him. "What is martyr?"

"You mean someone like Thomas Becket?"

"Yes."

"From what I've learned in church, a martyr is someone who dies for something they believe in." I pause. "Deletes." I list a few examples from our story time sessions—Apostle Paul, Stephen, Peter, all the sorts of stories that prove dying isn't always the best plot twist.

He leans forward, digesting the new word. "What is word for someone who deletes for something they do *not* believe in?"

I shrug. "Never heard of a word for that. Why?"

He mutters something about sparrows, but when I press him further, he drops the subject and heads toward a stone stairway to an outdoor garden.

* * *

Poppies and broken columns grow in the green patch of land. An elderly man paces between a wall of hedges with his hands behind his back. It smells green outside. We don't have that scent in Arizona.

"Your temples have gardens." Homer ogles the flowers. He kicks a displaced rock with his tennies.

"Churches," I correct him. "And sometimes. But I imagine they pay the workers to upkeep the land." Unlike the people in Palikari.

I feel a sharp jab in my side. I turn to see Mom has sidled up beside me. "What the heck, Mom? You know I hate it when you poke me."

She reddens. "Sorry, but Uncle Laran thinks he has an idea about Henry Whitley."

My frustration ebbs.

We could've figured this out sooner if we plugged him into a Google search. But, no, we had to use our internet as little as possible here, even with Mom checking her emails for the tour group every day.

My arms hug my sides to form a barricade. "Well?"

Mom and I slide onto a stone ledge that leads into the gardens while Homer meanders around the grounds, admiring various flora. I check over my shoulder for a guard to see if anyone will yell at us for doing so. No one in a uniform lurks nearby.

"He recognizes the name from his dissertation studies. Apparently, Henry Whitley's membership to a professional archeologist organization was revoked after he attempted to smuggle some of the artifacts from a Palikari site into his hotel. Namely, the fragment from Herodotus, the one with the date of the Festival of Sparrows."

Sparrows. Homer stopped talking in the Becket room when he mentioned those. Wonder if there's a connection.

"Do you think Henry wants Homer because of the Festival of Sparrows? Since he stole an artifact that had to do with that?"

She sighs, clutching her arms. She used to have a lot of bruises there. Not anymore. All that remains is pale skin. "I don't know. But unless Homer is finally willing to tell us about that ceremony, our hands are tied."

Chapter Sixteen
Why the Clock Gathers Stones

WE STRUGGLE TO PAY ATTENTION TO our guide when we reconvene in the courtyard. Not to mention, he rates worse than our last hotel on his ability to make us want to stay. One out of five stars at best—and not Arizona stars, mind you, London stars.

"We'll now be visiting The Canterbury Tales Museum. For those who are unfamiliar with the history behind *The Canterbury Tales*, Chaucer penned the story during the fourteenth century—"

I hoist myself on tiptoe, scanning the tops of the heads of everyone in our group for the ginger archeologist. If he found his way to our new hotel in Paddington, maybe he followed us to Canterbury.

My thoughts drift back to the old hotel. Bet he managed to bug our room and film our every action like that creepy Big Brother show. I cringe at the idea and shake the thoughts away. No, Harper, otherwise he would have waited for you and Homer to leave for Camden Market and nabbed Homer right there.

Shades of brunette and dishwater blonde flood me with relief. Nothing ginger stands out in the crowd. I drop down onto my soles.

Our large group funnels into a narrow alleyway of shops on the way to the museum. A child licks a cone from a frozen yogurt store. Saliva spills into my mouth at the thought of something cold and creamy, even on a day just peaking above sixty degrees.

Construction noises from a building undergoing scaffolding interrupt my thoughts.

"Why do they have to renovate everything here?" I wipe my nose with the back of my wrist, the scarred one. "Big Ben, soon the Houses of Parliament, the cathedral we visited. Why?"

Mom's shrill voice stings my ears from behind. "Even the buildings need a break from time to time." She catches up and tosses a warm smile my way. "You like your introvert time. Well, so do some of these places."

"Seriously? A building needs to be alone?"

She shrugs, the bag strap sliding down her shoulder. "People have visited some of those places for hundreds of years. Trodden down the stone steps until they bent, touched things they shouldn't have. Even popular attractions need a season of solitude."

Touch, touch, touch. Huh, even the buildings hate that.

Red flags dangling off a building signal for our group to cross from one end of the sidewalk to the other. The banners read, "The Canterbury Tales." Our tour guide stops us at the entrance of the squat building to give us a boring history of the Chaucer book.

I elbow Mom, but her blouse is so flowy it takes me a while to make contact.

"What?"

"Just wondering if Uncle Laran knows what Henry wants with Homie. If he's been discredited as an archeologist, no one will listen to him if he claims he found someone from the past. Why bother going through all the trouble when you risk getting arrested for kidnapping? Or worse."

"He'll get media attention, Harper. Back in the eighties, a man claimed to have traveled from the year 2003. Claimed Reagan would stay in office a second term."

Our tour guide raises his voice to stifle our conversation. "—the Father of English Literature, at least in a modern sense,

Chaucer is buried in Poet's Corner at Westminster—"

"Didn't Reagan do two terms, Mom?"

"Well, yes. But the man also said cars would run on salt water by the year 1993."

With a slight look of annoyance, our tour guide waves his umbrella and ushers us inside the brick building.

Wax figures in the shape of people greet us as we pass from room to room. Red illuminates the pasty face of a man in noble's clothes on a white horse. A servant wax figure that clutches a broom waves us forward with a single finger up a flight of steps scattered in hay.

"Chaucer penned these tales during a time of social and political upheaval." Our tour guide's face glows rosy as he steps toward one of the exhibits. "The Black Plague wiped out a significant portion of England's populace."

The second Dark Ages, my history teachers have called it.

No wonder Homie likes stories so much. They serve as a kind of escape for him.

I picture him huddled in a circle with the other temple slaves around a dim fire, exchanging tales of unruly visitors—the same way my friends in fast food share experiences about terrible customers.

"*A man brought in a sparrow to sacrifice,*" I imagine one would say. "*When I tried to tell him we only accept lambs, bulls, and pigeons—all the Old Testament stuff—he had such a conniption, I thought my manager would fire me on the spot.*"

"*Don't even get me started when we can't accept sacrifice coupons.*" The fiery glow would highlight the dark circles under the eyes of someone else. "*Not my fault no one invents paper discounts until at least the 1800s.*" Or at least, so Laran told me during one of his "teachable" moments.

I make a mental note to ask Homer about temple stories.

Maybe we can learn more about the Festival of the Sparrows and why Henry wants to kidnap him so much.

"Chaucer's stories embraced themes such as the nature of humanity, from the kindhearted to the greedy." Our tour guide gestures to a wax man glinting his eyes at the ceiling beside a dead knight. A single spotlight flashes on him in the dark room.

Before I can take a closer look, a bright screen flashes in front of me. Mom's phone.

"Uncle Laran replied. Henry predicted the laver would eject a Palikarian in May or June of this year, depending on the calendar interpretation. Twenty-eight hundred years after the Festival took place."

"How can he predict that?"

"I asked Laran a few seconds ago. Explains why Henry told me a man had visited the museum every day for weeks, months. Henry must've been waiting for Homer to emerge. Guess you beat him to it."

That historical document must not have provided the exact time of day when the laver would work its magic. Henry had gotten distracted by a Dark Age weapon when I first met Homie.

That could explain why Henry wants Homer so bad. Because he waited so many months to kidnap him in the first place—to do what? I wish we knew more about the Festival of Sparrows.

"Lucky that I was there at the right time, then, huh?"

"There's no such thing as luck, darling. Only divine providence."

I hug my arms. "Well, let's hope that whatever is keeping Henry at bay keeps it up."

Because knowing my luck these past few months, we don't have a whole lot of good fortune left.

Chapter Seventeen
Why the Sparrow Cries

BECAUSE MOM REFUSES TO ALLOW US to pull up Skype inside our hotel, Uncle Laran made me conduct Homer's lesson for today. No use in him taking a two-hour commute to get here. He scolded Mom and me for skipping a day of teaching on the train ride to Canterbury.

"Guess we'll have to cram in cosmetics and political institutions in one day," he texted to Mom when we dined at Pret a Manger.

"Cosmetics?" I had squinted at the glowing message. "Why would Homer use makeup?"

"Laran claims Egyptian and Greek men both wore makeup of some sort. At least, the Greek men loved to lather themselves in olive oil."

"Wow, to think they make fun of some of the theater guys for wearing eyeliner at my school."

"Apparently unibrows were the rage for men and women in Ancient Greece."

I winced, thumbing the bridge of my nose where my eyebrows would connect. Glad fashion evolves quicker than most things.

Mom leaves the room at seven in the morning to conduct research on time travel in a coffee shop. Our tour group heads out around ten for our next destination, so that gives me three hours to ask Homer about the topics Mom wrote down on a list for me.

"Uncle Laran's desired areas to ask Homer about. Please

write his answers in the blank spaces below. Use the back if needed.

1. Ask him about the Festival of Sparrows

a. He will not answer you. Press him once, and then move on.

2. Specifics about the Underworld—we want to flesh out some of the fuzzy spots in Palikarian religion, so ask him about:

a. The Room of Judgment

b. The importance of funeral pyres and the role they play in the Underworld

c. Palikarian Scarabs

3. Next cover the—"

I lean over the bed and nudge a figure on the ground with my toe. Homer unravels himself from the plaid hotel blanket and peers at me through sleepy slits.

"Sorry, Homie. Uncle Laran wants you to do a lesson today."

Knuckling his eyes, he yawns and sits up.

"All right, so first order of business, you want to tell me about the Festival of Sparrows?"

This appears to jolt him as his eyes spring wide, and he sucks in a sharp whiff of air. He pries open his lips. My heart thunderclaps in my chest. Does he trust me with this information that Uncle Laran has tried for months to get?

Homer clamps his mouth shut and shakes his head. Light dies in my chest.

"Homie, why not?"

"Bad."

"True, but sometimes we have to talk about bad things to get good things." At least, so my therapist told me all those months ago.

He chews on his lip and scrunches himself into a ball. His stance reminds me of a Muslim classmate back home when he prays toward Mecca.

"Hard story." Homer unbends himself and rubs his hands up and down his knees. "Bad story."

My gut squeezes with unease in my abdomen as a signal to move on. Why press him further on a painful subject?

But he almost told me. He *almost* trusts me.

I pat the bed and motion for him to sit beside me. He gazes at the covers and hesitates. Mom refused him access there during the night. My stomach sours at the thought of him being treated like a dog not allowed on a couch.

"Come on, up here."

He obeys and parks at the very edge of the bed, as far away from me as possible. His fingers massage the white comforter.

"Tell you what, Homie. If I tell you my most painful story from my past, will you promise to talk about the Festival of Sparrows?"

"You tell bad story?"

"Yes, if you'll share yours."

He stares at his bare feet for a moment. Calluses stick to his soles like rocks. Then, he shoots his arm toward me for a handshake. "Promise."

I shake his hand and hold on longer than necessary. "Good. Travel with me back a little over a year ago. You won't need electromagnetic wormholes for this one."

* * *

What Led to the Incident in Phoenix

My younger eyes peek around the corner of our stone-white walls into the kitchen. A brown lizard a few feet above me slithers toward the direction of my parents having an argument, standing on opposite sides of the glass kitchen table.

Mom heaves a black trash bag onto the table with a clatter of noise from within the container. She pulls out a beer bottle and waves it in front of my dad's face.

"Take a guess where I found these, Alex."

I spot traces of blush underneath my dad's tan skin. He waits a moment, and then a humorous smirk hides underneath his ruddy mustache. "I wanted to run a glass recycling plant in our basement. Collected them from all the neighbors."

Mom's hands plant on her hips. Even though Dad towers above Mom, she somehow seems taller. "Uh huh. And all the neighbors drink nothing but beer."

"Guess they live like the ancients. Did you hear back about that job with the touring agency?"

Leaning forward, Mom clicks the bottle against the table and glowers at Dad. "Alex, how quickly did you go through all of these?" She jiggles the bag.

He rubs his fingers against his temples. "Bet they'll contact you any day now. I know how much you and your brother love history."

With her free hand, Mom plants a fist on her hip. "You drank this within a month, didn't you? You went through hundreds of bottles just in February alone."

He shrugs. "Had to get in what I could before Lent. I know how seriously you Catholics observe it. Now, tell me what the agency said."

"How long?" She grasps the bottle in her fingers and thrusts her hand at his face, almost as if she's about to hit him with the glass. "How long, Alex, did it take you to build this collection?"

His face hardens as he presses both palms against the table, leaving handprints.

"One week."

The bottle drops from my mom's hand and shatters against the wooden floor.

* * *

Why the Incident in Phoenix Happened

The scene dissolves to the kitchen table once more, a few months later, with the sun filtering through the wooden window frames. Mom scoots her chair back and draws the blinds over the windows.

"Too hot in here." Beads of sweat glisten on her neck and on her bruised arms.

I emerge from my hiding spot in the hallway to grab cereal from the cupboard. Grasping the Lucky Charms, I reach for a bowl.

"Those are dessert." Mom slides into a chair by the tale.

"Not according to this." I tap the "part of a balanced breakfast" part of the box with a finger. "Or Dad."

"Harper, get yourself a bowl of multi-grain Cheerios. I won't tell you again."

Sighing, I grab the other box and pour myself a clump of unsweetened cereal. But, to spite my mom, I dig up a few marshmallows from the Lucky Charms and bury them in the mixture. And, to further the injury, I swing open the blinds, letting oven-hot sun spill through the room.

"Close those." She shields her eyes with her hand.

"Oh, but look at how the light shines upon all the earth."

"Harper."

"But Mom, I can't see as well with the curtains drawn."

Standing, she lunges forward and presses the two curtains together. She hisses and removes her hands so fast it's like the cloth had burned them. She freezes in place for a moment as if thinking about something. I take this time to park on a chair at the table and crunch on the marshmallows before she returns.

Sneaking the green-colored sweets into my mouth, I spot a slip of paper on the kitchen table. More paperwork for Mom's new job she got overseas, I think.

"When do you leave for England, Mom?" My voice is muffled by the marshmallows.

"In a couple weeks. The tour group technically starts this week, but the company took so long with the paperwork, I won't participate in all the attractions. Maybe next year, though."

"Next year seems so far away." I glance at the paper again.

I lose my breath when I read the headline of the packet on the table, heart pounding in my ears like a distant war drum.

In bright, bold letters read the words, "Petition for Dissolution of a Non-Covenant Marriage (Divorce) with Minor Children."

* * *

The Actual Incident before the Phoenix Incident

Fast-forward to the month of October, when I spy a roadrunner in the yard as I complete my geography homework. A hawk moth the size of my head, lands on the window, blocking the sunlight from streaming through.

"Go away." I growl. "It's only sixty degrees outside, and

Mom won't turn on the heat yet."

The creature remains put. I sigh and pull out my phone to call Dad. The dial sends me to voicemail. "Hey, Dad, just wondering if you could drop off my Halloween costume at Mom's place. The Cleopatra one. I know you just moved in and all, but I think I left the outfit in one of your boxes. Should be in the same one with the God Bless This Home cross-stitch thing-y. Let me know when you find it."

I hear Mom's heels click as she enters the kitchen. Pressing the red hang-up button, I return to identifying Greece and Rome on the world map.

"It's official today." Her voice is as hollow as a tunnel. "It" being the period of time before the divorce finalizes.

"Good for it." I trace the heel on the boot of Italy with a red crayon. "You know, Stephen King refers to It as an evil clown. We never did see the remake."

She frowns at the hawk moth in the window. "I know your dad used to watch the old version of that movie. Didn't like it when he had you see it with him. What is with that man and eighties movies?"

Her cell phone rings to the tune of "Splish Splash." *Mom, forever stuck in the fifties.* She clicks a green button, and I shade in the Mediterranean Sea with a light blue pencil.

I hear a sharp gasp and her phone hits the floor. Rolling off my chair, I flip over the device, the screen now a spiderweb of fractures. Mom crumples to her knees, face in her hands, yelling obscenities. She cries out the name of God over and over again.

At first, I think she's taking the Lord's name in vain—something that would never pass her lips—but I see her shrieking at the heavens. It's not a curse, rather a prayer.

"Mom?" I scream, trying to shake her. All I can smell is her peach perfume. She put on too much today.

She remains stiff for several minutes. I pick up the phone, but the person at the other end hung up. Or Mom did. Can't tell.

"Mom? What happened?"

Her sobs transform into shudders until she at last unrolls and faces me with a pink tear-stained face.

"The hospital." This comes out so stony and low, it sounds as if someone else inhabited her body. "Your Dad—"

She doesn't finish her sentence. I wrap myself in a corner and sob. She doesn't come over to hug me. Deep down she knows I won't let her.

* * *

Canterbury, Present Day

Homer has his arm wrapped around me as I scrunch my face to block any potential tears. I lean into him and shiver for several moments, suppressing any sobs.

"Pancreatic cancer." I massage the area underneath my stomach. It feels warm. "A kind of disease here which knocks out forty thousand people a year. It deletes them."

He rubs his thumb on my shoulder for comfort. "So *disease* delete your father, not your Mom."

I inhale. My diaphragm spazzes. Hold it together, Harper. "Sort of. I don't think it's a coincidence he died the same day the divorce went through."

"Harper." He sounds sad.

"After Mom signed the papers in June, he quit all activities. Used to play on a church softball team, led a Boy Scout troop, anything—he stopped doing all that. I think he gave up on living.

Thanks to Mom."

He hovers like a bird with his wing wrapping me in silence for a moment. Why do I like his touch so much when I hate all other human contact? Maybe he's not human. He's too good for that.

"All right, Homie. Your turn. Tell me about the Festival of Sparrows."

* * *

The Festival of Sparrows, as Told to Me by Homer

His story takes me to a Palikari temple, an outside portion of it beside the gardens. Steel clouds above flash with lightning and the occasional thunderclap. Rain drenches Homer as he shudders, despite the warm June air.

Ahead, the laver is mounted on a rocky pedestal with priests hovering over it, squeezing something scarlet and thick into the tub.

Something else snags my attention in his story—the laver. He says a copper wire winds around the tub's base with one end pointed toward the sky. Homer explains the priests use the wire to capture lightning and send the contents of the laver to our present day.

"This year?" I say.

"Yes, we have other name for it. The year they believe Underworld come to Earth. Consume everything. End of everything."

"Why did they think that?"

"Greeks threaten to invade. End of Palikari is end of our world. They hoped to appease the gods."

Lovely. "So, they were sending you to the Underworld?"

"Yes."

He continues the story. Glass-shattering shrieks emit from the general direction of the laver. A high-pitched alarm and then nothing. Again and again and again. Homer doesn't say what the screaming is. Who is doing it.

Two priests lead Homer toward the laver, each with a firm grip on his arm. Although Homer doesn't struggle, a pained expression stamps itself into his face. The entourage pauses midway to rub Homer's legs and arms with oil. According to him, it feels smooth and warm.

The high priest stands on a stone pedestal beside the laver and proclaims about the disasters the gods wreaked upon the lands in recent years—famines, earthquakes, invasions from the Greeks.

"We must appease the gods before we invoke their wrath again." His shouts grow hoarse above the screeches at the laver.

Quivering, Homer turns his gaze to the priests spilling the scarlet stuff into the laver. They crush something small and brown to extract the liquid. He won't tell me what it is.

"Homer?" My voice trembles in my throat. "What do they have in their hands?"

Even though he is describing everything to me in the hotel room, I feel as though he has transported me to the very event. He imitates the shrieks, the painful, painful, shrieks.

He swallows. "Sparrows."

I suppress the urge to puke as the priests dig sharp blades into the throats of the little creatures. Each lets out a series of chirping before the priests delete them.

"This is just awful, Homie. They must kill hundreds of birds to fill that thing."

He nods. "Thousands."

I tuck away any questions about how long it took them to collect all the sparrows, as Homer plunges with eager vigor into the story, perhaps to be done with it all.

"Filling this laver with the blood of sparrows"—the high priest's eyes jut wide and flash with lightning—"we will send their blood to the god of the Underworld and pray the gods relent."

Homer shakes as if someone forced him into a seizure.

"Homie, what role do you play in this ceremony? What's your duty?"

He winces. "I play the human sparrow."

I clutch at my throat. "You mean they cut—"

"No, keep listening."

With a jabbing finger, the high priest gesticulates at Homer as the two who flank his sides escort him to the laver. The priests hold up the last sparrow. This one, for some reason, does not utter a cry. Maybe the man who holds it clamps his thumb too tightly onto its throat, but the bird refuses to lift a shout to the heavens for salvation.

Man alive, say something, little guy. You won't get another chance.

Slicing its throat, the priest drains its blood into the tub and tosses the carcass off the platform into the pile of other bodies. When Homer reaches the top of the platform, the stench of blood overwhelms him. Darkness coats his vision, and the two guards have to hold him up.

They lift him and place him in the thick scarlet liquid. He describes the substance as warm and sticky. Without the two guards balancing his arms, he feels as though he'll slip into the metal tub.

"We now present the god of the dead with the human sparrow." The high priest gestures in front of the platform. A female dancer in less clothes than acceptable at a public school dances and chants.

"Our most despised and plentiful kind of bird in the temple. May the god accept this lowly human offering. If we remove him from the land, may the gods see this as a symbol of purging all that is impure in Palikari."

Man alive.

The dude starts to chant something, but Homer's hearing goes out when the priests, gripping a hand on each shoulder, plunge him into the blood. The metallic taste fills his nostrils and mouth, suffocating him. He thrashes, trying to surface, but the grip continues to hold him down.

Breath growing shallow and darkness forming a film over his eyes, he at last feels the weight on him release. Pushing against the slippery bottom of the laver, he emerges to gasp a breath. When the liquid drips from his eyes, draining down the laver, he finds himself in the British Museum.

* * *

Canterbury, Present

This time, I wrap both of my arms around him and rock back and forth.

"You win for the worst story, Homie."

His lips quirk in a sad grin, and he snorts once. "More terrible for the sparrows than Homer."

I shake my head, screeches filling my ears despite the air conditioner in the corner of the room blaring at full blast. "I can't stop hearing those birds shrieking. You imitated them really well. If it's any consolation, you're a great storyteller."

"Homer always hear them. The sparrows."

Sniffing, I blink several times to stop a river of water from spurting out of my eyes.

"Homie." My toes dig into the short carpet. "Why do you think that last sparrow remained silent? Why didn't he cry like the others?"

He doesn't answer. My little sparrow doesn't answer.

Chapter Fifteen
Why the Devil Lion Prowls

THUNDER GROWLS IN THE SKY AS our bus approaches Dover Castle, the stony building in a haze of fog. Mom alerted us that the weather dropped to the lower fifties, so Homer and I both wear a hoodie today. Him in green, me in red. We look like a perfect July Christmas.

As we roll up to the parking lot, our tour guide tells us we will spend two hours at the castle before driving home, arriving in the late afternoon.

The bitter aftertaste of the raspberry motion sickness pills still lingers in the back of my throat. I can only imagine how Homer feels. Mom made him take double my amount in case. He stares at the carpeted pattern on the ceiling in a dreamy sort of state. With his tongue lolling out, I worry he might have overdosed.

First the communion wine, now this…

Screeching, the bus doors open, and we exit into a drizzle of cold rain.

I pull my hood over my head and shiver, knees wobbling, as our guide motions for us to huddle in a circle around the vehicle.

We couldn't have this meeting inside the bus? With all the heaters?

Shoving my hands under my armpits, I hunch over, and my legs tremble. Even Homer, in his tranquil state, tremors with water dripping down his pointy nose.

Why didn't Mom buy any umbrellas here? Or rain jackets? This is England.

"Welcome to Dover Castle." He motions to the blocky building, barely visible in the fog. "Well, what you can see of it." A halfhearted laugh ripples through the group. "Here you'll find tunnels used during World War II, a Roman lighthouse, an Anglo-Saxon church, and of course"—he gestures to a blocky, stony building, where a single British flag waves on a cubic spire—"a castle, built in 1066 after the Battle of Hastings."

You could've said all of this on the bus.

"I plan to lead a tour around the grounds, but you can feel free to roam around and take in the sights of the castle."

Mind soaring back to the British Museum, I think through the most obscure places he mentioned. I can breathe in areas with fewer people.

Then again, with Homie by my side, I could suck in a healthy gulp of oxygen back in Phoenix during rush hour.

"There's also a chap who's offering tours of the World War II tunnels in the area." He points toward a hazy stone path that dips into a tunnel. "He's a bit more of an expert in that area, so you might want to meet with him. I believe he begins his tour in an hour."

He checks his watch. "Meet back here in two hours, or you might find yourself walking back to London."

The tour guide hands out neon wristbands for entry into the castle. I strap one around my already drenched arm and tap Mom on the shoulder. She turns to me, raindrops dewing on her hair, which she pulled into a tight bun earlier this morning.

"You taking the tour, Mom?"

"Have to for my job. I need to evaluate how this guide does at every spot. Lucky for him, the tour company doesn't let him do many talks. Sounds almost as boring as your uncle in his classroom lectures."

A smile tears up my cheek at Mom's insult toward her brother. I wipe it away along with a swath of rainwater and rub my pale hands together.

"Are you joining me on the tour, Harp?" This comes out in a stern sort of voice that sounds more like a statement than a question.

"No, I think Homie and I will peek around at some of the more obscure sights. I imagine everyone will be rushing to get into the castle."

Sure enough, clumps of our group travel in hunched masses of raincoats and umbrellas toward the security gate near the actual stone gate of the fortress.

Mom squints at Homer, who now spins in circles in the rain with his neck arched back and tongue out to catch the water. "You sure you can handle him alone? The tour group would be much safer, you know."

"I hate crowds, Mom. And something tells me Homer wants more of a chance to roam around the grounds, having been cooped up for over two weeks." I add the last part hoping guilt will well in her chest.

She sniffs, shivers, sighs.

"Fine, Harper. I will allow for both of you to wander the grounds." She unzips her coat pocket and pulls out my phone. "But please keep in constant contact with me. And I expect you at the bus ten minutes before we leave."

My cold skin burns with anger. So she had the phone in her pocket the whole time. We could've listened to music on the bus ride to calm Homer's stomach sickness.

Shoving her hand into her pocket, she pauses for a moment and then pulls her fingers out to grip my arm.

"Do *not* lose him, Harper."

I flinch. "Stick to him like toffee. Got it." My stomach growls. Aside from the hot chocolate, I can't remember one of the last desserts I had. And Uncle Laran made a mean sticky toffee pudding on one of our first nights here. Reminisces of butterscotch dance on my tongue.

Mom releases her grip and joins the crowd for the tour group up the walkway. I wait until the mist obscures her before I pull Homer out of his endless spinning. His neck snaps forward, and he frowns at me with his tongue still out.

"Water." His voice comes out thicker than toffee pudding.

"It rains all the time here, Homie. You want to visit an Anglo-Saxon church?"

He pouts. "Why?"

"Maybe they have wine there," I tease.

Hugging his arms across his chest, perhaps imitating Mom when she crosses hers, he shakes his head. "Stay outside."

My hoodie clings to my skin. Knees buckling, I sigh. "Why, Homie? F-freezing out here." My teeth chatter.

"Water."

"That's not a good reason."

"Miss outside." He gestures in an indistinct direction of grass. "Miss garden. Miss home."

Guilt curdles in my gut. I wipe my nose from rainwater and drape a soggy arm around him. Even with the poor conditions back in Palikari, we have torn him away from friends. I chew my lip. Maybe even a girlfriend. Even if they didn't have those back then, he might love a girl back home. I tuck my arms into one another.

"I know you do, Homie. We can stay outside. You've seen plenty of churches anyway."

Who knows? Maybe he'll keep me warm. Every time I stare

at him, my neck catches fire.

We amble around the perimeter alongside stone walls and large mounds covered in grass. Trudging up one of these, and avoiding two near-slips, we run into a cannon that drowns in puddles. Someone has stopped the mouth of the weapon with a red peg.

Homer kneels by the cannon, soaking his jeans, and rubs his hand across the smooth black surface. He presses his ear to the thing as if expecting the weapon to whisper a secret.

"Duty of this?" He raps his knuckles against the metal. His eyes bulge when he hears the tinny tap of his fingers.

Images of him during the Wonder Woman movie flash across my mind in the leaden lighting. Considering the people who built this place situated the cannon near a cliffside, if I tell him what the weapon does, he might react and tumble down to his death. The weird, drunkenness of his walk—from the pill overdose—wouldn't help either.

"People rode it like horses," I lie. "See the wheels on it? Like a chariot."

"Horses?" He climbs on top of the cannon and straddles the base. I glance over my shoulder to make sure no security personnel lurk nearby. No one appears in the mist.

Everyone has gone to the castle, I guess.

Homer bounces on the cannon as if trying to coax the weapon to move. "No go."

"Of course not, Homie, it's—it's dead. Deleted a long time ago."

With a quick motion, he slides off its back and lands in the mud—very, very close to the cliffside. I race forward and grab his hand. How do his fingers remain so warm in such cold rain?

"Why dead horse out in rain?"

"Save these questions for Uncle Laran, Homie. He knows far more about history than I do." I tighten my grip to ensure he won't stray any closer to the cliffs than needed.

"Harper smart, too." He trips over his feet, half due to the puddles and half because of the pills.

"Sure, Homer. Everyone's smart. Look at you. You learned the English language in just a couple months, thanks to your handy-dandy oral tradition or whatever."

"Harper *good*."

I freeze in place and stare at him through the sheets of water. He only uses "good" to describe the most wonderful things in life. A toothy white grin glows in the blurred lighting. Fire ignites every part of me. I break eye contact.

"You took too much medicine, Homie. I'm not a good person."

His head jerks side to side. With his free hand, he jabs a finger at me. "Good. So, so good."

In a sudden motion, he cups my chin and plants a kiss.

Man alive, I did not expect that.

It feels innocent and a little awkward. I don't think he's done it before—after all, I never have—but something about the gesture warms my face and stomach. And then I don't feel the rain anymore. Time pauses.

He releases, and I manage an "Oh" before craning my neck toward my feet. "We should get out of the rain before we catch a cold."

I don't think sicknesses work like that. Hugging myself, I angle toward the castle.

The medicine relaxed him, Harp. It made him drunk or something, I reason to myself as we take the slippery hill one step at a time. Maybe kissing means something else in Palikarian culture. People greet each other with holy kisses in the Bible.

But *holy* cannoli, what a kiss.

Wow, wow, wow, did that happen? Our lips just touched, touched, touched, and I didn't hate the feeling.

I try to force the thoughts away, but they boomerang back every few seconds.

We reach the entrance of the castle.

Blue and red banners display on jutting poles as we pass through the stony archway. Trailing a line of people, we follow a sign that points us to the high tower and wind up an old staircase. Everything smells warm and wet. I realize, as we pass into the first room, that I still have my fingers wrapped around his.

I unclasp my hand and pretend to admire a scarlet curtain with a golden lion stitched into the fabric. Even glazed in cold water, my cheeks blaze like hot coals. "I think they set up these rooms to look like medieval times or something." As I pass murals on the wall of knights, I motion to them. "Warriors, hundreds of years after Palikari. Lots of people deleting in things like the Crusades. At least, that's what my history teacher says."

A realization strikes me. Homer told me in the hotel this morning that he thought the laver would transport him to the Underworld. At least, the end of the world where the Underworld consumes everything. Maybe he thinks he's still there. The dim lighting in the castle doesn't help to dissuade that impression.

Has he thought he's been in the afterlife this whole time?

"Homie, do you think you are in the land of the dead?" If so, he just kissed a zombie, or whatever they have in their mythology. Gross, that ruined the moment.

He shakes his head, rubbing his finger along a painted blue bench. Tightness disappears from my chest.

"How did you know that you hadn't traveled there? That this

isn't the end of the world?"

Swiping the remainder of the rainwater glaze from his face, he rests his chin on his hands. "Because high priest say Underworld full of mean spirits. Mean things. Bad things. And Mom and Uncle Laran kind, not mean. Harper good, not bad. So, Homer not in Underworld."

I wince at the words *kind* and *Mom* placed side by side but decide not to dampen his spirits. Everything grows hot from the use of the word "good" by my name. I realize my lips have crawled so far up my cheeks they could touch my ears. I try to force them down, no use.

On the way through the rooms, my heart jolts in my chest when I spy a tourist with ginger hair, the same shade as Henry's. But, when he turns his face, I realize the person is a she, no older than twelve, with a heavyset build and short haircut.

Relax, Harper. Henry's way taller than that. How would he have figured out how to follow us here anyway?

Homer squeezes my hand and my anxious thoughts dissolve.

We traverse through a few more rooms, one with plastic bread loaves to represent the medieval diet. My stomach burns from within me, and I clutch my abdomen at the fake food.

"Getting hungry. Probably won't eat until we return to London, huh?"

Homer, not seeming to hear, holds the loaf to his nose and sniffs. He recoils at the lack of a warm, toasty scent. The whole castle smells like stone.

"How about we try to get food after we visit the top of this castle, Homie?"

"No money." With a sigh and pout, he grips a long spoon placed in a cauldron. He peeks inside, I assume to see if the workers left any soup in there.

"I still have some left over from the day in Camden Market."

His expression brightens at that, and he shouts something along the lines of racing me to the top of the tower. Before I can object about asthma, he whooshes out the room and up the winding steps. I remember Mom's warning to keep an eye on him. Despite myself, I force my feet to pound the stairs, fast as they'll go.

I take a breather halfway up, letting a couple tourists pass me. Amidst the heaving, wheezing breaths and burning lungs, I hear a yelp. I force myself to stop breathing, but the noise has stopped. The sound has triggered a memory of Homer's shrieks in our hotel room, when he imitated the sparrows.

A group of laughing girls passes me. Must've come from them. Crazy tourists—I hate how much noise bounces off these stone walls.

Continuing my race up the flights, I pass stone hallways which lead to rooms ranging from places to sleep to an armory. Focus, Harp, get to the top. You can take mental snapshots later.

At last, I reach the roof and crumple to my knees, lungs aflame, herds of people scooting around me to get a view of the grounds in the hazy mist.

Pushing myself up, I scan the crowd for a Palikarian who will flash a toothy smile at me and, rainwater dripping from his curls, announce he has won the race.

I spy no green hoodie caked in mud anywhere.

My heart thunders. One hand clutches my burning side, the other my chest. I make a mad scan of my surroundings, and my eye catches on the flailing British flag hoisted on the roof. "Homer, where did you go?"

A few tourists crane their necks at me for a moment and then return to the edge of the building to take in the lack-of-a-view. Green foliage on the ground level pokes through the fog.

Fear freezes my veins, and I feel tears well in my waterline and spill down my cheeks to join the other droplets of rainwater. This time I can't blink them back.

What happened?

"Did you get lost in the castle, Homie, on your way up here?" The words crack in my throat like glass. My squishy sneakers squeak. That has to be it. He sprinted into one of the rooms we passed along the way. He gets distracted sometimes.

I feel a hard tap on my shoulder, and choke on a sob in my throat.

"Oh, Homie." I double back. "I thought you—" My voice trails off as the girl in the short ginger haircut withdraws the hand she just poked me with. My skin recoils at the touch.

"A man told me to give this to a girl in a red hoodie." She speaks in a shrill British accent. The kind of voice I could be content to never hear the rest of my life. Her tone reminds me of the whistle my mom used to blow as a volleyball coach. She got most of the bruises on her arms from that, which helped to hide any suspicion from the players' parents about our home situation with Dad.

"He also said to give it to someone with blue hair, but—" The girl's brown eyes flash at my pixie cut. Most of the blue has faded throughout the course of summer. Mom didn't want to pay a hairstylist to retouch the roots.

"Larger kind of guy?" My voice cracks so much I feel it shatter in my throat. "Hair same shade as yours?"

"Yes." With a gloved hand, she passes a book to me with the title *The Pursuit* emblazoned in green letters. "He says thank you for the gift." She makes direct eye contact. "He'll treasure it."

A yellow sticky note on the book's cover burns my retinas. But I don't need to read the note to know what the message says.

Part Three: August

Are not two sparrows sold for a penny? Yet not one of them will fall to the ground outside your Father's care. And even the very hairs of your head are all numbered. So don't be afraid; you are worth more than many sparrows.

—Matthew 10:29-31

Chapter Nineteen
Why the Lightning Strikes Twice

ALTHOUGH THE PALIKARIAN EXHIBIT CONTAINS FEW visitors, the guards still fill the room. Knew we shouldn't have visited the British Museum again.

Uncle Laran motions for me to follow him into the half-room. I do so with caution. Perhaps they remember me from the video cameras posted around the room. Do they have a screenshot of my face from the day Homer emerged from the laver?

I massage a nervous index finger and thumb through my hair.

Most of the blue dye has vanished. If the cameras videotape in color, they won't recognize my blonde roots underneath. And from what I can remember in the TV shows I watch, CCTV streams in black and white most of the time.

Plus, I forced myself into the tight olive dress from Primark today. Last time at the museum, I wore a hoodie, so maybe a dress will throw them off.

Uncle Laran, seeing me lag, pulls me into a whisper. I hate the way his beard scratches my ear, like Dad's. "They won't remember you. Homer arrived two months ago. Besides, I think they are more worried about the artifact that escaped. Probably didn't pay any attention to you."

At the mention of his name, my lip trembles and tears well. Ever since Henry took him, I've cried more times than I care to count. And I hate this. Man alive, I hate this.

What did you do to me, Homie? You broke me. I was made of stone. And you broke me.

A gentle nudge from Uncle Laran drives us toward exhibit. We stand back at the other end of the room from the laver, not to draw attention to ourselves. Even if the guards eye us with suspicion, what can they do? Yell at us for looking at an artifact?

A.K.A. the world's weirdest time machine.

"Homer told you they used to have a wire wrapped around the laver?" Uncle Laran pretends to look at a black scarab amulet in another glass case. The specimen reminds me of a large beetle.

I nod, coughing into my sleeve. I wince at the taste of mucus in my throat, nothing like a summer cold. Mom says that with all the stress I've endured, my immune system had weakened.

"Made of copper. At least, he pointed to a pence and said they made it out of the same material."

Uncle Laran tosses a quick glance at the laver and back to the amulet. "Well, the lightning must have burned the copper clear off the laver when the vessel transported him here. Or perhaps the wiring rusted and fell off over time."

"Why lightning?"

Last time I checked, the tub didn't travel eighty-eight miles per hour like the DeLorean in *Back to the Future*. Dad and I used to love watching that movie.

"You need a powerful current of some sort to create a wormhole of magnetic fields according to Thornean and Einsteinian theory."

I frown, staring at the iron laver. In an automatic motion I shove my hands into my hoodie pockets. "But how did historians dig the laver up if the tub transported from his time to ours?"

A guard with dreadlocks nearby shoots me an odd look of suspicion and leaves the room to garble something into her walkie-talkie.

Observing this, Uncle Laran ushers me out of the room.

"The laver transported *him* and the blood, not itself. I'll explain downstairs."

We pass a crusty brown head of a statue of an Ammonite king—kind of reminds me of some artifacts from the *Titanic* when they'd stayed underwater so long—and fat, flat statues from a group known as the "Sea Peoples." Uncle Laran informs me this group of people wreaked havoc around the time the Greek Dark Ages started. Supposedly.

"Could've also been a number of natural disasters that made the entire Mediterranean plunge into a dark time. Too hard to tell. Don't even know if Homer had a grasp of the history during our sessions. It was a Dark Age to him and us."

Winding down the stairs, I remember Homer leaning against the corner of the wall at the bottom his first day here. How I had to wrestle the hoodie over his onion-scented head and sneak him out of the museum. Onion and pine—I miss those scents.

We enter the atrium. Uncle Laran finds two open seats by the café and suggests we grab something to eat.

I shake my head, the unholy taste of the apple and mayo still fresh in my mind from the sandwich I ate two months ago.

"We should grab some lunch." Uncle Laran pats his stomach where a button from his oxford bulges. "I usually eat two hours earlier than this, but because I cancelled my class for today, schedule's a bit off."

Uncle Laran would have made the visit to the museum earlier, but the first half of the week was spent trying to figure out Henry Whitley's location. The man left no traces on social media, and when Mom placed Henry's email in an online tracer, the website revealed he used a forged header to send the message. She mentioned something about a VPN. In either case, we'd gone back to square zero.

When Mom suggested turning the case over to the police, Uncle Laran rejected that proposal. "Too risky. They'll want to know our relation to the boy. He's not family."

"We could report him as a missing friend."

"But if they find him, they'll be curious about his history. And if they discover where he comes from, back to the British Museum. And who knows what will become of him if that happens."

No, we had to stick to Plan A, all while keeping Henry and any other tomb robbers away from him. Once we retrieved Homer, we'd return him home.

After a week's worth of efforts, we leave Mom to do the researching after she spends the day with her touring groups.

"Want me to fetch you something at the café, Harper?" Uncle Laran doubles a glance when he spies the Malteser cakes. He winks at me.

I sneeze into my dress sleeve. Uncle Laran unfurls a tissue from his coat pocket and offers the cloth to me.

"I'm not hungry." The word hungry gets cut off by me blowing into the Kleenex.

"Harper, you've barely eaten these past few days and have walked outside aimless in the rain for the last three of them. No wonder you're under the weather."

I wave the air as if trying to brush away any remaining sneeze particles. "Fine, Uncle Laran. I just hate the food in the British Museum."

He steps back. "You certain? I could grab you something small, like a muffin or pastry."

The idea of a dessert would've sounded delicious with Homer here. Now, everything tastes like mulch when I eat it— cupcakes and carrots alike.

"I'm good. You can grab yourself something if you want."

With an awkward bob of the head, Uncle Laran departs toward the trailing line at the checkout. While he orders, I pull out my sketchbook to draw the papery red poppies in the garden in front of Uncle Laran's apartment complex. After smudging two lines on the paper, I shut the notebook, feeling unmotivated to pencil anything.

My chest heaves with a heavy weight, as if someone has dropped a millstone on my sternum, and my eyes shutter to slits from the weight of crying so much.

Uncle Laran returns with a small bowl of parsnip and potato soup. The broth smells of carrots and some other earthy vegetable. Tears pop from my eyes over nothing and everything at once, and I bury my head into my arms on the table. The sobs sear my raw throat, shredded by the mucus of the cold. And my nostrils inflame from the overuse of tissues and sniffling.

"Harper." I feel Uncle Laran's hand hover over my back for a moment as if to give a pat of comfort. He thinks better of the gesture and withdraws his arm. "You cry more than the clouds above London."

I lift my chin, wiping the glaze of briny water off my cheeks. "You would, too, if you lost Homer at Dover Castle." I bang my head against the table three times. "You're so, so, so stupid, Harper."

"Well, you *did* lose him…" Uncle Laran admits.

He stirs the spoon in the broth, pauses, lets the silverware slide from his grasp.

Uncle Laran props his elbows on the table, in deep contemplation for a moment. "My mom once left me and your mother in an airport when we were kids."

Laran, now's not the time.

He doesn't catch onto my glare. "Due to a long layover, my sister and I fell asleep on the airport floor. When we awoke, Mom had boarded the plane and the flight had departed. Granted, the eighties were quite a different time, and security less tight at airports."

He glances upward at the ceiling, lost in the memory for a moment. Laran thumbs his chin. I realize now how much its shape reminds me of a gourd.

I blink, a few tears streaming down my quivering lip. I lick the salty taste. "Uncle Laran, I don't think that story helped me feel any better about the situation."

"Sorry, I meant that we've all lost something important to us before. Most institutions have lost and found boxes or rooms for this reason." He claps a hand on my back for a brief second. The air escapes my lungs. "We went hard on you. And I blame part of the incident on your mother for letting you go off on your own that day. But we'll find him and bring him home."

"And if we don't?"

"Rather dislike that word 'don't.' Heroes never seem to use it in all the great books."

As my shaking subsides and tears dry up, Uncle Laran siphons his milky soup into his mouth. He tilts his head from side to side to indicate the first bite is "so-so" in quality. Something tells me the museum spent most of the funds on artifacts instead of culinary prowess.

"Any updates from Mom?" My trembling chin nods at his bag, which holds his phone.

He unbuckles the satchel and pulls out the device. "Nothing yet."

I slump in my seat, back arching over the table in defeat. Great.

"Says she just returned from her tour group an hour ago. Hopefully should have more of an inkling by the time we return to the apartment."

When he drains the last of the soup, he motions for me to follow him into the gift shop. We pass by Egyptian cats on keychains and a toddler reaching for a rubber duck in knight's armor.

Uncle Laran takes a black shopping basket made of fabric and unfolds it to make a cylinder shape.

I fold my arms and lean my hip against a display case full of stuffed animals. "Have you two figured out how he even got here in the first place?"

Uncle Laran taps his nose. "Ah, I was waiting for this. I know how you get about my…lectures." He holds up the basket. "Pretend this is a laver." He hands me it and grabs a red wooden chess piece with a knight on a horse. "And this, Homer." The horse and his man fall into the fabric container.

"For the blood, what will we use?"

He finds a red t-shirt with the Rosetta Stone on it and tosses the souvenir on top of the knight. "There, happy?"

"Not really. I hated when Homer described the ceremony."

He claps his dry hands and rubs them. "Now, to create a magnetic field, one needs an iron vessel."

"Yeah, still don't get why."

"Allow me to finish. Iron is magnetically charged—ferromagnetism, I believe my colleague called it. Such an object has the capability of creating a magnetic field through which a wormhole can tunnel."

I squinch my eyes for a moment, and then nod when the information clicks like a camera snapshot. Iron forms a magnetic field. A hole pops up in that field.

"Okay, so the laver, made of iron, can do that. Why did they need blood again?"

"The iron content in the blood helped the effect all the more." He grabs a green tartan scarf and ties it around the basket. "And with a copper wire wrapped around the laver—"

"Why copper?"

"To conduct the electricity, of course. That comes from the lightning. The electricity charges the magnet field to form a tunnel to our time."

With a free hand, he grips a pencil decorated with a London bus to play the part of "lightning" and strikes the "wire." He digs into the bag and pulls out the "blood" and "Homer." After a moment, he looks at me.

"Understand, Harper?"

Lightning hits the wire and forms the hole in the field. You need the lightning and the iron vessel to make everything work.

"Sort of? I'm assuming you mean the laver stayed in place, in 800 BC Palikari, and Homie, and the blood"—I add with a shudder—"slipped through a wormhole or something and landed in *England*? Wouldn't he end up in modern Palikari?"

"Well, from what I understood from my colleague, wormholes break through *both* time and space—"

Kind of like the Doctor's TARDIS. Okay, I think I've got the hang of this.

"—so he must've taken a tunnel route from ancient Palikari to modern England."

I scratch my neck, trying to absorb the information. A clerk's scanner beeps as my brain juggles this.

"But do we have a guarantee that if we whip up any old iron tub and toss him in, he'll just magically transport to the time and destination he needs? What if he ends up in some horrible time, like the era of the bubonic plague or something?"

Uncle Laran frowns. "Perhaps a link exists between the two lavers—the one in his time and the one in ours."

"In that case, we're in trouble. No way we can pour a bunch of blood into the British Museum laver, take the artifact outside, and hope a thunderstorm hits it with lightning before the cops come arrest us."

This stumps Uncle Laran, and he paces around in the shop between wooden elephant instruments at the back. A child grabs one and blows into the mammal's rear. The wood makes a high-pitched elephant trill. Like a sparrow's cry. Oh, St. Olga, here come tears.

"Mummy, you have to see this." The child grins wide and warm as the Arizona desert. Something about his Scottish accent makes my lips twitch.

Uncle stops in place, eyes brightening, and returns.

"Homer mentioned a supernatural chant during the Festival of Sparrows, right?" His voice grows rapid, excitement flashing all over his face. "What if we repeat the chant and use a cast iron bathtub as a substitute for the laver?"

"A bathtub? Seriously?" I try to envision the Doctor hopping into a tub as he traverses the reaches of time. Eh, I wouldn't put it past the eccentric characters on that show.

"A cast iron one shouldn't differ much from the predecessor. Same iron content."

"You said a *professor* told you this information?" Someone needs to get rid of this guy's tenure.

He ignores me and fiddles with the wooden knight from our time traveling model. The bauble rolls in his hands for a few moments, then he clutches the souvenir. "Perhaps it's the supernatural elements that transported him via time *and* space. The chanting and all that. Palikarians did, like most ancient cultures, dabble in magic. The magic had to have been an important catalyst to get him here."

Dark magic, Mom will *love* the sound of this.

He hunches into himself with his arms outstretched like a mad scientist revealing a plan.

I shake my head at him. "Two reasons why that won't work. First, you'll work a miracle if you can convince Mom to recite a chant from a different religion."

"We'll just have her say, 'In the name of the Father, Son, and Holy Ghost' at the beginning of the ceremony."

I smirk at him and quirk a brow. The beep from the scanner up front interrupts our moment.

"Funny, Uncle Laran, but no. Even *I* feel a little uneasy chanting something in another language. We could be calling up demons or something. I don't think it's safe to mess with that stuff."

Safe? Oh, come on, Harper, you sound like your mom.

Maybe that's not always the worst thing. At least she didn't sell you to a brothel, like Homer's mom. Why are we going with Plan A again?

Right, because of Henry.

"Is that the second reason for why we can't transport him in a tub?" Uncle Laran scratches his whiskers. "You and your mom disapprove?"

"No, that's reason one. Second, the priests dunked Homer underneath the blood before he could hear the words they used. Even if we found him and created the laver time machine in the yard of your apartment complex, no one could say the chant. No one knows it."

Without another whisper of an argument, Uncle Laran shuffles his brown dress shoes and curves his spine in a defeated fashion out of the shop.

"We would need a plan B, then." With a sigh, he wipes his forehead with his palm. "Much as I would love for Homer to stay in my apartment, even after you and your mother leave England, he needs to be outside. And that could risk a run-in with Henry. Besides, there's no guarantee I could protect him when I'm away teaching at university."

My chest deflates. "And he can't come to America with no passport."

Also the main reason we can't just ship a tub to an ancient Palikari site, located in modern-day Greece. You need the proper documents to get there as well.

We shuffle out of the building and into a cold drizzle of rain. Uncle Laran pulls out a black umbrella from his bag and lifts it above us. The rain claps on top of the fabric, sounding like metal beads rattling on a roof.

"I guess we can figure out all the time travel kinks once we get Homer back." I inhale the mixture of smog and wet.

He sighs, passing a group with a selfie stick on the stone stairs to the museum. "Only so many opportunities to test the hypothesis. Not too many thunderstorms in the near future, according to the weather forecasts. Just one in eight days."

Uncle Laran whips out his phone. The device glows underneath the curtain of the dark umbrella. He furrows his brows for a moment, scrolling on one of the apps. He shoves the screen in front of my nose and points at a text message from Mom.

"She thinks she found Henry Whitley's apartment."

Chapter Twenty
Why the Revenge Is Best Served Never

BEFORE WE SLIP OUR SHOES OFF at the door, Mom grabs us by the arms and pulls us into the kitchen. My protest against human touch bobbles in my throat. She releases us and shows us her phone. I see a map to the house where she claims she "found" Homer.

"Look at the red dot on the map." She slides the phone into Uncle Laran's hands as he fumbles with his jacket. She runs some fingers through her wild hair, eyes crazed and almost bloodshot. "Henry lives on the outskirts of London. Barely any neighbors around him. Sounds like a prime spot to hide an artifact with not too many people around."

Uncle Laran lets out a low whistle. "Eighteen miles away, Livy. That will take us at least two hours by train."

When Laran explained how long transport takes to go a short distance on one of our Skype calls, I laughed. In 'Zona you can drive for hours on end without passing through any major cities.

I slide into a hard chair at the table, out of breath. Uncle Laran made us speed-walk the whole way home. I cough into my sleeve and dig in my pocket to use the tissue Uncle Laran gave me at the British Museum. Swallowing the metallic taste in my mouth, throat dry, I rise and grab a glass from the cupboard and fill the cup with sink water.

Not that I don't trust her lack of tech savvy, but… "How did you figure out the location, Mom?" I down a sip of lukewarm liquid. Minerals swirl on my tongue.

"I found his mother on Facebook. At least, I think I did."

"You *think*?" Uncle Laran frowns into his salt and pepper beard. "For a two-hour train ride, you'd better *know* at this point, Livy."

She explains that she looked under all the profiles containing Whitley to see if Henry had any relatives online. She stopped when she reached a woman with a vague hint of ginger hair in her white tresses. "Same eyes as the man in the museum."

Scrolling through past posts, she found one photo from 2009 with the address number in one of the pictures. The woman had taken a photograph of herself and her husband in front of the house with the tagline, "Waiting outside Henry's door to surprise him for his fortieth birthday." Mom shows me the picture. The woman's crinkled face behind bug-eye glasses does bear the same sharp cheekbones as Henry. She has looped her arm around a man with a hunched back and balding scalp. Her husband, I assume. On the ruddy brick house, the address gleams in tarnished golden letters—936.

"Wait a minute, Mom. So you have just the number of the house? Not the street name or anything? 936 isn't exactly anything to go off of."

"And Henry is a rather common name here," Uncle Laran adds.

"Plus, 2009 happened a long time ago. He could've moved out since then."

Spider fingers crawl onto her hips. We hadn't let her finish. Uncle Laran mutters an apology, and she continues. "I scrolled down her feed a little longer and found she re-shared an article her son Henry had written years ago about Palikarian temple practices. That sort of gave away his position. Granted, he'd taken the article down, maybe to cover up his digital footprint. But her caption told me everything I needed to know."

Oh, guess she has found him after all.

I park onto the armchair in the family room, letting the information sink in along with my backside into the cushion. Gravity overtakes me.

"But you still don't have the full address." I take another sip of the water. My throat still burns. Can't wait for this sickness to end.

"Right, so I reached out to her to get that information." She pulls up the message, smoothing her free hand on her pencil skirt and reads it to us. "'Hi, Elizabeth. I found your son's wallet at Paddington Station. I tried to find his username on Facebook, but he doesn't appear to have one. Do you happen to have his address, so I can deliver it to him?'"

My lips twitch. Much as the woman drives me crazy, I want to applaud her revenge for what he did to her on email.

Cold realization stops my breath. "But maybe Henry warned her ahead of time." I inhale. "Or she might've messaged him afterward to see if he'd lost his wallet. Or she wanted you to send her a picture of the wallet."

Mom shakes her head and reads the response. "She said, 'Oh, thank you for reaching out, Livy. You will be able to find him at 936 West Greenwich Drive. Please let me know when you deliver it to him. He never tells me anything. All I know is he attends services at St. Mary's every week, so not too many complaints here.'"

Man alive, he attends church. Guess people of the faith can do all kinds of nasty stuff. Has anything changed since the time of the Palikarians?

"And I said, 'No problem, Elizabeth. Children can—'" She pauses midway through the message. "Well, what happens after that doesn't matter much. We covered the address, and even though she posted the picture in 2009, she appears to think he still lives there."

Uncle Laran's face darkens as he peers over Mom's shoulder to read the rest of the message. He raises his eyebrows.

"Bit harsh, don't you think, Livy?"

She blanches and shoots Laran a warning look, but I pop up from my spot on the armchair. A little too quick as my legs and head throb from walking so fast today.

"What does the rest of the message say?"

"Doesn't matter, sweetie."

"It has something to do with me, doesn't it? You mentioned something about 'children can.' Can *what*, Mom?"

Hesitating, she clacks her heels once, twice against the hardwood floor. "I tried to gain her trust, Harper. The more children break their mothers' hearts, the more moms can relate to one another."

I bite my cheek, forcing back a comment about how mothers do as much a bang-up job at breaking the hearts of children. But, instead, I grab the umbrella by the door and return to the table.

"We going or what?" I twirl the umbrella string with my finger. "The sun only stays up for so long. Let's get Homie."

Mom and Uncle Laran exchange wary looks. Arms crossed, Mom sucks in her cheeks. "Sweetie, we need you to stay here. For safety's sake."

Yes, her favorite word stings my ears once again.

My jaw sinks to protest. "Three of us, one of him, Mom. No way Henry can take down all of us at once. Especially if he's not expecting someone to show up at his door and force him to give up Homer."

"Sorry, Harp." Uncle Laran scrunches his forehead. "We risk enough with just your mother and me going. She doesn't want to risk losing you and Homer in the same trip."

Forming an O with my lips, I start to object, but tears form a river down Mom's cheeks. I regret ever wanting to hug or make amends with her. Too many motion sickness pills must've polluted my mind that day.

"Harper, I know you want to be brave and to rescue your friend after losing him. But you remember how you felt after the day at Dover Castle? How everything inside of you felt like breaking? How you had no idea how you could still breathe air when your lungs drowned in sadness? Multiply that by ten, and that's what will happen to me if you fall into any danger."

Yes, I know the feeling.

Guilt burns in my gut. I slump onto the family room carpet and arch my back over the couch. "Fine." I sigh. "Only because I can't hurt anyone else on this trip. Who knows what I put Homer through?"

Mom and Uncle Laran wish me a solemn farewell and pass through the creaky door, making sure to lock it. I return to my laptop to scroll on Tumblr for the next few hours. Clicking on the internet icon, I notice Mom left the Facebook browser open, without logging out.

I click on the message bubble and read the rest of the conversation.

Livy: No problem, Elizabeth. Children can be hurtful sometimes. Once they discover you're human, they don't trust you anymore.

Elizabeth: Gracious, well, I suppose. Shame they cannot see us like angels, the way they used to as children.

Livy: Maybe. Guess if they kept believing that they'd never want to leave home.

* * *

After hours spent skimming through my summer reading of *Hamlet* and taking notes on my computer from SparkNotes, I hear the apartment door slam. I hurtle off my bed, shoving the sheets onto the floor.

Oh, please tell me you found him.

I rush to a weary-looking Uncle Laran and Mom. With a feeble smile, Mom opens her arms to hug me, but I brush past to look behind her. No third figure of Homer stands beyond them.

"He wasn't there?" Tight, my throat stabs me like a dagger. I hack into my sleeve.

"Your coughs sound worse." Mom kicks off her rainboots by the front mat.

I ignore her. "What happened when you got there, Uncle Laran?"

He shuffles into the kitchen and grabs a beer from the refrigerator. I thought Mom had cleared him out of all alcohol since she disapproves of the stuff, but I suppose he acquired some during our hiatus at a different hotel.

"When we arrived at the house, we knocked at the door, and a little girl answered." *Click* goes the beer bottle cap. "Said she went by the name Clara. We asked if she had a father named Henry, and she said no. Your mother pulled up Elizabeth on Facebook, showed the girl the picture, and asked if she had a grandmother by that name."

Feeling the hope deflate in my chest, I collapse onto the family room couch. "Let me guess, she said 'no.'"

"Correct. And when your mother asked if any adults were around, she said yes, her father Richard Thorpe, but he was sleeping upstairs, and she wanted to let him rest."

Mom leans against the wall, her bun disheveled. All the lights go out in my chest and in Mom and Laran's faces.

"We tried to wait on the stoop after the girl closed the door." Mom slumps even more. "We knocked on the door an hour later, but no one came. We thought the child was worried we wanted to kidnap her or something. Even though there weren't any neighbors around to give us odd looks, we felt awkward staying there, so we came home."

Uncle Laran pours the beer into a glass and sets the vessel on the kitchen table.

"Mind if you grab me one, Laran?" Mom nods at the amber liquid.

What?

He cocks his head, but he obeys and clicks open another bottle. The scent of fruit and alcohol fills the air. Cradling the new drink, Mom drains half the contents in one go.

"So now what?" The question hurts my throat.

They both shrug. "Now," Uncle Laran says, "we hope for a miracle."

Warm anger flushes through my neck, through my balled fists. "That's it? You just plan to sit and let him disappear?"

"Now, Harper."

"No." I jab a finger at Mom. "You have no room to talk."

I hear Uncle Laran protest behind me, but I ignore him. I don't care. They cooped me up in here all day and gave up after looking at one house.

"Not after you let Dad disappear, too."

Before I have a chance to observe the line I crossed, I rush into the bedroom and bolt the door. I can feel the trip wire of my words snap under my foot. I can even hear the explosion they set off if I listen closely enough to the ringing in my ears.

Chapter Twenty-One
Why the Man Is Very Good

STUMBLING INTO THE KITCHEN AROUND NOON the next day, I spy a sack lunch on the countertop. I assume Uncle Laran forgot his meal for school. A letter lies beside the bag, and as I yawn, my throat aches. The sickness sticketh closer than a brother.

A cursive "Harper" in blue pen is etched across the envelope.

I open the note and read, "Thought you could use a meal, saw you haven't eaten much as of late. I know it hurts—not just your throat—but try to eat half the bag's contents. Sincerely, Mom."

In surprise, I squint at the signature for a handful of seconds. Mom? Mom who slept on the family room couch because she wanted to avoid me in my room last night? That Mom?

After I cough into my Deadpool shirt sleeve, I rummage through the lunch sack and pull out the contents. A cucumber and cream cheese sandwich, an odd tropical juice box with guava and pineapple flavoring, salt and vinegar chips, and a small piece of candy in a shiny pink wrapper. Most of those food won't help my throat out much, but I know we're limited in what the convenience stores here have available.

"Mom packed me a dessert?" I wince as my voice comes out hoarse.

Gripping my throat, I grab the juice box and carry the drink to the family room. Might as well try to cool the searing pain somehow. I slurp through the plastic straw. Tangy juice stings my esophagus. I gag when a glob of guava puree lands on my tongue.

Hate foods with weird textures, like peaches.

Setting the juice box down on a side table, I pull out my laptop and renew a search on Henry Whitley. Google, as always, yields pictures of tombstones and obituaries of men with similar names who died in the 1960s.

Nothing there. This confirms our hypothesis that Henry cleared his digital footprint so others couldn't track him down.

Uncle Laran had mentioned he stole part of the Herodotus scroll or something. Why did no news sources document that? Maybe they printed the information but never posted it online. Who knows? Must've done that way back in the '80s or '90s, before the internet became a big deal.

Pulling open LinkedIn—Mom's account is still logged in— I search through the database for his name. Maybe he works at a company of corrupt archeologists. Nothing except for a man who's employed at a legal firm in Kentucky appears in the results.

Heat flushes my face.

Why didn't I see it before Homer got kidnapped? Homer's shoulders had scrunched up all the way to his ears in Hyde Park that one day, and we'd bolted as soon as I took their picture. And that little girl having some project where she "needed" to take photographs with "strangers" for "inclusivity" purposes. Bet Henry grabbed some random girl and paid her to say all those things.

And at Dover Castle too, when another ginger girl handed me a book.

Wait a second, both those girls had the same eyes, and the same sharp cheekbones. Henry's cheekbones.

Did he have a daughter?

I try Facebook and scroll through Elizabeth Whitley's photos down to the one from 2009 with her and her husband in front of the house. In the picture, she wears a patterned headwrap, old once-ginger hair popping out, and a red raincoat. I scowl at her sweet smile.

Bet Henry warned her ahead of time about Mom and Uncle Laran coming to his house. Either that, or she hasn't heard from him since 2009.

Feeling my chest deflate, I set the computer aside and crush the juice box in my hands, letting the yellowish liquid spill over my sweatpants. Everything feels cold and wet.

"How did Henry find us at Dover Castle?" I ask the blank television screen in the cabinet in front of me. "I can see how he found us, otherwise. Followed Uncle Laran to our hotel. Booked a room. But we gave him no warning about our trip to Dover."

Only Homer, Mom, her tour group, and I knew about us going.

Gut squirming like a snake in my abdomen, I pull up Mom's email server in the browser. Probably illegal, or at least deserving a stern talking to. My cheeks inflame with a mixture of fear and shame as I click on the inbox button. But Mom should be more careful to log out of her accounts.

Most of the emails come from a man by the name of "Jacob Snodgrass." Fantastic name, bet his kids love him for it.

His tone reads manager-like in the bodies of the messages. "Dear Ms. Hesiod" and "Sincerely, Mr. Jacob Snodgrass" materialized in every email. Mom's boss?

I read through a few, and by the time I reach the third one down, my heart pole vaults into my throat.

"Dear Ms. Hesiod,
Please remind the guide tomorrow that there is a man who plans to conduct a tour in the World War II tunnels at Dover

Castle. The last time our guide had an opportunity to yield the tour over to someone at Westminster, he had forgotten.
 Sincerely,
 Mr. Jacob Snodgrass"

I click on Mom's reply.

 "Dear Mr. Snodgrass,
 Thank you for the heads up! Any idea who the guy is who's giving the tour of the tunnels? I love World War II history and don't want to miss that portion of the tour.
 Livy Hesiod"

Of *course* she would like that time frame, five years shy of her favorite decade.

The next reply from the boss arrived late, around midnight. By that point, Mom would've fallen asleep at the hotel. And because she refused to use the hotel's Wi-Fi, for fear of Henry Whitley tracking the signal down, no way she could've seen his reply until after we took the tour at Dover.

 "Dear Ms. Hesiod,
 I apologise for the late response. I do not know the man, but his name is Henry Whitley. He inquired about the tour group's next destination, claiming to lead tours for free in most parts of London. When I replied, "Dover Castle," he answered, "Wonderful. I'll be in the area, visiting some relatives."
 Ordinarily, I do not share such information with third-party tour guides without proper references. However, after you submitted complaints about our tour guide's mediocre performance this season, and we received such replies from others in the

group, I decided to take hold of the opportunity. Our guests might reuse our services if we provide them with compensation, such as a free tour through the Dover Castle World War II tunnels.

Sincerely,

Mr. Jacob Snodgrass"

Doubling over, I hack until I taste metal.

"That sick, sick—" Another cough robs the insult out of my mouth. Even if we rescue Homie, this guy can find us anywhere we go.

And something tells me he won't stop until he makes sure we can't get Homer back.

Helplessness wells in my chest and throbs in my temples. I try to divert myself by turning on the television. A British comedy comes on, but no mirth bubbles in my stomach. Knocking a pair of knuckles against my chest, I swear my ribcage sounds hollow. Lead pumps through my veins, the gravitational pull of the earth yanking me deeper and deeper until I disintegrate into the ground.

Casting a sideways glance at the leather loveseat, I find myself wishing to see Homer arching his back over the arm. The desire to have Uncle Laran lounge in the armchair, eyes bright as he elucidates about the Underworld of the Palikarians or something boring. Even to want Mom in the corner, on the border dividing the kitchen and family room, shaking her head at the madness of everything inside the apartment.

I sigh. Alone at last, and I can't breathe. I can't breathe.

Chapter Twenty-Two
Why the Angry Sun Sets

One Month Ago

"I Wonder Woman." He pronounces it "woo-man."

Suppressing a giggle with my hoodie, I peek out from the arm sleeves to watch Homer try to pull down my Wonder Woman crop top over his midriff.

Bored out of our minds in the smelly hotel room, and after going through too many stories from the Bible, we decided to try on random clothes I'd packed in my suitcase.

He laughs and tears off the shirt, handing the top to me. "Harper turn."

Heat floods my cheeks. "Oh, no, Homie, I haven't worn something like that since middle school. Don't even know why I packed that thing." My arms wrap around the folds of my stomach. "You know how it is with overpacking. And with Mom not paying for laundry. I guess we dug that up. Like archeologists."

"Harper turn," he insists.

I chew on my lip.

"Okay." I duck into the bathroom, peel off the hoodie, and shimmy into the crop top. Fresh pine wafts from the fabric. Huh, I guess we did do the boyfriend/girlfriend hoodie thing after all. My gaze flits away from the bathroom mirror and I hug my abdomen to hide the rolls when I exit the bathroom. "Ta-da."

Homer cocks his head forty-five degrees, reaches forward, snags my arms, and spreads them apart like a bird. I can't hold anything back now. Now he can see me. No more Hide and Seek.

"Beautiful."

My shoulders drop. I didn't know I'd been holding them so high. "Really?"

"Harper Wonder Woman."

"Okay." Curse this pale skin, because I bet I've turned to a hot pink shade by now. I twist around to face my suitcase. "Let's see how you feel about trying on neon yellow leg warmers."

* * *

I watch an episode of *Doctor Who* to ease my mind from, well, everything.

Uncle Laran returns and has brought back takeaway from an Indian restaurant a few blocks down. A strong whiff of curry and naan hits my nose when he swings open the apartment door.

"Good Moore, what a long day at the university. Figured we'd have someone else prepare dinner for tonight."

He places the bag on the counter and pulls out the plastic containers with the meals. Steam clouds the clear coverings of each.

After affording this one crane of the neck, I continue to stare at the screen as a blue TARDIS spins across the scene. Having not seen Uncle Laran since last night, when I slammed myself into my room, we left things on terms poorer than the beggars by Hyde Park.

In the kitchen, he pauses when he finds the lunch bag Mom left for me today. He rustles his fingers through the sack and discovers I consumed nothing in there except for the juice box. Scratching his chin, he opens the refrigerator and puts the contents inside on one of the shelves.

"Beautiful day outside," he remarks to no direction in

particular when he shuts the fridge door.

"Uh huh." The *doo-wee-oo* of the TV show theme song overpowers my words. "Nice."

"Today I taught my students about the Battle of Delium. Riveting discussion, just riveting. Everyone enjoys a nice Boetian victory."

I swear he doesn't speak English half the time. "Nice, Uncle Laran."

"Would've taught a far superior lecture if my lesson plans were not interrupted last night by your mother's crying."

A lump forms in my throat. I choke a swallow and manage another "nice," forcing my eyes to stay on the screen. Darkness absorbs the picture as the TV makes a crackling sound from someone hitting the power button. Uncle Laran looms above me with the remote in hand.

"Suppose we have a chat about what happened last night."

Mmm, or let's not suppose at all. Back to the TV, please?

Squirming on the leather couch, I try to keep my face tight and hard. "Dunno what you mean."

He presses his palms on his knees and winces as his bones crack as he takes the other end of the sofa. "Harper, seeing how you interact with your mom has dissuaded me from ever wanting to parent a child."

"You're welcome."

"You ignore her. Disrespect her. Call her a murderer." He smudges his weary face with a hand. "She has urged me not to intervene and that she can put up with you on her own. But a twin brother can only handle so much before he must step in."

"I don't need to hear this from you." A rumble vibrates in my throat.

"Well, I don't quite care for what you want. Now sit and

behave until we iron all this out."

The condescending tone, the fact both adults had pitted themselves against me—it causes ants to crawl up and down my neck. Without a Homer to protect myself, they've plunged me into a battlefield outnumbered.

Anger pumps through my chest. With each heartbeat, I feel the toxin pulsate through me like a thorny fire. In a huff, I jump up from the couch and start to head to the room.

"You're the queen of leaving conversations." Uncle Laran's knees crackle again as he rises. "We have a word for that here. Coward. Perhaps you're familiar with it."

Fingers grasping the icy door handle to my room, I drop my arm and face him. The blaze has reached my eyes, and I could burn him in place right now.

"Go ahead and lecture me." My arms wave in the air as if caught in an explosion. "Not like I haven't gotten it from a dozen therapists after Dad died. Or our pastor who always sided with Mom—*always sided with her*. Or every one of her relatives because she's incapable of doing anything wrong, and I—I'm just a stupid teenager who doesn't understand anything."

Purple spreads across my cheeks. I see the color in my periphery.

I jab a finger at him. "And you haven't even heard my side of the events. Everyone thinks Dad died because of pancreatic cancer, because of all the beer he drank. But strange coincidence he died the same day the divorce went through, huh?"

"Harper." Uncle Laran rolls his fists.

"She knew he was sick. *She knew*. If she waited until he recovered, I might've forgiven her—"

"Harper!"

"—but she went ahead anyway. She could've waited until

he was cancer free, but she just couldn't. Could've just continued the separation until he got better. But she went ahead. And so he died."

When the last words cross my lips, I crumple onto the floor. I hear the explosion this time. My body shakes, legs and arms convulsing. Choking on air and diaphragm spazzing because of all the heavy breathing, I gape my mouth as wide as it can to let in fresh air.

Two thick dress shoes step onto the tile in front of me. I refuse to follow their trail up to the face of what I imagine to be a furious Uncle Laran. Instead, I bury myself into my shaky arms. Images of Homer crying in front of the mummy in the British Museum flash through my mind.

"Homie. Why do you think that last sparrow remained silent? Why didn't he cry like the others?"

Now I know why the sparrow cries. Why the Homer wails and the Harper dissolves into tears. Because we hope something or someone can hear us. Before we die—on the outside, inside…everywhere.

Crack go his knees again. Uncle Laran squats next to me and drapes a stiff arm around my quaking shoulders. At this point, I don't care about the touch.

Something tells me Phoenix didn't do this to me.

"Harper." He sighs. "Your mother never knew about the sickness."

Huh?

It feels as if someone's attached jumper cables to my brain.

"What?" I ask through a snotty nose and mouth. The word comes out more like "Bwat?"

"Your father, after they separated, never told her about the illness. He seemed to hide many things, not only his alcohol consumption. Your mother discovered his deadly secret the same day you did, the day he passed away."

I wipe my face on the hoodie sleeve and hug my knees. "She knew nothing?"

"She held the marriage together with all her might, Harper. You must believe that. Relatives noticed bruises on her arms, and she would have mental breakdowns at work. The parents of the students on her volleyball team complained to the administration."

I nod and knuckle the corners of my eyes.

His nostrils flare as he exhales. He smells like beer. "When they fired her, it served as a wake-up call. She wanted to wait until you went to college for better timing. I suppose there's never a good time—"

"—to break up a family?"

"—to do the unforgivable and save your life."

"My life?"

"How soon would the bruises on your mom's arms find their way onto yours?" He nods at the scar on my wrist. "They already had. She shielded you so many times."

Splotches form on my skin. It feels as if my lungs had been full of Arizona sand, blocking me from breathing, but now someone had dug out the dirt, and I can enjoy oxygen again.

I clasp my hands into fists, digging my nails in. No, Harper, you can't let her get off that easily. Not after months of refusing to look at her, not letting her touch you.

"T-that doesn't e-excuse everything sh-she did."

"No, and I agree she took some rather rash actions such as sending Henry Whitley my apartment address. But how long will you let this bitterness rip you apart?"

My front teeth bite hard into my lip. To my dismay, I draw

no blood, but my chin begins to tremble.

Uncle Laran takes another stab. "What would happen if we rescued Homer, and he never spoke with you again?"

In goes the dagger.

I sigh. "I know what kind of answer you're expecting." Gravity pulls at me, threatening to tear me in half. "That if he did that, it would crush me."

"But he will forgive you. Because you're both human, and he allows for faults. Why not you?"

Why not me…why *not* me?

I can yield no reply. Forgiveness it is, then. To rid my chest of this icy guilt, to at last live and breathe again.

"Something smells delicious. Indian food?"

The apartment door swings open and Mom halts when she sees both of us crouched by the bedroom. Smoothing her pencil skirt and bun, she furrows the wrinkles on her forehead. "What's going—"

I hobble onto my feet and dart at her, covering her in a hug. The embrace feels like electricity. Mom jolts backward at the impact.

"I forgive you, Mom." Tears drip from my face onto her suit jacket. "So, so, sorry. For everything."

Her shoulders lurch and begin to shake as she joins in the tear fest. Shuddering breaths and briny water fill the space for the next few minutes.

At last, she runs a pair of fingers through my greasy hair. "Oh, honey. That's all I ever wanted to hear."

* * *

Weary from losing a lot of water in two nights, Mom retires to bed early. Uncle Laran shuts himself in his room to do some lesson planning for tomorrow, Friday, his last day of lecturing for this week.

The clock strikes ten, and I refuse to go to bed any earlier than midnight. Otherwise, I will have to forfeit my rights as a teenager.

Distracting myself, I microwave the leftovers from the Indian curry and eat them at the table. The garlicky and spicy tofu mixes well with the cold naan from the fridge. I grab myself a glass of apple juice and down that to douse the spiciness lingering in my mouth.

Scrolling through Tumblr, I find myself growing bored, my eyes losing all of their moisture. Right before I close out of the browser, a ding from Facebook Messenger sounds.

Why would that happen? I never use my Facebook—only people older than thirty do.

Clicking on the link, I spy my mom's name in the blue line that runs across the top of the page. She forgot to log out again. For all her security with taking away our phones and laptops, you would think she'd remember to sign out of her social media accounts.

A message blinks at the bottom of the screen from Elizabeth.

Elizabeth: I forgot to message you the other day. Did you manage to return my son's wallet to him? I would have asked him myself, but he has not called me in months.

I bite my lip and crane my neck toward the crack in the bedroom door. Hoisting myself from my spot in the armchair, I tiptoe across the tile toward the room to wake her up.

She looked exhausted before bed. I freeze mid-step. I should probably let her know sometime in the morning.

Then I remind myself how Mom and I plan to leave in less than two weeks. We don't have that much time to recover Homer and reach a thunderstorm.

Still, I should let her sleep. Like Uncle Laran said, I've pushed my luck with her most of the trip. Even though she forgave me, I shouldn't add any more offenses.

I return to the couch, where my fingers hover over the keyboard. *Shouldn't reply, not my account.*

Then again, she might know about Homer's location. Maybe I can extract the information from her somehow. I let my fingers dance across the black keys in the darkness of the family room.

Livy: I'm afraid he wasn't there. In fact, no one was there at the house.

After I click Enter to send, I add more to the message.

Livy: I wanted to stop by again to return the wallet tomorrow. What time does he return home from work?

As I await the response, I toggle through Elizabeth's pictures to get some more clues. I did this during one of the days Mom and Uncle Laran left the house, but I got bored after scrolling all the way back to 2009. So, this time, I start at 2009 and start to travel backward in time. Another ding of a message halts my progress.

Elizabeth: That's a shame he was not there when you arrived. Did you see Amelia when you stopped by the house?
Livy: No, I didn't see her.

Amelia, I know that name.

With rapid speed, I scan through the photos, looking at the labels for Amelia. I stop at one with the tagline, "Spending the day with our granddaughter, Amelia, at the Natural History Museum."

A girl with fiery red hair, about four or five years old in the picture, scowls at the camera in front of a stegosaurus skeleton. Elizabeth and her husband flank her sides.

I squint at the image, recognizing her face from somewhere.

Images from Dover Castle flicker across my vision. Add eight years to the girl's face and grow her hair to her shoulders—instead of the bob cut in the picture—and she looks just like the one I saw the day Henry captured Homer.

The one I spotted in the castle room and at the park.

The one who handed me the book.

The one Mom and Uncle Laran said answered the door to the house.

She's Henry's daughter. She must've been the one to answer the door when Mom and Laran arrived and lied about her name. Called herself "Clara." Henry had warned her, hadn't he?

A new message blinks on the screen.

Elizabeth: How odd. You must have arrived in the early afternoon. Henry comes home an hour after his daughter returns from school at four o' clock. At least, those were the times I was able to catch him for a call, whenever he chooses to answer his mobile. You will have better luck finding them at those times.

My heart races. Four? But Uncle Laran teaches class tomorrow and Mom leaves with her tour group. Neither gets back to the apartment until then. And, even if we wait till the weekend, we don't know Henry's schedule, or Amelia's.

Sure, we could wait until next Monday, but who knows what could happen in that time? Maybe Elizabeth will reach out to her son asking about his wallet. Then, he could rent a hotel somewhere far away and take Homer with him to escape us.

The realization pummels into me. I have to go tomorrow and do it alone.

Forehead creased with a slight panic, but also determination, I reply to the message.

Livy: Wonderful! I will make sure to stop by tomorrow.

"In the early afternoon." I lick a sweaty lip. "Before anyone comes home."

I hope.

Chapter Twenty-Three
Why the Shepherd Leaves Ninety-Nine

IN THE MORNING, BEFORE MOM WAKES up, I slip a twenty pound note out of her wallet into mine for the train ticket to the house on 936 West Greenwich Drive. The icy guilt surfaces again. The feeling will go away after he's back and all is explained. I hope.

Hopping onto my computer, I see a new message blinking from Elizabeth on the screen. She had sent it not long after the other ones, but I drifted off not long after I mailed the last reply.

Elizabeth: How daft of me! I remembered Amelia's term does not begin again until September. If you stop by the house any time today, she will likely answer the door.

Pressure builds in my temples as I read the message. I feel like a soda can about to burst. So much for arriving at an empty house. All of last night I researched how to break into homes.

But man alive, with Amelia there, she could call the police on me.

Too late now. Either Homer comes with me today, before the thunderstorm on the ninth, or I risk letting Uncle Laran try to rescue him. Mom and I leave on the twelfth.

Part of me wants to ask Mom to accompany me, but I didn't give her enough of a heads-up so she could inform her boss she can't come in today. Uncle Laran already left to teach class. And something tells me neither has much experience in espionage. Mom's voice alone could warn a guard dog from a mile away.

You'll figure it out when you get there. You have a two-hour commute to think of the worst possible scenarios.

The door to our room clicks shut as Mom emerges, wiping the sleep from her eyes. Her silky nightgown hugs her knees.

"Slept in." She yawns. "Luckily my boss has us touring the exhibits at Windsor later in the afternoon today."

Unluckily, that puts my trip on a delay.

I fight the urge to exit early in the morning because Mom would raise questions. But that means waiting until all members of the apartment evacuate.

Distracting myself, I prepare breakfast. Setting a bowl on the counter, I pour the Special K grains into it. The sweet wheat smell tickles my nose, and I sneeze into my dark black sleeve.

"Careful not to get your germs on the food." Mom waves a fork at me from the kitchen table. "Otherwise, we'll have to re-stock Uncle Laran's groceries. You're still contagious, since you've only had this for a few days."

"Okay, Mom." My throat still feels raw, and the cold shows no signs of disappearing. Something tells me it'll make great friends with asthma.

I reach into the fridge and grab an orange, a tub of vanilla yogurt, and a banana. Returning to the table, I dollop the yogurt on a plate and proceed to gulp down large quantities of food. Even with the buildup of mucus in my stomach, some of the hunger remains and shoots pain in my abdomen. The meal appears to quiet the gastrointestinal beast a little.

Mom cringes as I slurp the milk in my cereal. "Haven't seen you eat like that recently. Do you feel any better?" She reaches forward to feel my forehead with her hand. Although still getting used to the touch thing again, I can breathe at last when she does so.

"Your temperature seems normal."

Not sure how accurate we can deem the palm thermometer readings. "I'm fine, Mom. Thought eating would maybe keep the sickness at"—a series of coughs—"at bay."

She eyes my plate with uncertainty. "Don't know how much good the dairy will do."

I need the protein for today's journey.

Not pushing my luck, I push aside the bowl of cereal and dig my fingers into the orange peel. Bits of the white citrus-y stuff find their way underneath my fingernails.

"You look like a ninja or something." Mom eyes me up and down once.

What else do you wear when you rob a house? A wedding dress?

"Running out of clothes. We haven't done laundry in a while. It was this or the Wonder Woman crop top, and believe me, you don't want to see me in that."

She bobs her head over a cup of steaming tea that hints a strong ginger scent. "Sorry, sweetie. I figured since we're leaving in eight days we could make the clothes stretch over that amount of time. You wear sweatpants so often. I figured most people wouldn't notice if you re-used a few outfits."

I sniff my t-shirt and crinkle my nose. Even with the cold, the thing still invades my clogged nostrils with a body odor stench. I miss Homie's pine scent.

Eyeing the clock on the stove, my heart droops in my ribcage. It sags against the bones like the remains of a popped balloon. If Mom doesn't leave for her tour soon, I'll run into *both* Amelia and Henry at the house.

"So when do you head out, Mom?" I pluck the white veins of the orange and place them next to the dejected yogurt.

"Soon, dear. You think you can handle today on your own?

Windsor is a decent drive away."

"I'll be fine. Just gonna stay here and watch telly, as Uncle Laran likes to say."

Nodding, she unclasps her bag and pulls out her wallet. Paralysis strikes me. She never pulls that out unless paying for something or getting money out of the ATM.

"What are you doing?" My voice shatters in my throat.

"Double checking how much cash I have left in here. I want to buy some relatives souvenirs today—my mom likes the china they have at the Windsor shops. Want to get her some nice plates or a teacup."

"Oh, I'm sure you have plenty of cash. Teacups can't cost that much." I toss a wave of dismissal, knocking my spoon off the table. The silverware clatters against the hardwood with a loud ding.

"Just filled up yesterday at the ATM, but once the machine shortchanged me."

The cavity in my chest misses a beat for a moment as all my veins freeze. Hope those Camden Market churros were worth it if she catches me in the act now.

"Just making sure they gave me the proper amount this time."

I watch in horror as she licks her thumb to count each note. When she reaches the end, her features darken. "They did it again."

Not the best at acting, I try for a look of shock. "Are you kidding me?" Pain sears my throat. Maybe my wince has convinced her.

She jerks her head in an emphatic motion. "No, and I counted the notes after they came out of the machine. I could've sworn I got it right—it was the right amount yesterday, but I thought I counted one twice. So I wanted to double check."

I place a hand on her back for comfort. My croaking voice tries for a hint of sympathy. "Sorry, Mom. That's awful."

Groaning through her nose, she tucks the wad of cash back into the wallet. "Guess I'll need to use the debit card more often. I just like to pay in cash more, you know? It feels more old-fashioned."

The wallet makes a thunk when she drops it into her leather bag. She swings the strap over her shoulder and heads for the door.

"Have a wonderful day, Harper." She kisses me on the forehead. The wet from her lips burns even moments after. Maybe I haven't gotten used to touching entirely, or maybe my guilt causes the prickles inside my skin. "Now, don't get into any trouble."

She screeches the apartment door open—they really need to oil that thing—and dissolves into the fluorescent hallway lights.

I wait until she's long gone. "No promises."

* * *

I arrive at the house half an hour before four. I swallow, but the spit gets caught in my throat. Clenching and unclenching sweaty fists, I panic as my vision grows blurry from my heartbeat thundering so much in my chest.

Oh, Harper, how in all of Arizona's stars do you plan to do this?

Tucked between bushes and creeping emerald vines, the brick house shrouds itself behind large hedges and a winding stony driveway. Moss plays Hide and Seek between the cracks. Even if neighbors reside close by—they don't seem to exist within two hundred meters of this patch of land—the looming hedges and cloud-like trees in the front yard block all but the door from an outsider's view.

Laran and Mom guessed right. Henry chose a perfect place in solitude to hide a kidnapped artifact.

Rocks skitter around my black shoes as I slink up the path. I approach the front windows padding on my tiptoes to see if I can spy Amelia inside. Pebbles scuttle against the driveway and a pigeon warbles in a nearby tree.

At last, I crouch by the windows near the front door and peer inside at an empty family room. Two vacant red chairs sit side by side in a silent conversation.

Coast clear, I hope.

My fingers fumble with the bottom of the window to slide the pane open. Squatting in a patch of peonies, I grunt, but the screen refuses to budge.

Plan A—break into the house via the front window.

Status—failure.

Now for Plan B—check around the house for other windows. I spy one high up, but the tree closest to it has thinner branches that wouldn't support even a skinny woman like Mom. So I creep around the perimeter. Nothing on the sides of the house, so toward the back, I guess.

Hands in sweatpants pockets, I shuffle toward the backyard. I pass spiky thorn bushes that line the sides of the house. So many trees and shrubs cover the backyard, an entire army could hide back here without anyone noticing. A huddle of pine-tree-like shrubs span a good ten yards.

Worst case, I can bolt behind those trees if someone comes to investigate the house right now. We'll call that Plan Z. St. Olga knows I created enough schemes on the train to fill the whole alphabet.

When I reach the rear of the house, before I check inside the large sliding door windows, something in the backyard arrests my attention.

In the middle of a patch of grass gleams a bathtub with some sort of shiny wire wrapped around the basin. Attached to the wire, a lightning rod of sorts, a tall, sharp needle point, juts toward the cloudy sky.

Moving closer, I notice several large white bottles surrounding the tub. Inside the clear cases, a sluggish brownish-golden liquid jiggles when I wiggle the jugs back and forth. In the glint of sunlight, the label reads, "Liquid Iron."

Man alive, there are enough of these to fill the whole tub.

Then it hits me. In the Festival of Sparrows, the iron content from the sparrows' blood filled the tub and helped Homer travel in time. At least from what Uncle Laran explained at the museum.

Maybe Henry wants to recreate the process without the use of animal blood. Where would you even buy animal blood? From a butcher or something? Do those still exist?

Why would Henry want to send Homer back to Palikari in the first place?

It would get rid of the evidence of his archeological 'find.' I thumb the rigid cap of a liquid iron battle. Then, I shake my head. No use wasting time on this. Figure all the info out later. I pull out my phone and notice the little battery bar on the top blares a red three percent.

I thought I charged this last night. A wad of cotton forms in my throat when I glance at the time. I have fifteen minutes remaining till Henry arrives home.

Focus, Harper. Let's get Homer out first. Speculate later.

Rushing to the sliding doors, I peer into a kitchenette area and spot no one by the granite countertops and the ceramic jugs in the windowsill. Time for Plan C. I recall one of the YouTube videos I watched last night.

Plan C, push up on the latch until the door unlocks from the inside.

Right before I enact the third part of the mission, I wobble the door with my palms in case. Of course, it doesn't open. Henry wouldn't make this part of the plan that easy. With the door handle in my hands, I crouch and attempt to force the thing with all my might off the track.

"Augh." I release the door and stare at the purple indent in my palm.

They made this process look so easy in the video.

"Come on, Harp." I grit my teeth and crouch again. "You got no time left."

Lifting again, I watch the inside lock rotate a little. Another try, another, and at last the lever inside gives a benevolent click. I slide open the doors and creep inside, reminding myself that Amelia could lurk around any corner.

The wooden floor creaks as the almond-y scent of soy fills the space between the kitchen and living room. Smells like yoga and abduction in here.

If I had a kidnapped person and hid them somewhere, where would I keep them? Come on, Tumblr, don't fail me now.

A basement comes first to mind. Since, well, I watch too many movies. Then, second, if the basement plan doesn't work out, a door with a lock.

Sounds like a plan with a letter attached to it.

Cringing as my boots clunk against the floor, I press my ear to a door on the main level. When I hear no noises inside, I click the handle and enter a study filled with the smell of old books and an empty desk where a laptop would go. For a moment, my eyes trail over the other objects on the desk—in particular, a photograph of Henry and his daughter in a white confirmation dress. They each flash brilliant smiles. Henry holds up his thick shoulders. His expression glows with pride.

I know that look. Dad gave me those so many times.

Beside the photograph lies a pink handmade card with two stick figures—a girl and a taller man. A rainbow arches over the two. The card reads, "Happy Birthday to the Best Dad."

I feel my pulse punch my ribcage. Cotton once again fills my throat. *Harper, you're breaking and entering the house of a dad. The house of a good, Christian dad, and his little girl.*

Screwing my eyelids, I force myself to inhale and exhale until my thoughts outdo the chorus of my heartbeat.

True, Harper, but good Christian dads can bruise people, too, and blame the marks on bicycle accidents—like yours did. They can stalk foreigners and abduct tourists.

Now, get your life together and find Homer before Henry tacks on another awful thing a good Christian ought not to do.

Besides the bathroom on the main level, no other doors exist. Especially not one to the basement. Carpeted steps face me to the upper level. I have no choice but to go up.

Two steps into my ascent, sweaty hand on the railing, I hear a shriek followed by a shrill, "Stupid! You let the Creeper destroy the courthouse."

The voice belongs to a girl, perhaps in her tween years. I hazard a guess—Amelia.

Then, a string of curse words spills out in such a quick succession, like a staccato of notes from a wind instrument. They remind me of the ones the orchestra for the Annie performance back in middle school played. It takes me a moment to realize they came from a twelve-year-old proper British lady.

Yep, the *sweet* child who wrote the card downstairs curses like a sailor. I regret nothing.

"Honestly, they let anyone play Minecraft." Her keyboard thunders, full of the rage of her fingertips. "Even mental people."

Dropping onto my hands and knees, I crawl up the stairs and spy three rooms. One in the middle with the door wide open hosts Amelia's occasional screeches. Flanked on each side of that room stand two white doors, each closed.

I shimmy up the rest of the steps—and feel a slight carpet burn—toward the nearest door, the one out of Amelia's sightline. Forcing myself upward, I tuck my knees underneath me and reach for the handle. It opens with a click and a whine.

"Shhh." *Did I just shush a door?* In a scurrying motion, I rise to stop the door from making more noises and peer inside. Nothing, only an empty master bed with a red comforter. Belongs to Henry, I bet.

Mouth dry, I realize that means I have to check the other door across the hall. Which entails crossing in plain sight in front of Amelia's room.

I press myself against the wall and shuffle with ginger steps until I reach the entrance. Heart playing the maracas inside my rib cage, I dash across the doorway, reach the other one across the hall, and unclick the lock on the knob.

All right, plan whatever letter we've reached…say, H, for Homer. Let's hope you worked out.

Without reserve, I swing open the creaky door and find a figure in a blue tunic, sitting cross-legged on the sheets of a small bed. When he sees me, his eyes brighten, and he bolts onto his bare feet.

"Harper!"

He lets out a happy wail as he collapses into me. Smells like onions, but I'll take anything right now. Chest exploding with ecstasy, I motion to shush him, but a pattering of footsteps behind me causes me to freeze in place.

"*What* is going on here?"

I spin around and spot a girl with dragon-red hair wearing computer headphones with her arms crossed. Her ruddy eyes widen when she sees the door open to Homer's former room. She blanches and turns on her heel to sprint down the steps.

Man alive, to call the police I bet. Or worse, Henry.

Homer appears to read her mind as he catches up to her and wrenches his hands around her arms. She shrieks, voice tearing into my ears like glass, reminding me of a sparrow shriek. With rapid speed, Homer shoves her into the room where they'd held him captive and shuts the door. I turn the lock and fight a wave of nausea in my stomach.

What did we just do?

Amelia pounds her fist against the wood and screeches. "Let me out. *Let me out this instant.*"

Before I have a chance to reply, Homer slips his fingers into mine and we race down the steps. As we bolt outside and sprint a hundred meters away from the house, I glance over my shoulder—and watch as Henry's car pulls into the driveway.

Chapter Twenty-Four
Why the Bird Wanders

I DON'T KNOW FOR HOW LONG we run, but fire pumps from my sides and lungs, and I halt on the sidewalk by a white cottage. Puffing out heavy breaths, I try to focus my blurry vision on the wooden picket fence and blocky hedges.

Welham Green, miles and miles away from London.

But at least I have found my sparrow.

Steps ahead, Homer stops and stares at me as I inhale the warm smell of the sun glaring off a rusty red car parked on the side of the road. I don't know why the sun has a smell, but to me, everything does. It stands for everything good in this world. Warmth, comfort, promise.

"Why Harper stop?"

"N-need a b-breather." I gasp. "S-stupid asthma. Besides, I think we l-lost Henry's car."

Face molding with sympathy, he comes over and pats me on the back. I imagine this gesture will help. It doesn't, but I don't mind his touch. His *pat, pat, pat* at last feels welcoming instead of like a warning.

I cough into my sleeve. Cool, clear snot dribbles out of my nostrils. Okay, maybe he shouldn't touch me when I'm in this state. When will this stupid cold end?

I force my attention onto the brick building across the street to avoid the burning sensation in my lungs. A white sign in blue letters declares, "Welham Green Dental Practice." My tongue glides over my teeth, and I wince at the gritty texture of them. Mom gave me no time to brush my teeth this morning before I made my escape.

Parking on the sidewalk, I peer at Homer in his blue tunic. Splotches stain the fabric and the cloth smells as bad as the first time he wore it. How long ago did Henry make him put on that thing?

"Sorry I didn't bring more clothes." I motion to my all-black attire.

He lifts and drops his shoulders and takes a seat beside me. I wrinkle my nose and attempt to block out the urine scent. Still, I wrap him into a hug. Elation fills my stomach.

"So sorry. We wanted to find you sooner. We tried, but Henry hid you well."

He buckles his chin to his chest and absorbs the words. "I know."

"Did he make you do stuff you didn't want to do?"

"Ask lot of questions." He smiles at a small pine tree shrub. "Homer not answer most."

"Good." I pat him on the back and pull myself a little closer.

After a few moments, we rise and I scan the area for any street signs I would recognize. I spy one for Welham Dixon Road, the path to the station. Lightning bugs glow in my chest at the utter remarkability that we managed to get Homer out of Henry's house with few complications.

"How far away? Home?" Homer scratches at some perspiration on his neck.

"Well, it was two hours by train—we're back at Uncle Laran's apartment, by the way—had to hop onto the Northern Line, which had an extra fee, then Victoria, then—"

Sweat stings my eyelids as my eyes bulge. With a frantic hand, I dig into my bag and pull out the wallet.

"Oh, no. I forgot to steal enough for ticket prices when we

came back home."

"Home."

"Yeah, when I looked up train times, they hadn't mentioned processing fees or…" My fingers jiggle the remaining pound coins in my wallet. "This won't be enough to get us home, at least not on the train."

At the news of no train ride, Homer perks up, his features brightening. I wonder if images of his first time on the Tube play through his mind.

"No, Homie, this is bad. It would take six hours to walk back. London's seventeen miles away."

Unfazed, he steps barefoot on the rock-littered sidewalk. "We walk, then."

Holding up a hand, I pull out my phone. "Let me get GPS up, in that case. No idea where to go after we reach the station."

When I click the top of the phone, the screen remains dark. I click again. Nothing. Again, again, again.

I curse. Not as much as Amelia, but enough to fill ten seconds. "I think my phone died on me." It was less than five percent at Henry's house. "How? How does the battery drain so fast here?" Our phones, like the old buildings, need a break, I guess. Mom explained a month ago that many cellular devices didn't fare well overseas.

The sidewalk ends into a patch of tall grasses that itch our legs. Homer continues forward with confidence, and I trail behind because I figure Ancients followed stars and stuff like that to get to destinations on ships.

Except we're not in water. And the sun doesn't set until ten here, six hours from now.

Hugging the side of the road, I lean to the left as cars race past. I pry out information from Homer about his stay at Henry's.

From what I can tell, even as a corrupt archeologist, Henry treated Homie well as a prisoner, probably due to his British genes.

Detainee treatment included three well-stocked meals a day, an occasional tea hour, and Amelia even let him watch her play Minecraft once in a while under the supervision of Henry. Man alive, sounds like better conditions than what he received in our cramped hotel.

When Homer mentions how Henry never made him take a bath, his words call up images in my mind from the backyard with the bathtub and the liquid iron.

"I think he built you a laver in the backyard. Maybe after you answered enough questions, he'd film you going back in time. Better to have that information to himself than let any other archeologists try to steal you away from him."

Did Henry also worry what the authorities would do with Homer? That they would take him away forever?

I secure my hand in Homer's and squeeze tight. Not this sparrow, Henry. You won't steal this one.

Homer understands "laver" in that sentence, but not much else. He tells me so.

"Of course, he would've been disappointed." I grimace as some dry grass scratches my legs. "Because you never heard the chant during the Festival of Sparrows. And, Uncle Laran thinks that helped to get you here somehow. So I have no idea how he planned to do the ceremony in the first place."

Ahead of me, Homer remains silent. He knocks over a sprout of white wildflowers with his foot.

"Right, Homie?"

"No."

"No?"

"High Priest try festival one other time."

He describes the event in the same amount of detail as the time they used him as sacrifice. But during the first trial run of the Festival of Sparrows, Homer watched with the other slaves a great distance away. During a thunderous storm, he observed a friend-slave as they paraded the first human sparrow toward the laver as the cold rain pellets stung his skin.

"Close friend." He arches his neck at a cloud shaped like a bird. "Almost like brother."

I plunge into the story with him.

He explains that two guards dragged a young man, into the laver, and plunged him underneath the blood of the sparrows. The figure struggles, and the guards begin to pull him up.

"No." The High Priest waves a frantic arm at them. "He must stay under until the lightning strikes. We will then know if the gods accept the offering."

So they hold down the sparrow. Homer winces as he continues the tale.

Lights form jagged images across the sky, like a camera flash, as the High Priest recites the chant in a low, throaty voice. His eyes roll into his head, curls covering a laurel wreath.

A minute in, the High Priest ceases his hymn and glances at the laver.

The lightning never comes.

So the High Priest approaches the laver in his draped tunic. He digs his fingers into the sacrifice's garment and pulls Homer's friend out of the basin. The figure is so heavy, the two guards aid in pulling the body out of the laver.

Dead.

They drape the human sparrow on the rocky platform and glower at the corpse, then at the skies.

I cut the story short. "Homie, that sounds awful. No wonder

Henry's house seemed nicer in comparison to Palikari."

"Nice. Not *good*."

I suppose he made a good distinction between those words. Nice people can kidnap, under the right circumstances. Good people won't.

"And no wonder when they made you the next sparrow, you freaked out. They held you under the blood until lightning struck."

Will we have to replicate that? And how will we get the timing right with the lightning? You never know when it strikes.

Cross that London Bridge when we get there, Harper. For now, I need to focus on getting him home and safe.

"But you did say you remember the chant?" We reach a sidewalk with a metal railing that bars us from the woods. Here the road forks. Homer takes a left, and I shadow behind, hoping he made the right decision.

"Yes, I remember."

His auditory culture comes in handy.

Besides the walls of fragrant green trees and the stench of car exhaust, we find nothing on our long journey to set our sights upon. I try to entertain him with Bible stories and fairytales, but what feels like two hours in, I grow out of breath, esophagus still raw from the cold, so we continue to pace in silence.

What seems like another two hours after that, worry sprouts in my insides as the sun dips low on the horizon.

"Homie, you sure you know where you're going?"

Darkness covers the shadows underneath his eyes. "No."

Umm, what? "You have no idea where you're leading us?"

"Yes."

I stop in the middle of the sidewalk and crumple to my knees, massaging my sore calves. Too tired, I can't muster any frustration or emotions apart from weariness. Besides, I can't be mad at him anyway, not after everything Henry put him through. "Dunno how much longer we can keep wandering. The sun goes down in less than two hours."

"Find place for sleep, then."

A sneeze tickles my nose as I motion to my bag. "No mo— *achoo*—ney. Without any cash or credit card, a hotel won't let us stay for the night."

He drops to the ground and folds his legs underneath him. "Sleep here, then."

"What? On the sidewalk?" My palms press against the gritty texture of the pavement. "Like a homeless person?"

"Yes." He flits, for a brief moment, a look of warning at me. I've never received that glower from him before. Let's hope it won't resurface.

Discomfort bubbles in my stomach.

Clutching my abdomen, I realize I haven't eaten since breakfast and walked who knows how many miles. But with the sun bleeding pink behind the trees, and the air growing cooler, I know I can't last much longer without rest.

We shuffle into a patch of grass by the sidewalk. I make sure to put plenty of space between him and me, since Mom would in no way approve of me falling asleep within several feet of a male. Waxy grass scratches my neck, hair, and ears. I try not to think about any ants or creepy crawlies that skitter in the dirt beneath us.

"You ever slept outside before?" Let's hope no jogger will trip over our feet resting on the edge of the sidewalk.

"Yes, for long time." His long eyelashes flutter shut. Even from several feet away, I can feel his warm breath. "In Palikari, many sleep outside."

Despite the chilly wind that ripples through the shrubberies nearby, I feel heat crawl up my neck. No wonder he took so much pity on that beggar we passed. How many times did Homer sleep on the Palikarian streets at night? Before his mother sold him, did his family live without a home?

Night owls hoot and frogs chirp. As I drift off, I wonder if the ground in Palikari hurt his shoulders as much as it hurts mine now.

Lead fills my brain. As soon as the world goes black, Homer shakes me awake a minute later.

Drowsy, and with a bad taste in my mouth, I blink at the silhouette in the light of an almost-full moon. He's on his feet and offers me a hand to help me rise. Everything feels stiff. A groan exits my nostrils in a hot breath. "Homer, it's not morning yet."

"I know. We go to follow stars."

"Huh?"

"Like I did first night here. When I run away from man."

He slants his chin toward the dark blanket in the sky dotted with traces of clouds and weak, shining lights. Stupid light pollution from the cities nearby.

Blinking the sleep from my eyes, I shiver. The temperature outside must've plummeted at least ten degrees. "Can you tell with all the clouds and the terrible lighting? It's harder to see the stars near cities."

"Yes, we go now."

Soreness aches in my muscles when I hobble onto my feet, following behind the shadow in a tunic. I shiver and tuck my fingers into my armpits for warmth. But cool sweat coats my fingertips and makes me quake more.

The walk seems to take hours as Homer pauses on several occasions to seek help from the skies, forming L-shapes with his fingers as if measuring the backdrop of the night with them. When he appears to find a star, like a point on a map, his legs march forth in giddy glee. I stumble behind and take turns between rubbing my hands and breathing into them.

We pass by houses with cold, barren windows and lighting poles with craned necks as if the burden of the electricity has become too much for them.

It feels as if someone has stuffed a bag of rocks in my calves, and each lift of the legs grows more painful than the one that came before.

My heart flutters within me when we enter another town full of shops. At first, I think we've reached the outskirts of London, until a swinging sign for Hampstead glistens in weak lamplight.

Man alive, my body aches with cold and sweat and fire all at the same time. If we go for longer than another five miles, I think I'll tear myself apart limb from limb. *Great, the wind picked up.* Feels like that Robert Frost poem out here.

And miles to go before I sleep.

And miles to—

A skyscraper looms on the horizon as we approach city lights. My pain dissolves as I force one foot in front of the other, matching the stride of my guide. Even the smell of cigarette smoke rushes my adrenaline at the prospect of arriving home within the hour.

From our entrance to London, it takes us a while to locate the apartment within the city limits. One street looks familiar until the road trails off into an unknown alleyway. At last, in the darkness, I spy a recognizable building. A rainbow flag dangles in front of the doorway.

Tears rush to my eyes when we bend around the familiar block and spy the apartment complex.

For a few minutes, we have to pound our fists against the door. "Mom, Uncle Laran, it's us. Let us in."

We must've woken up some neighbors.

The door swings open to Uncle Laran in striped pajamas. Unable to control myself, I collapse into his arms in a hug, and Homer follows. We stay in that formation for three long pauses.

He clears his throat. "You have your mother almost sick to death. Called the police force, the Queen, and anyone else who could pick up a phone."

"The Queen?" It's wild to believe that in 2017, she's still kicking. Who knows how long she'll continue to be on the throne?

"Of course not the Queen. I thought you spoke in only sarcasm, Harper."

Hearing the commotion, Mom emerges from the room and her lips tremble seeing us huddled in the doorway. She piles herself into the embrace and sputters through tears, "Don't you ever stay out later than nine o' clock again, young lady!"

There goes my dating life, in that case. If I can stick with this sparrow, though, I don't know if I really mind.

I wrench myself from the knot to cough. "Brought, *cough,* a surprise, *cough.*"

Mom releases me and goes right to Homer. She squeezes so hard, I'm afraid she'll break him.

"This smart guy brought us home using the stars. Phone died, so no GPS." I wave the dead device. "And I have one more surprise. Turns out, we don't need to build a laver time machine for Homie. Henry already made us one."

Chapter Twenty-Five
Why the Bronze Snake Bites

WITH WARM TEACUPS IN HAND, WE cluster around the kitchen table with Google Maps pulled up on the laptop screen.

"A bathtub, you said?" Uncle Laran points to the date the satellites captured the images. 2010. No wonder the backyard looks empty, except for shrubs and trees that could hide a small army. "Cast iron, perhaps? It's not quite the same as wrought iron."

"How so?" Mom presses her cup to her lips.

I follow suit and find the black tea brew bitter. Reaching across the table, I grab the creamer and pour a stream of white cream into the cup. My shoulders relax as I watch the two liquids swirl before they blend together.

Uncle Laran leaves his tea black. "From what I can remember, one of the irons is harder than the other, but can't remember which."

The tea trickles onto my tongue in a blend of sweet watery spices. I place the cup on the table. "You think we could still use the tub to get him back to Palikari?"

With a cup to Laran's nose, the "mhmm" comes out muffled. "We'll have more problems with finding a time when Henry isn't home. Worst case scenario, we put Homer in the tub, and he goes nowhere."

"Henry works until five. So the only issue you'll run into is if Amelia spots you and calls the cops." Guilt pangs my gut. I still can't believe we left her locked in a room. "If you two can get off work, we should be able to arrive there on Tuesday—the day of the thunderstorm—hours before Henry gets a hint of what we're up to."

"How do you know his working times?" Mom clinks her cup against the table a little too hard.

Man alive, I almost forgot about the fact I sneaked into her Facebook account to get that information.

"I—uh—saw a work schedule on his desk when I snuck through the house."

Heat from her glare rests on my face and neck. Mom digs into her bag and pulls out a phone. Scrolling, she clicks on her Facebook messaging and flashes the message between her and Elizabeth at me.

"Look familiar?"

"Teens know a lot about social media, Mom."

"I mean the fact that my Facebook messaged her of its own volition, inquiring about times when Henry would be at home."

"Technology has gotten smart throughout the years."

"Harper."

Biting my lip and swiping a clear snot trail from my nose, I sniff.

"You left your account logged on, Mom, and she messaged you. I wanted to wake you up, but after everything that happened that night, I thought it best to let you sleep."

"And venture out on your own, on a train alone, to rescue him? Why didn't you wait until the weekend?"

"I thought Amelia was in school. Elizabeth told me the opposite in the morning, but it was already too late by that point."

Her eyebrows form a slope on the bridge of her nose. "So that's where the twenty-pound notes keep going. And they went missing once before. Did you use that for some other little excursion?"

Scenes from Camden Market flood my mind. Reminisces of the garlic curry float on my tongue. Racks of vibrant faux fur coats in the middle of a hot midsummer's day, the sweet fried donuts bubbling in a vat of oil, all the scents and scenery flash before my eyes.

As my mouth pries open for what I hope will be an adequate explanation, a cough comes out. Not from me, but the hack comes from another end of the table.

In a borrowed ASU sweatshirt from Mom, Homer hacks into the navy sleeve for ten seconds straight. He stops to take another breath, followed by a series of dry coughs. Sweat glistens on his forehead and turns the navy armpits of the sweater to black.

"Ah, poor Homie." I let a sip of cooler tea scald my still-sore throat. "I think he caught my cold." Figures. Even though we slept a distance away from each other on the sidewalk, germs can travel great distances.

Uncle Laran's waxen face melts into one of horror. Eyes wide and forehead creased, he presses his hand on his head and mutters something about temperature. Mom beats him to the punch and has her palm pressed against Homer's skull.

"Warm."

Her brother swears. Not the word itself, but the fact Uncle Laran cursed at all jolts me like a lightning bolt.

"What?" My heart catapults into my throat. "It's just a cold. Sure, it lasts forever, but you learn to deal with it."

Homer grips his head with both hands and lets out an animal-like moan. His fingers alternate between his temples and his neck. He slumps onto the table and groans into his soft placemat.

"Homer." Mom touches him lightly on the shoulder. "Why don't you go lie down on the couch over in the family room?" She tugs his arm, which sends another series of whimpers. She glances at Laran, who makes a motion with his arm of carrying something.

Mom nods and scoots Homer's chair backward. Uncle Laran rises and his knees crack when he bends to hoist the Palikarian on his shoulder. Grunting, he succeeds and turns in the direction of the family room, with his load bearing fresh tears on his trembling cheeks.

He sets Homers gingerly on the couch. "Liv, go to the pharmacy."

"And buy *what* medicine?"

I sniff. "Guessing NyQuil will do the trick. He and I could split the bottle since we never used any medicine to treat this cold."

Uncle Laran ignores me. "Whatever you can carry, Livy."

With that, Mom opens the kitchen cabinet and pulls out a large shopping carrier. The stores charge for bags here, after all. Then, with a quick churning of the hand, she motions for me to follow, and we bolt out the door to the sound of an agonized wail from the couch.

Down the fluorescent hallway, I struggle to keep up with her quick pace.

"Poor Homie can't handle headaches well." Short pants trail from my lips while I pump my arms. "First the time he drank too much communion wine, and now with this cold. Don't get me wrong, the headache hurts. But maybe not *that* much."

He comes from Palikari, after all. You'd think after all they put him through there, he would have a stronger resistance to pain.

Granted, different time periods have different pains. Maybe they don't get many colds where he comes from.

Mom doesn't answer as she skirts around slow pedestrians

on the sidewalk and crosses the street even though the crosswalk displays a red "do not cross" light. A silver car blares an angry horn at us as we make a mad dash to the other side.

"Mom, they could've run us over." My pants have reduced to rasps. Why did she have me come with her again? Won't I infect others in the store? She must not have had much time to think about any of this.

"Need to hurry."

Once through the glass doors, Mom plucks various medicines off the shelves without a second glance at the labels and forces them into my arms. Her eyes rim with a certain red madness, and I clamp my jaw shut. She'll ignore my questions anyway in this state. We race to the self-checkout, and the barcodes beep in such a quick succession it sounds like one fluid noise.

Dumping the bottles into the bag, Mom takes off again to the rattling of pills and her high heels clacking. My legs, stiff from walking all yesterday, scream at me as I jog to keep up with the woman who crosses the street, yet again, to the red no-crossing man.

Fire forms a cloud in my throat as I wheeze, rushing up the steps to the apartment. When she bursts through the door, Uncle Laran snags the bag like a racer grabbing a baton in a relay. Before I can enter, Mom yanks my wrist out in the hallway and shuts the door.

"Now to answer your questions." She brushes the wild hairs behind her ears. "Even though the cold you have may not affect you much, this sort of sickness doesn't exist in his time. Maybe he'll endure it like you—but for all we know, a cough could mean the death of him."

Death? My chest freezes.

I killed him.

I press my back into the hallway wall and slide down until I reach the carpet. My diaphragm spazzes as I try to choke down tears.

"I had n-no idea. I thought colds were only contagious for the first few days. And I've had this stupid cold forever." Would this knowledge have prevented me from going to un-kidnap him?

She places a gentle hand on my shoulder and squeezes. "Not your fault, Harper."

Her calming words fade as the thought *murderer* strikes me again and again like jagged ice that carves into my skin, cold and then hot and then blood. *You killed him, Harper. The one thing that made you afraid to be close with people.*

Now goes the last sparrow, without so much as a cry.

* * *

His symptoms worsen over the next twenty-four hours. Chills rack his body as he paints the couch in sweat. Mom places a cool cloth on his head to stem the fever, but this causes him to shiver.

The dry hacks and sneezes keep me up all night, and he empties an entire tissue box from his runny nose. Even when we enter the family room, everything smells the way a hospital does.

I kneel by his side of the couch and let the tears stream down my face. They wet my jaw.

"I'm so sorry, Homie. I'm so, so sorry."

In a daze, he glances at me with a weary smile smeared with sweat. The pleasant expression fades as another headache darkens his face like an inkblot. Veins surface like vipers that crawl across his forehead.

"In Underworld," he says in a hoarse voice between coughs, "Homer never be any good animal. No bull. No ram. No even sparrow."

Such a terrible thing to look forward to. To have no idea

what happens to you after you die.

He grimaces. "Tell me story, Harper."

Dust fills my throat. "I don't know how many Bible stories or fairytales I have left. Anything in particular?"

"Tell me story about Underworld. Tradition for Palikari before they die."

The wind leaves my body for a moment. I forget how to breathe for two seconds. Then oxygen surges into my lungs. I roll my fists.

"You're not going to die, Homie. I won't let you."

"Tell me story anyway."

I grip his sweaty hand in mine. His fingers have frozen over. "My Underworld is different than yours, Homie. I think you might like to hear a story about it."

He perks up when he hears this. "Your Underworld?"

"It's a little place called Heaven. They pave the streets out of gold up there. And they say no sickness, no sadness, and no tears exist up there. So I guess all three of those things happening tonight would be over."

Breathing hard, he props himself up on his hands to attain a better sitting position. "How do you go to this Underworld?"

I smile at him as the sweat dampens his curls to stick to his forehead. "Well, for one thing, there's no sparrow sacrifice involved."

* * *

By morning, most of the symptoms appear to dwindle.

He threw up five times last night but seems to keep down liquids this morning. Throughout the late hours, the three of us took turns watching him for any signs of improvement. Mom debated calling a hospital when blood surfaced in Homer's vomit, but she wasn't sure what to do about Homer's medical records. After all, he lived in another period of time. Plus, according to Uncle Laran, getting inside British hospitals was harder than the American equivalent.

Uncle Laran and Mom, for the first Sunday all trip, stay home from church. We watch a sermon online from our pastor back home, and Uncle Laran substitutes sandwich bread and grape juice for our communion.

Worn out from the events of the night, Homer sleeps through the "service," but I promise Mom to fill him in later, especially since Pastor tells good stories. This time, he calls someone up to the stage to eat a salty cupcake for an example of falsehood of outward appearances.

By Monday, the day before we would go to Henry's house during the thunderstorm, Homer gains enough strength to walk around the house. His talking facilities improve a tremendous amount as well.

"The night Homer sick"—he plucks some dirt from underneath his nails —"Homer had dream."

In the vision, a black bull with red eyes told him his day had come to visit Leinos in the Underworld. The bull wrenched open his large jaws to latch onto Homer's head. But just before the teeth clamped down, the sound of a shrieking sparrow pierced the air. A small bird landed on the bull's head and pecked its eyes out.

Oh, lovely, thank the Arizona stars Homer tells me this as I take a bite of my Special K.

"That was when Harper wake Homer. Harper is sparrow that save me."

Swallowing the cereal, I glance at my shoes and smile, and wonder whether he or I was the sparrow in that dream.

Chapter Twenty-Six
Why the Heaven-Thunder Roars

"UNCLE LARAN TELL HOMER STORY?"

"What's that, Homie?" I pause my pencil on the outline of a man by the Peter Pan statue. My last ten sketches have included all human subjects. Glancing over my shoulder at a bench flanking my side, I toss a quick wave at Uncle Laran. Glad he let us visit Hyde Park one last time before Homer leaves our time forever, even if it required adult supervision.

"Who tell Homer story when Harper no here?"

I frown at the sketch as the rotund man I've been drawing skulks away toward another statue. "You mean, who is going to tell you stories when I leave for Arizona?" Does he assume that our replication of the Festival of the Sparrows won't work?

He shakes his head and stretches his arm around me on the bench, like boyfriends do in movie theaters. "Harper tell other people about Homer? Tell stories of Homer? Write down?"

Laughing, I twirl the pencil in my hand. It falls and clatters off the iron bench.

"I'm not really a good writer, Homie. You'd better talk to Uncle Laran. He's a historian. Historians tend to tell history best."

Homer frowns at a chartreuse bird as it hobbles near his tennies. He sucks on his teeth, then blows out his lip.

"Not sure if that true, Harper."

"I mean, some historians are really boring, so people might fall asleep when he talks about you, but he could at least tell your story better."

His arm encircles me. I lean in an avoid Uncle Laran's one

eyebrow-lifted gaze.

"Harper?"

"Mmm?"

"No of-fense"—he sounds out the phrase—"but his-tor-ian terrible storyteller."

"Uncle Laran, you mean?" Well, he did bore his students in his lectures.

"No, all historian."

I sit up and squinch my eyelids as a breeze catches my eyes at just the right moment for forming a glaze of tears. Even the wind makes me cry now.

"What'dya mean, Homie? Historians know history best. Hence *history*-an."

He scrunches his nose. "Laran study Palikari history for many year. But Laran did not know many thing until Homer told him." He leans in very close. My heart flutters, and I try to mirror Homer, while avoiding Uncle Laran's eyes.

I shrug, barely able to inch my right shoulder up with his hand on it. "Well, true, but the events happened a long time ago. Historians can't always get the facts right."

Now I wonder how often they *did* get it right. How many Palikarians went through history unnoticed? Or other historical events—did they play out how we learned them in school?

"Uncle Laran know many thing now." He ducks in close, and our lips touch. Oh, St. Olga, I'm going to miss this when he leaves. "But he don't know that."

"I would hope not." I suppress a giddy laugh. "If you kissed him, I think we'd have other problems."

He flashes a grin. "Yes, but, I mean, he don't know Homer like Harper. So he can't tell as good story as Harper."

Placing the back of my head against his chest, I sigh as I

watch a boy in a red t-shirt hug the base of the Peter Pan statue. I smile. Most humans aren't so bad.

"I'll try, Homie. It might take me a lifetime, but I'll figure out how to tell your story right."

Returning to my sketchbook, I try to recollect the hook in the man's nose, the subject of my drawing. An instant later, Homer grabs the sketchbook and flips back to my illustrations of Hyde Park, the ones without people. He taps one etched with swans. "Nice."

"Thanks, can I have it back?"

He flips to one I drew this morning of him peering out the window at London. The caption underneath the picture, in cursive, reads "Sparrow."

"This."

"Yes? That's you."

He points at the drawing and then flips through all the others I have outlined of people. "Beautiful."

* * *

"Run through the plan one more time for me." I park in an open seat on the morning train ride to Henry's house.

We picked an early time to ensure plenty of hours before Henry returns home from work.

"We don't have a clue when the lightning will strike." Uncle Laran's knuckles grow white as they grip the pole in the middle of the train car. "So the more time we spend at his house, the better chance the lightning will hit when Homer is submerged in the liquid iron."

Underneath a long rain jacket, which cuts off at his legs, Homer appears to be wearing no pants. Inside the coat, he's dressed in his Palikarian tunic to avoid any confusion upon his reentry to his home country. But for now, we try to dodge any odd expressions from the Brits on the rail line.

Uncle Laran switches his grip to the yellow strip dangling from the ceiling to maintain his balance. "As soon as we arrive, we'll pour the liquid iron into the tub and put him in. Every ten minutes, we will hold him underneath the mixture for thirty seconds in hopes the lightning strikes. We'll repeat as long as necessary."

"Making sure to say the chant Homer taught us last night," Mom adds in a hushed whisper. She stands by the glass barrier right by the doors.

Seriously? The dark magic chant? My jaws sinks at her.

"You're fine with saying something from another religion, Mom?"

She gazes out the window as we pass by an outdoor area with a field full of sheep grazing in a gray haze of a thunderstorm. I spy a slight reddish tint on her pale cheeks. "Of course, we'll ask the Lord God for His help before we start the chant. Worst case, we'll ask for forgiveness later."

"Mom."

She tugs her bag, which keeps sliding off her shoulder. "What? Might as well take as many precautions as necessary to get your friend back home. Otherwise, Henry'll kidnap him again, and who knows if we could ever retrieve him after that?"

And there we have our two options—get rid of Henry, or get Homer home.

Plan B no longer exists. Homer and Henry can't both stay in England. One needs to go.

I've mulled over these options in my mind on the way over. Because if Henry lives and Homer doesn't return home, Henry will stop at nothing to kidnap him again. He has followed us everywhere, after all.

But we obviously won't go for that killing option, so Homer *must* get home.

A chill runs down my spine.

What if Henry does go for that killing option?

I try to shake the thought away. I saw his desk, the sweet card from Amelia to the "Best Dad Ever." Surely he wouldn't try to kill us for sending this precious artifact back home.

Then again, much as I loved my dad, he had his faults.

The doors swing open underneath an alcove for a station. I tuck my feet as close to the seat as they'll go as passengers pack into the train. Everything smells wet and moldy from the rain.

Thank goodness most people get off well before we reach Welham Green. Almost no one lives there.

I squeeze Homer's hand. "Uncle Laran, you sure we can't keep him somehow?"

He steps closer to me as a passenger in a gray hijab reaches for a pole to stabilize herself. "I wish, Harper. No one wants to send him back to slavery or to a time with such a low life expectancy. If Henry wasn't on his trail, I wouldn't think twice about letting him stay with me. Expenses and all, he's become like family."

Uncle Laran at last could have a son. But Henry took that option away from him.

Hunching into my stomach, I place my cheek on my fist and watch Homer with his hands wrapped tightly around a pole. His knuckles blanch. He grits his teeth and clamps his eyes shut for the first half hour. But, when he realizes the journey takes three times as long, I make him swap seats with me until enough people filter out of the train's stomach for me to flank his side.

"Ready to go home, Homie?"

He looks at his sandaled feet. "Bad," he manages, and then, "good."

"Home? Bad and good?"

His head sways from side to side in a noncommittal fashion. "Yes."

"I guess every place is a little bit of bad and good. What do you miss most from home?"

"Which home? Here or Palikari?"

Something jabs me in the chest like a spike on a Greek shield we'd seen at the museum. London—with its thick smog and loud rattling rails, with its four-story tea shops and beggars blocks away huddled in sleeping bags. Its bleeding stained glass cathedrals and flashing rainbow lights from strip clubs. The way its cucumber sandwiches refresh a dry mouth that's inhaled cigarette smoke all the live long day.

London has become our second home.

"London or Palikari?" Homer pulls me out of my daze.

"Palikari. What do you miss most about it?"

He draws in a rattling breath and coughs into the coat sleeve. He still hasn't overcome the cold. "Miss games we would play at temple. Toss disks into jar female dancer held. Also miss dishes of fig, left over from sacrifice to Leinos. And seeing many star at night."

Agreed, I will rejoice when I escape London's light pollution. "You happy to go back then?" My heart sinks as I ask the question.

Before he can reply, the train brakes and swings open its doors to a grating *ding-dong-ding-dong*. We exit the car. Raindrops pelt us and clear trashcan bags billow in the breeze by dark blue benches. Mom pulls up the GPS on her phone and shields the screen from the cascading water. She planned to use her phone battery on the way here. With mine off in my bag, I'll turn the device on and guide us home.

Worst case we can walk back. I cringe. *Don't even joke about that, Harper.* Besides, no one can read stars like Homer can.

Without thinking, he and I lace our fingers together, and Mom eyes the two "kids" with a mixture of amusement and sorrow. I have a hard time discerning the expression in this dark haze outside. Maybe Amelia won't notice any strangers in her backyard amidst all the shadowy lighting out here.

On the train ride, I mentioned that she was playing Minecraft when I had come to retrieve Homer from their house. With her headphones on, she almost didn't hear us in the hallway, even with the door wide open.

"Have a kid in my high school who loves that game. He plays for hours at a time. Maybe we'll get lucky and she'll do that while we try to catch a lightning bolt."

We still have a backup plan in case she decided to ditch the video game for today. If she calls the cops on us, we'll scatter in three directions, with Uncle Laran directing Homer by the hand. I've already picked my hiding spot, the clump of pine bushes behind the property. Sure, the police might find me first—I chose the closest hiding place to the house, after all. But better they take me away than find Homie.

Plus, when I researched punishment for trespassing in England last night, worst case, I'll deal with a five-thousand-pound fine or imprisonment for a handful of months. Who knows? Maybe they'll go easier on me as a minor.

We reach Henry's house. The bricks have darkened to a near brown with all the rainwater.

Uncle Laran's dress shoes squelch in the mud when he steps onto the grassy path. He pauses, perhaps disgusted at the very un-British predicament. He sighs and continues onward.

Guess he'll be an American today, God bless.

When we skirt mini lakes in the backyard, Uncle Laran heads for the bathtub and rubs his fingers across the smooth outer rim.

"Anything wrong with it, Uncle Laran?"

"Nothing, just…an odd substitute for the other one. Come, let's pour the liquid iron in."

Although a bit of rain residue rests in the bottom of the tub, Uncle Laran says to leave it. Liquid iron has plenty of water in it anyway.

Crouching, we click off the white caps and heave the bottles, dumping the thick brown liquid into the tub. It takes several minutes to pour all the containers in, and not a single one is left unopened. The mixture wafts a pungent sort of scent, reminding me of a marriage between alcohol and metal.

Homer takes my hand as we help him step into the slippery time machine. He continues to lace his fingers with mine in a tight grip, as though afraid he'll slide into the liquid iron never to re-surface.

Won't let you go, little sparrow.

"Shall we begin the first ten minutes?" Uncle Laran glances at his watch.

A lightning bolt flashes across the sky. It turns the clouds orange.

"Sounds like a yes." Mom clenches her eyelids shut and raises her hands to the heavens. "God, forgive us for what we are about to say. Somehow turn this Palikarian chant into an anthem of praise for you, and"—she chokes on her words—"please get our Homer safely home."

With that, Uncle Laran's voice loses all its color as he intones the chant.

Mom stands there and contributes nothing. Laran had suggested she play the part of the dancer to "make the ceremony as close as possible to the real one. You don't have to dance exactly like her. Just flail your arms a bit." Mom and I gave that a hard pass. The human eye should not see that kind of horror in one's lifetime.

Homer's arm quivers, and he grips my hand tighter until my fingers turn purple and jut in odd directions.

"Ready, Homie?"

"No. Push me down anyway." His ribs expand as he takes in a large gulp of air.

I place both hands on his shoulders and shove him underneath the surface. Then I release my grip, in case lighning strikes. Don't want to get electrocuted. I count thirty seconds in my head. I find myself speeding up the last ten seconds, wrenching my arms under his armpits to pull him back up before I reach "three, two, one."

Digging my feet into the mud, I shout for someone else to help me lift his body. I feel him kick inside the tub to get a strong footing. Must be crazy slippery in there.

The hum of Uncle Laran's chant ceases as he and Mom grip onto part of Homer's tunic to pull him up. We manage to haul him up as he lets out a loud gasp. He rubs the liquid iron from his eyes and squints at us.

"London?" His features dim in a somber sort of way. He knows the answer.

"London."

We let Homer catch his breath and wait another ten minutes

to try the process again. Homer's spirits appear to dampen, but we remind him that the first Festival of the Sparrows didn't work on the first try. Two seconds later, I regret bringing this up because the person who played the "sacrifice" for that festival died.

In my periphery, I spy an upstairs light flickering on. "Amelia?" Cold shock ripples through me. *Please tell me she didn't spot us.*

Uncle Laran raises his eyebrows at me, and I point at the upstairs window.

"Don't see the blinds drawn. Besides, even if she does open them, it's rather hard to see out here. She might just miss us."

Let's hope.

The ten minutes elapse, and I hold Homer underneath the liquid iron again. Another chant, another spider web of lightning…nowhere close to the lightning rod attached to the bathtub. It takes twice as much effort to tug Homer out from underneath the brown waves. Raindrops dapple in the muddy lake as he inhales long, exasperated breaths.

"Maybe we should try another day." Mom's face wrinkles in worry. "I don't know how much more Homer will be able to handle. Recovering from sickness and all."

Homer coughs into his muddied sleeve as if on cue.

"You leave on the twelfth, Livy," Laran says. "I can try again, but Henry will notice we used his machine, seeing as we dumped all the liquid iron into the tub. I can construct my own, but that would cost thousands of pounds. And something tells me my landlords will not agree to a tub stationed outside the flat complex."

"One last try after a ten-minute break." Mom nods at Uncle Laran's wristwatch. "And then we give him a longer rest period."

"We can only take so many breaks before Henry comes back

home," I remind them.

When we reach the full ten minutes, I ask the sparrow one more time if he's ready, but he looks off in the distance as if paralyzed by something. Perhaps the idea of having to go under again. After so many dunks into magical disappearing blood and liquid iron, I would feel numb about the process too.

"Homie, are you ready?"

No response.

"Okay, well, I need to dunk you under for another half-minute. But we'll let you take a longer break after this. Okay?"

Right as I grab his shoulders and feel him slip to the bottom of the tank, I spot a shadow emerging from the huddle of pine tree shrubs. Lightning flashes and catches the glint of a knife in the hands of Henry Whitley.

My breath holds for so long my lungs burn.

He's gonna kill someone.

Mud squelches as he races toward Uncle Laran with the knife poised. I scream, lifting Homer with all my might, and Uncle Laran ducks out of the way. Mom rushes over to help me pull Homer out of the tub, but silver dazzles in my eyes amidst another flash of lightning.

I shove Mom out of the way as Henry swipes at her with the large kitchen knife, but just before the point can reach me, Homer surfaces, smelling of metal. He grips the side of the tub but slides a few times before he catches his balance. He wipes the brown liquid from his eyes, and Henry freezes with his dagger poised inches from the Palikarian's nose.

Whites show in Henry's eyes.

Won't hurt his specimen—smart. That means he's reserved the murder weapon for the rest of us.

I eye his knife, but fear paralyzes me. I couldn't even grab it from him if I tried.

With lightning speed, Homer snags Henry's arm—the one with the knife—and clamps down hard to wrench the blade out of his grip. Henry leans his head back to let out a groan of pain but continues to hold onto the handle.

"*Enough,*" Uncle Laran cries from nearby. "Henry, drop the knife. You won't hurt him. He's too valuable to you for that."

With his other hand, Henry raps his knuckle against the tub. The cast iron makes a *cling.* "We have ways of teaching others who won't cooperate." His voice comes out a lot deeper than it had in the park. Back at Kensington, it sounded light, but now it carries a din of desperation. He bends his wrist and slices Homer's hand. Homer lets go, and Henry raises the blade again.

"Amelia wanted to call the cops, but I told her not to bother." Rainwater drips off his sneer. "Even prison for six months won't keep you off my trail. We end this now."

My heart thunders hard against my ribcage.

He cranes his neck toward me, and his lip snarls. "Heard you're the one who broke into the house."

Dust fills my throat. I open my mouth, but nothing spills out. Can't. Breathe. *Grab the knife, Harper. Grab the dang knife. Or run.* Why can't I move?

"Ladies first?" He dives across the time machine, knife aimed for my chest. I shriek and leap back, but he falls into the tub before he can reach me.

Wait. I blink. He doesn't fall.

Homer holds him down. Black blood from Homer's hand trickles into the liquid iron.

Paralyzed, we look on as the mass in the tub thrashes around. Homer winces and lets out cries of agony for the next several moments until the liquid stops forming waves. When the water stills,

Homer limps out, aided by my hand. His arm feels cold, wet, and sticky.

Even in the dark lighting, I see deep cuts dug into his leg from the knife. Henry must've plunged the sharp blade into Homer's skin in the tub to free his grip.

"Mom, Laran, help! He's injured."

We lay Homer on the muddy patch of yard and bind his cut calf in my wet hoodie.

A jagged flash of light blinds me for a moment as it hits the lightning rod on the tub. Sparks fly off into the wet grass, orange glow dying the instant they reach the ground.

Dead pause.

"Did the tub send Henry back in time?" I clutch at my throat and wince. It's raw from the cold and my screams.

Uncle Laran sneaks forward and fishes his hand in the brown mixture still in the bathtub. "We found a life form." He lunges as if to help Henry to his feet.

Henry Whitley's pale face surfaces. I feel my stomach squirm, choking down a fresh vat of vomit. Definitely not a *life* form.

"He's dead." My voice has lost all color. I should not be this calm about this.

My therapist said everyone deals with traumatic events in different ways. Maybe the emotions will set in when my heart stops racing.

"Afraid it came down to that, yes." Uncle Laran releases his grip on the corpse, and Henry slides back into the tub. "Let's head back to the apartment before Amelia senses something amiss and calls the authorities."

We help Homer to his feet. With his arm on my shoulder, we hobble into the hazy mist of the rain.

Chapter Twenty-Seven
Why the Merry Tent Collapses

I WINCE AS HOMER UNWRAPS THE gauze from his leg, and I hand him a new roll. At least the blood has dried by now.

"Thanks." The word catches in my throat. "For…you know."

He grabs the back of my head and presses my forehead to his. Maybe this means something in Palikarian culture, but I won't complain. He pulls away and finishes wrapping the bandages around his knife wound.

"Sparrows save sparrows."

"Yeah, but you also had to delete someone in the process." I shudder, blinking away images of the tub. "I keep getting flashbacks…I keep seeing his backyard. Seeing him."

"Me too." He bites his lip as he slides up the pant leg of the sweatpants. I really should pack those for tomorrow, but I figure I can stop by a thrift store any time.

Besides, Homer needs plenty of new clothes to start his new life living at Uncle Laran's flat.

I slump onto the loveseat next to him and let out a long sigh. "Too late to run away?"

He smirks. "Harper really bad at following stars."

Harper really bad at a lot of things, kid. "Okay, fair. But maybe I can take you with me on the run."

Shaking his head, he laces his fingers in mine. "Harper have school. Have life. And Harper mom be sad."

True. For the first time in a long time, I wouldn't want that.

Pressing myself into his shoulder, I gaze at our reflection in the blank family room TV. "You gonna be okay staying with boring old Uncle Laran?"

His shoulders bob up and down in a laugh, and a bit of a cough from the cold. "Uncle Laran teach me more English. We see what Homer do in few years. Maybe help Hyde Park garden."

"You'd be a fantastic gardener. And you can have those birds in the park carry back little messages for me." I peek at his face quick enough to catch his eyebrow furrow. Yep, they didn't have messenger pigeons in Palikari. "Just remember me, okay?"

With soft, warm hands, he cups my face and kisses me long and hard. He releases and presses his forehead to mine again. "Always."

* * *

My suitcase skitters as we enter the Heathrow airport. Although I packed almost nothing in addition to what I brought here—give or take a Primark dress or two—the luggage feels twice as heavy.

Even in the early morning hours before the sun threatens to emblaze the sky, people buzz from the baggage check to the security point around the corner past the food court. But I know I can breathe in here. My little sparrow helped me in crowds, and now I only have asthma to worry about.

Mom stops by the kiosk to scan our passports. Today she wears a hoodie and sweatpants. *How very 1950s of her.* Even Mom can't stand sitting on an airplane for nine hours in a dress.

Uncle Laran stands off to the side in a tie and business suit.

He has to make up for his muddy clothes from the day in Henry's backyard.

"Uncle Laran." Slow and steady, my eyelids pry themselves open—a miracle during these early hours. "Something kept me up last night, but I didn't want to wake you. Why didn't the time machine work in the backyard? Is it because we didn't say the chant when the lightning struck?"

I hear a growl from Mom as she slides the passport the other way to place on the machine's green glitchy scanner.

"To be honest, that kept me awake as well, Harper. I suppose a number of things could have contributed to its lack of function. Perhaps cast iron made a poor substitute for wrought. Maybe he wired the copper wrong, or we truly did need sparrow's blood. Or, like you said, perhaps the dark magic chant propelled Homer forward."

We'll never know. But I'd rather leave some mysteries unsolved.

The walkie-talkie from a security guard nearby garbles something incoherent. He wears a hat with a checkered brim and carries a gun. Oh, yeah. Mom said only the law enforcement people carry arms here. Explains why Henry used a knife. I shudder. Flashbacks dart across my mind.

"Y-you don't think they can trace the murder back to Homer, right, Uncle Laran? I mean, he can argue it was out of self-defense."

Except, we did trespass. Whoops.

Homer sits off in a blue chair by the doors, fiddling with the bandage wrapped around his leg. He gives me a sad sort of smile.

Uncle Laran scratches his scruff. "Doubt they'll arrest him. They have no fingerprints or records from a man out of time itself. And with such a covering of trees in the area, no neighbors could have witnessed the event."

Not to mention, the neighbors live so far away.

"And what about Mom messaging Henry's mom on Facebook? Can't they trace that conversation?"

"From what I can tell from her messages, Henry had not contacted his mother in a while. Amelia likely hasn't spoken to her grandma that often. Even if she remembers us coming to her doorstep and asking about Elizabeth, we didn't give her any names. England's a lot bigger than you would think."

Images of Amelia with her Minecraft headphones reel in my mind as they did last night. I pictured her tear-streaked face, slapped by rainwater, as she raced out into the yard and let out a wail when she found her father dead. Of course, we didn't stay around long enough to see her reaction. But some part of me wishes we had. So we could understand what we had done.

And no girl should have to live life without her father.

"Wonder if Homer's ever killed someone before." I should've asked him the other day on the couch. Our goodbyes had kept us busy.

"I think we've all murdered someone at least once in our lives," Uncle Laran answers in a hushed voice, eyeing the guards nearby. "Just most of us haven't done so physically."

Before I can prod Uncle Laran further, Mom returns with the long, white tickets. She slips one into my fingertips. I frown at the faded ink. "Middle seat both flights, huh?"

"I can switch places with you if you'd like."

"Please."

"Ready to check your bags?" Uncle Laran claps his hands together.

"Laran, the airport made us come three hours before our flight. We can take our time through security. At this time in the morning, we'll get through in less than an hour."

Fiddling with his fingers, Uncle Laran insists we begin for his health and sanity. Mom relents and motions for me to follow. Before we reach the baggage check area, a guard stops us to double check our passports and ask us why we had visited England in the first place. London must have a couple extra security checkpoints before the real one where you kick off your shoes.

I answer, "Sightseeing."

"Where all did you visit?"

"Oh, all over." I knuckle my dry eyes. It's too early in the morning for an interrogation. "Museums in London, some cathedrals, Dover Castle."

"How long was the drive to Dover Castle?"

My eyebrows form a bridge across my nose. I don't know. I wasn't paying attention. Why does this matter? "Umm, an hour and a half, I think."

With this, he sends me through to the man at the baggage check station. We reach the worker behind the conveyor belt who motions me over with a jerking wave. I hand him my passport and boarding pass. He scans each for a moment as I heave my suitcase onto the scale. It weighs almost nothing. I could've fit ten books in there and still made the limit.

"Light luggage."

"I'm not one for souvenirs." Can't stick a Homie in there, at least.

He eyes the bag for a moment and then lifts it onto the conveyor belt. I follow his brushing away gesture to leave the station. While Mom checks her bag, I join Homer on his bench as he watches a woman in heels dart toward the security checkpoint.

"Everything move so fast." Homer gestures at the woman with his chin.

"People think they can outrun time. They're usually wrong."

We waver in silence for a moment as he shoves his hands into the hoodie I gave him, the one he wore the first day in the British Museum. Figured I have plenty and won't need to put on a warm jacket in Page until winter.

His tongue licks his chapped lips. "I see you again?"

"Uncle Laran plans to FaceTime us once a week, so you will see me. Just not here." How to explain such complex technology to him? Then again, he's braved trains. "But meeting in person. I—I don't know if Mom has the money to fund a trip to England every year. This summer alone drained her, even with a paying job."

He stares at the arching spines of light on the ceiling. A man whizzes by with his tea steaming from a plastic cup. The brew wafts a warm herbal scent.

Suddenly, Homer grips my hand in his. "Tell me a story."

A nervous laugh bubbles in my throat. "I mean, I can. Ran out of the ones from the Bible. But why?"

"Palikari tradition. When man leave, for war or to set up tent elsewhere, he tell a story."

It seems the Palikari tell stories on every occasion.

"A story, huh?" I watch Mom heave her suitcase onto the scale. Looks like the bag weighs almost as much as Homer. "All right, I think I have one you'll like."

I talk about a warrior—the bravest in the land—who encounters a witch, who sends him to a faraway kingdom on a quest to find the mysterious Armor of Truth. Along the way he meets a sage, an annoying minstrel who won't stop singing, and a sparrow who refuses to chirp a single note. They embark with him to find this mysterious armor, fighting dragons and gorgons and anything else that ends in an "on" that comes to my mind.

In my periphery, I notice Mom and Uncle Laran huddling by a distant bench, letting the two of us have our space for the last story.

The heroes encounter additional obstacles on the way—

otherwise the story wouldn't last very long. They battle through raging thunderstorms, capsized ships on the sea, and even catch a plague from Crete islanders whom they thought had the armor. They were wrong, of course.

On his quest to find the armor, a mad wizard chases after the warrior to turn him into a silent sparrow, unable to speak the truth he finds once he discovers it. The group finds the armor inside a volcano's stomach. But, alas, the wizard beats them to the ledge inside the cone of the magma machine.

The wizard lunges for the sparrow first, but the warrior dives at him and plunges the villain into the magma pit. The warrior almost dies in the fall, too, but he lands on a ledge nearby, un-scathed. He then dons the armor, and the sparrow transforms into a princess whom he carries off into a Hollywood sunset.

Although he doesn't understand "Hollywood," Homer seems to grasp most of the story. "Best tale yet. Back in Palikari, hero dies at the end every time."

Well, glad to know I have a lot to look forward to when we read *The Iliad* and *The Odyssey*. "Homer, don't you see the story is about you? I thought it was obvious."

His eyes widen. "Homer not warrior."

"After what you did at Henry's house, the Queen should knight you."

I stop mid-sentence as he plants a kiss on my lips. He really does appear to be a fan of kissing, but again, no complaints from the Harper department. My cheeks flush at the mental image of Mom and Uncle Laran watching from nearby, but I brush away the thought and enjoy the moment, hoping it will last forever.

It doesn't.

We break apart, and Mom—after giving us a few seconds to recover—ventures over with my carry-on book bag and stretches out a hand.

"Sweetie, we need to start going through security. Even with the extra time, we can't risk missing the flight."

I ignore her hand but nod. Time to go home.

Weaving his fingers in mine, Homer leads me all the way to the security checkpoint where I spot girlfriends embracing their guys in suffocating hugs. Even Uncle Laran squeezes me in a death grip.

When I hug Homer, I feel his hot tears spill down the back of my Daredevil t-shirt. A river Thames forms in my eyes, and I return the favor to him. But I doubt he'll feel it in the thick hoodie.

"Time to go, Harper," my mom calls, her voice a million miles away.

"Coming."

I squeeze his fingers one last time and let go. I approach the blaring yellow sign that reads "All Departure Gates." A cry from behind me stings my ears as I hear Homer wail. I force myself to keep my gaze forward as I hear.a thump hit the ground. I assume it's his knees. He cries as I snake through the line.

It's traditional in Palikari for people to wail, according to Laran. Homer must sense the tense body language Laran's known to do though and quiets his sobs.

But I still hear them. Even in the silence.

I hear you, little sparrow. I hear you.

AUTHOR'S NOTE

Three Years Later, in 2021

When I started this book, my parents were in the middle of a heated separation that had begun in August of 2017. I wrote the book in February of 2018, and by the time I hit Chapter Nineteen, my dad gave me *the call*.

The one that I'd prayed would never come ever since I was four years old, in the car, and asked Mom, "Are you and Daddy gonna get a divorce?"

She never answered me. She just cried.

When I hung up, I sobbed into my pillow. The friends in my dorm didn't know what to do. After all, I hated touch (author's note in 2023: most likely because I have autism, a discovery that took place five years after writing this book). So they stood in my room in awkward silence until I lifted myself from my bed and worked on homework. Because college work never rested.

Little did I know that I had years of healing to look forward to.

2018 had been a wild year, and Sparrow kicked it off.

I hadn't found my author's voice until I wrote this book. Never before had I "pantsed" a book—instead of plotting anything ahead of time—or written a book in first person. That is, if we ignore some horrendous fan fiction I wrote back in high school.

So to say I didn't know what I was doing is the understatement of the decade.

A lot of publishers didn't understand Harper. Some said I made her too hard in the beginning and others said I softened her too much at the end.

Now, looking back three years later, after I've finished the sequel and found my forever home with Mountain Brook Fire, I realize a lot of why I wrote Harper the way I did, and why I wouldn't change her.

Don't get me wrong, I will receive and do a lot of edits on this book. I wrote this author's note before I sent it off to the editor, and I love how thorough Mountain Brook tends to be. A good editor sees the potential in a manuscript, shapes it, and steers it in the right direction.

But all to say, when I wrote this, I needed a Harper.

A girl who feared touch.

A girl who feared showing vulnerability.

A girl who was so, so hurt and needed healing.

Years later, I haven't fully healed, but I've scarred, throbbed a lot less, and seen everything in a newer light. I fully believe that God, prayer, therapy, and characters like Harper and Homer pulled me through to get to a much better place.

So thank you to all those who saw me, heard me, and like Homer, never let me go.

ACKNOWLEDGMENTS

To my Lord and Savior Jesus who hears me even when Time and History will forget to mention me. You love even the sparrows.

To the teachers who made history come alive—Dr. Johnson, Mr. Ling, Mr. McSparran, Mr. Samsonas. Especially Dr. Johnson who gave a voice to some of the voiceless characters in Ancient Egypt, Greece, Rome, and the Middle Ages. Even though Palikari is a made-up country—a conglomeration of Dark Age Greece, the Etruscans, and some elements of Ancient Egypt—I know that if they existed, you would have done them justice as well.

To Prof. Taylor, Mrs. Riordan, Mrs. DiPaolo and all the teachers who helped push my writing along the way. We don't live in the Greek Dark Ages, but it's still tricky to get our voices out there. Thank you for listening to my terrible first drafts and believing in the final ones.

To the British Museum who, when I asked about information regarding security measures and the tampering of objects, replied, "Thanks for your interest in the British Museum. Unfortunately, we are not able to share our security measures with members of the public. I hope you are not too disappointed and wish you the best of luck with your future activities." Hopefully my guesswork and insatiable scrolling through online articles and YouTube videos—which would give me barely an inkling of your security procedures—measured up to the current standards. If not, it's fiction.

But, seriously, I did enjoy visiting the British Museum the most out of all the attractions London offered. It truly is a historian's paradise.

To Miralee who saw the promise of this book. And to Nikki and Alyssa who never stopped fighting for the story. It feels good to be fought for, prayed for, and deeply loved. I am forever indebted to you three.

To Alyssa who has the misfortune of going through the content edit of this. I know you won't go easy on me, and I'm totally fine with that. I wrote this three years ago and had a lot to learn then. I still have a lot to learn.

To Tessa, Cyle, Sonya, James, Carlee, my family, and anyone else who heard me when no one else did and—most importantly—listened.

To Trey who showed up long after the writing process of this. Took you long enough, you goof.

And of course to my ever-patient readers. I know this is a departure from some of the books I've written before. Thank you for sticking with me as I experiment, play, and experience the story with you together.

www.ingramcontent.com/pod-product-compliance
Lightning Source LLC
Chambersburg PA
CBHW071542030726
47598CB00001B/190